Stevie Davies, who [...] historian and literary critic. She holds an honorary appointment as Senior Research Fellow at Roehampton Institute, London, and is a Fellow of the Royal Society of Literature.

Her first novel, *Boy Blue* (The Women's Press, 1987) won the Fawcett Book Prize in 1989; *Primavera* (The Women's Press, 1990) confirmed her literary reputation; and her shattering breakthrough book, *Arms and the Girl* (The Women's Press, 1992) received universal praise. *Closing the Book* (The Women's Press, 1994) was on the long-list for the Booker Prize, and the shortlist for the Fawcett Book Prize. Her fifth novel, *Four Dreamers and Emily*, described as 'poignant, funny and luminous . . . immensely enjoyable, lit by comedy and wisdom' (Helen Dunmore, *The Times*) was published by The Women's Press in 1996; and of *The Web of Belonging* (The Women's Press, 1997), shortlisted for the Arts Council of Wales Book of the Year Prize and the Portico Prize, the *Independent* commented, 'There are good writers, there are very good writers. And then there is Stevie Davies in a class of her own'. She is also the author of *Emily Brontë: Heretic* and *Unbridled Spirits: Women of the English Revolution 1640–1660* (1998), both published by The Women's Press.

Also by Stevie Davies from The Women's Press:

FICTION
Boy Blue (1987)
Primavera (1990)
Arms and the Girl (1992)
Closing the Book (1994)
Four Dreamers and Emily (1996)
The Web of Belonging (1997)

NON-FICTION
Emily Brontë: Heretic (1994)
*Unbridled Spirits: Women of the English Revolution
1640–1660* (1998)

STEVIE DAVIES
Impassioned Clay

First published by The Women's Press Ltd, 2000
A member of the Namara Group
34 Great Sutton Street, London EC1V 0LQ

This edition published 2000

British Library Cataloguing-in-Publication Data
A catalogue record for this book is available from the British Library.

ISBN 0 7043 4659 1

Printed and bound by Cox & Wyman, Reading, Berkshire

to Katherine Wyatt
for twenty years of friendship

> once again, the fierce dispute
> Betwixt Damnation and impassion'd clay
> I must burn through

(John Keats, 'On Sitting Down to Read King Lear Again')

> I am one that is of no sect or gathered people
> whatsoever, so I walk alone as a woman
> forsaken; I have fellowship with them that lived
> in caves, and in dens, and desolate places of the
> Earth, of whom the world was not worthy.

(Joan Whitrow, 'The Humble Address', 1689)

Part I

One

As a child I would hide troves of pebbles and fircones, and the following year, when the memory of my secrets had sunk almost to vanishing-point, instinct would draw me, roving the cherished spaces of the garden, to their place of interment. I'd hum or whistle, cruising absent-mindedly, circling a sanctuary at once familiar and obscure. Hunkering down, I'd begin to ferret with my fingers between stones in the rockery, or beneath the copper beech, not quite sure what it was I was looking for. Out would come a cone, a cache of plumstones, a twist of paper containing a coded message to myself. Each time it was as if a stranger had stored these treasures for me to gather, for the child I had been last year was outgrown, replaced. I invested these intimate hoards with awe and sanctity. Time's cyclical passage hid their existence even from myself; but just as their memory neared extinction, they came to light.

Now we dug in earnest, excavating a burial. Our spades rang off stones and broke the fibrous mat of roots that webbed the Cheshire clay. We shovelled earth from above her face, then feathered soil from a still hand which lay open to us. The throes of our labours delivered human kin. With the nest of bones – some shattered, others entire – we salvaged the gravegoods of her Calvary: an iron crown. As she had unconsciously waited, so I had been biding time unawares. Heart spasming, I reached down into the bed of clay to cover what was left of her hand with my right, my writing, hand; and she gripped me.

✳

'Be silent, Olivia,' were nearly the last words my Quaker mother addressed to me. 'Listen in yourself. To the truth that is in you.'

The message, delivered from the bed at Pinfold Farm where she and generations of us had been born and died, seemed an inhuman echo of some doom handed down from perishing mouth to mortal ear over centuries. I shrank from its rigour as from a reprimand, longing as ever for an intimacy foreign to her nature. I hunched in an adolescent ball of curdled grief and resentment on the uneven boards of the bedroom, my head just below the parapet of the pillow, under the great brown timber that ties the oak cruck of the house, so as to avoid the decaying power of her eyes. I kept silent parliament with a black beetle scuttering under the bed, in communion with the 'beggar's velvet' of the homely fluff collected there.

Many creaking comings and goings later, amid a murmurous empathy of soft voices, she herself was silenced. I cast open the window and stared out into a twilit wilderness of allheal and lovage, her planting. Minty and lemon scents ascended, complicated by resin from the lopped fir and contaminated by exhaust fumes; a pale glow yellowed the bank of evening primrose. I let in the mosquito-scream of suburban strimmers and the roar of the main road; the Crewe train shuddered our timbers from the embankment. A removal van hesitated on the corner of Cedar Avenue, where families constantly replace one another in drab commuter semis and no one is ever permanent. My mother's people have agelessly inhabited this straggling homestead, which, beginning as a Tudor yeoman's farm, has been extended by haphazard stages sideways, its timbers clad in whitewashed bricknogging, its meadows progressively sold, until only the building and a half-acre patch with an orchard remains.

My father came in behind me. 'She's gone, love,' he told me gently. 'She's at peace. She didn't suffer.'

The removal lorry, spying a gap in the traffic, sped away under the railway bridge. My father had tears in his voice. Needy pauper in the shadow of her blazing idealism, he expectantly but with hesitation solicited my fellowship. I said, as if bored, 'Oh. Right. I thought so.'

4

His voluble eyes stared in bewilderment at my absence of response. My mouth remained open, like a hole. The house in its aghastness veered sideways as I straightened up from the window, pitching me down on to the settee, to bury my deathly pale face in my arms.

Be silent. Listen to the truth that is in you. It denied me the milk I nuzzled for, the smelly, sticky, lovely warmth every jelly-legged calf has the right to expect from its mother. When, occasionally, I paused in listening to the void she had left in the house as her heirloom, and attended to my own silence, its hollowness echoed back only hunger and thirst.

My second mother was always telling me to be quiet, but that was not the same thing. Her 'Be quiet' contradicted my first mother's 'Be silent'.

Neither mother corresponded to the kind of woman I coveted. I wanted someone plumper than the first, more doughy and less yeasty; a hot-water bottle woman who'd let me snuggle, loaf and be comfortable. I wanted someone less aggrieved than my second mother at the perfections she suspected in my first.

'Try not to moon, lovey,' she instructed me, when I was still mourning. 'I'm your mum now.'

'We'll have to do something for her,' she said concernedly to my father. 'She's got ideas in her head.'

She wouldn't go into our garden. She took issue with it every time her scared brown eyes looked out of the window. Did she glimpse the ghost of my first mother, as I did, misty and gaunt, inhumanly abstract, pondering in the depth of the silence beneath the copper beech? I sat whole days with a book in my lap, beside the mound where we buried my mother in an unmarked grave, grassy and butterflied. When the counterfeit was out shopping, I hurled myself on the breast-shaped mound and howled.

My mother had arranged for a Green funeral and wanted to be buried in a cardboard box. No words should be said over her, neither should an inscription commemorate her. Dad, intimidated after her death as he had been for years before by the awful grandeur of her unworldliness, obeyed to the letter. The cardboard box, she had decreed, should be as cheap as possible, remarking that since there was no such thing as death, it would not be necessary for us to grieve. I cried on the mound as much in rage as sorrow. She had denied me, so it seemed, every right a fifteen-year-old only daughter might legitimately claim; and left the way open to this ass of a woman carping incomprehensibly about my hairstyle, fingernails and laddish slouch. To the first I was a vagrant soul; to the second a messy body.

But before we could bury my first mother, and replace her, we had to clear the site. She was laid aside for some time while this was done.

✳

I watched from my bedroom window on the morning my father and uncle began to dig. The summer heat had been fierce, and the lawn was parched, rock-hard. My flabby dad, his face red and puffy from forbidden crying, was not equal to the task in any way. His spade bounced back from the turf. He jabbed it down with his heel again and again, till sweat stood on his forehead and he had dinted the topsoil to a depth of no more than an inch.

'It's all these roots,' he explained to me as I came out. He sounded tangled up in himself. 'The whole place is a web of roots.'

'Let me have a go.'

'Oh gosh no, Ol. It's no work for you.'

'Why not?'

'Well – it's your mum, isn't it. Dan and I will manage. Bring us out a cup of tea if you like.'

'Quite. It's my mother. I think we'd do better with a fork.' No way was I going to be a tea-lady, ministering to the menfolk while they did the significant work. I was her heir. I was her only daughter and her only son. If anyone should fight the earth with a fork, to dig her last bed, I should be the person.

He was right, the turf was webbed with taproots from broom and rhododendron, and with multitudinous fibres from the roots, in themselves fragile but knitting a mat of soil. As you got deeper, the soil became easier to work, and

Uncle Dan and I made steady progress. My father sagged in to make the tea, like a lamed man. Together we cut steeply down, through the sour Cheshire clay, raising an odour that suggested not clean dirt, but rank and brackish pools where the freshness of rain never falls.

'You don't have to do this,' said Dan. Like all my father's family, he believed his brother had married an extremist whose idealism threatened the very foundations of the social organism: that easy-going mateyness which makes for human fellowship, whose sacrament is a pint in the pub before Sunday lunch.

'I know I don't have to – *but I want to*,' I riposted ferociously, and the spade I'd exchanged for the fork clanged on stone. 'Why shouldn't I anyway?'

'No reason at all.' *Chip off the old block*, I heard him think. But he stopped digging all of a sudden and fell to his knees at the rim of his end of the hole. 'What's that?' There was queasy trepidation in his voice.

'It looks like – a bone.'

Setting the tea-tray down on the lawn, my father knelt beside his brother, leaning forward as if they were praying in unison to something fearful down there in the pit. 'A dog's bone, I should think,' he offered. 'No, don't. Don't go down,' he warned me, lunging with his arm, unsuccessfully.

'It's a person,' I said, from the pit. Someone had got there first, into my mother's place.

The police came. The pathologist. Finally a team of archaeologists from Manchester University. Now my grave-digging activities were suspended, for exhumation would take time: patient daily brushing and sifting of dirt from bone. It seemed the bones might be ancient, and a valuable find. We could have gone ahead and buried my mother in another part of the garden but my father was superstitious about defying her authority. She had specified that spot, and he would not rest until she could rest.

Glazed, glacial, I prowled the team, observing their methods and studying their revelation. Someone was being delivered from an interment of – who knew how many centuries? So far we had the right hand and arm, part of the crushed ribcage and the twiggy collarbone. At night I'd go down and skulk around the shelter they had left to protect the skeleton. I'd burrow my own hand into the garden soil, as if to wash it in origins and rehearse a final undoing. I felt as if part of myself were being unearthed. And lay at night churning with the awareness that the green world I'd thought so vital was a surface skinning over rafters of bone, soft tissue rich with generations of flesh. Everywhere I was, somebody else had been; and furnished a meal for worms and maggots. They and we, we and they, went through and through one another. Down there, in those communal depths, who was who?

Beneath our house lay other houses, a dark sea in which the ashes of long dead fires sank, with smashed cooking pots, coins and all the people, plants and animals that had ever lived. The sea slapped against the foundations of my mind, like bilge beneath a pier.

I'd ridden my trike over that sleeping head; built Lego castles and stamped in a tantrum. Not knowing. I should have stepped tiptoe over ground at once sacred and terrible.

'Is it a man or a woman?' I asked the archaeologist with the pony tail.

'Hard to say just yet. I'd guess – a woman.'

He worked away with his brush, eyes screwed up. The fingers of her right hand were clarifying, little by little. I squatted down beside him, as he coaxed the details out with whispering motions of the brush. After a while, the horror began to ebb; it was replaced by curiosity and interest, an impulse at once scientific and quiveringly personal. The tacit hand spoke to my eye. Its lattice of bones lay in the curious gesture of one who is on the point of speaking, fingerbones apart, thumb somewhat raised; or in an attitude of what I now recognise as blessing. Crouching, I held out my own hand, elbow crooked, and looked from one to the other. The dead hand was smaller than mine, childishly small. Its complex architecture arrested me, the rhythm of bones that had sloughed the dress of superficial matter and lay in emergent nakedness so that I could ponder the fact, to me astonishing, that what she was, inwardly so was I.

'Could I have a go?' I asked the archaeologist.

He sighed patiently and, straightening up, passed across the brush. 'Go on then. Very delicately. We don't want to disturb or dislodge anything.'

I dabbed at the forefinger, tongue between my lips. A little dry clay fell away. As I worked, the relationship between my living hand sifting off the dirt and the shed life I worked to disclose absorbed me. I was diverted from the shock of mother-loss to the mystery of underlying and intrinsic shapes. I had often pondered the spiral forms of empty snail-shells in our garden with a similar forensic admiration.

'My mother's going down there – when she's gone,' I informed him.

He swivelled, jarred at my straightforwardness.

'Oh dear. I'm really so sorry,' he said. His hair and face were dust-tawny, as if he had family links with the world below.

'No, it's all right. She doesn't think she's dead,' I told him. 'She doesn't believe in it. We're to plant a cherry tree on her head.'

'That'll be nice,' he faltered. 'Lovely blossom.'

✳

It was a woman. And beside her was interred a strange helmet. None of the team had ever seen anything like it before. We were an overnight sensation: *Who is Cheadle Hulme mystery woman?* was splashed over the front page of the *Stockport Advertiser*, beside a picture of a skull and a cage-like structure. It was as if they expected someone to come forward to identify her. There was a smaller photo of the site of excavation in our garden, with myself posing in front of the archaeological team. There I stand, grave and stern, assuming my mother's characteristic expression of detached introspection, to disguise my inner world of moody confusion. It was the first time the face of the dead woman and my own were aligned.

Experts arrived from Oxford and London. They looked hungry as hounds. An American, a cultured and soft-spoken woman in her mid-thirties, blurted as soon as she saw our lady (in case someone should get there first): 'I know what that is. I'm afraid you'll be disappointed with her age,' she told the pony-tailed professor. He had wanted an Iron Age date. 'Sixteenth, seventeenth century at the earliest. But, look, unless I'm much mistaken, her neck is broken.'

'It would be, with that thing on her head. Must weigh a stone.'

'At least. But that wasn't what broke her neck.'

'What then?'

'My guess is, she was hanged. Wearing the brank.'

The newspapers were doubly delighted: with the hanging and the scold's bridle. *Witch unearthed in Cheadle Hulme garden*, ran another headline.

I crouched with the others, staring at the face and the rusted iron cage. Her poor jaw had been shattered by the bridle, and, where the spiked metal bit had been locked into her mouth, her teeth had smashed.

'On that hoop,' said the Washington woman, brushing off crumbs of dirt, 'they'd attach a rope – rotted off now, of course, to lead her round the village. Ride her, you see, like an untamed mare. It's a wonderful find,' she said, enthralled. 'I don't think many of these scold's bridles have survived. It will be interesting to see what kind of bit we've got here. Flat, turned down, spiked. Two, three inches long?'

'Her poor tongue,' I said, and the tears came.

'Oh, that was the idea,' returned the professor with biting sharpness. 'Shut her up for good.'

The evening before they took the silent woman out of the earth, laying her out on a stretcher, I seized the opportunity to be alone with her. Sporadic squalls of wind made the plastic shelter billow and subside, deflating in slow gasps as I sat in the inner twilight, shining my torch on the face – would you call it a face, I wondered? – of the person from the underworld.

No, I thought, it's not a face.

My mother was said to have had 'high cheekbones', a sign of beauty as my father used to say. I had the idea that the bones were the deepest secret of a face, the mysterious foundation, dictating all that one could read on its surface.

But the skull itself could not be read. I shone my torch like a searchlight into the sockets where the eyes had been, and saw right through to the shattered back of her cranium. By this time I had become so accustomed to the 'find', as the archaeologists called her, that I felt, if any prickle of fear, only the safe frisson you experience when gripped by an exceptionally powerful book. There was little of the ghoulish left in my fascination, which belonged to an intrigued reverence for the stillness and repose of the being who lay beneath my gaze, a cryptic sketch rather than a portrait.

My torchlight filled her eye-sockets one by one with luminosity, casting a glow that lit her interior with a strange beauty, so that the bone became transparent and the interstices seemed limned in light.

The space where her mouth had been did not, I was interested to note, grin as skulls were fabled to do. Only the poor smashed teeth and skewed jaw reminded me of the human agonies these bones had outlasted. I knelt in my pyjamas and dressing gown, sweeping my torchlight slowly up and down the calm remains. The ruined cathedral of the ribcage. The disjointed but aligned tibia and fibula. The slack jaw's soundless cry.

A squall sprang up and buffeted the tent, which belled and seemed to draw breath, sucking in a cold gust which invaded our interior space. It made me shiver and affected me like a ripple of sudden anxiety. Childishly I fancied the corpse sensitive to cold in her exposure, the fleshless rafters of bone open within and without to the rush of air. A queasy sense of indecency, of dishonour to the exhumed dead, dragged out piecemeal from the mothering earth, afflicted me at the same time, though I could not have given a name to it. With a gesture of fellow-feeling, I shrugged off my green towelling dressing gown and laid it gently down over the bones, mantling them until morning.

They came for her early, in a van. Alexander Sagarra was with them, the medical artist, shortly to become world-famous for his reconstructions of ancient figures. I remember him as absurdly boyish, with shoulder-length fair hair, a dark tan and very white, milky-looking teeth. He could have been a sixth-form prodigy, and it was hard to recognise in him the distinguished artist-cum-scientist whose name we had vaguely heard.

'We might just try to model her sometime, what do you think?' I heard him propose to my father, who feigned polite interest. Dad's heartfelt desire was to rid our household of skeletons, morbid preoccupation, archaeologists needing cups of tea. His need was to lay to rest a dear but overwhelming wife, whose peace-principles had in life elicited an unease equalled only by her posthumous ability to turn the very earth inside-out.

Alex wandered into our house, making himself at home, his good nature infecting even my troubled self. He browsed the stoneware pots that thronged the house, my maternal grandparents' handiwork, for both of them had been professional potters. 'Seriously good stuff,' said Alex. His hands cherished the glazed sides of my favourite jug, a great-bellied vessel whose colour wavers between auburn and ochre, depending on the light. 'Well, I'll be off. We'll see about a model, shall we?'

'In due course,' said Dad. He put a loving, relieved arm round my shoulders and squeezed, as we watched the van disappear in the direction of Cheadle Road.

'Are you OK, Olivia? I mean from all that bizarre...I mean, we should forget all that...unhealthy stuff.'

I nodded and seemed to acquiesce. I took a can of beer out of the fridge and broke the seal, taking a swig and handing it to him with a smile. For she was private to me, the companion of my most secret thoughts. I did not want him to know of this other world, in which she lay under my green cloak, in pure repose through the long night.

∗

We replaced her with my silent mother, filled the hole in and planted the young tree on the mound. No words were said over her: but the still earth declared her presence whenever I opened my curtains in the morning, and the cherry tree seemed to suck virtue from her chemistry.

Two

I became quiet, bookish, numb. Like a spectre at his fireside, I haunted my father with a frozen speechlessness that denied response to any overtures from a world newly rendered permissive. For, after a decent interval and a due allowance of regret, he throve. He simply couldn't help it. It was impossible to avoid noticing that my mother's removal afforded him freedom to revert to type. Genial and generous, he liked to enjoy material things. He was a man made for physical enjoyment, who had fallen headlong for his opposite in my mother. Her passion was reserved for the holding of candles at anti-war vigils, or at Greenham, where she had gazed unblinkingly into the eyes of the American military, through the wire netting.

He had respected that, but fundamentally I suspect her state of permanent protest and witness embarrassed him. Not that she had ever criticised his commitment to the things of this earth: *We should enjoy the world and each other*, she'd say. *That's what it was given us for.* Somehow, when innocent hedonism became a matter of principle and duty, it lost its relish for my sybaritic, slothful father.

A fortnight after we had got the burial over, sad though he genuinely was, he suggested we take out the yacht for a sail.

'Or wind-surfing,' he said, 'it's grand at the water park. Do you fancy a ramble in the Goyt Valley? Tennis? How about a swim at Cheadle Baths?'

I shook my head, scarcely raising my eyes from my book. 'You go,' I mouthed.

'Oh gosh, no,' he said, hunkering down by my chair and gently removing the book from my hands. 'I couldn't go on my own. I thought it would be good for us to go out together, love. Just do a few ordinary things, the two of us. I think she would have wanted that...don't you?'

I quietly reached out for the book, in which I had lost myself and forgotten his existence, her death, my pain.

'Look,' I said. 'All I want is to be left alone. You go. OK?'

He went, hangdog.

The next-door neighbour reported when he returned, looking relaxed and smelling of beer, that I'd spent the earlier part of the afternoon lying on the mound, my arms outstretched in what looked like a cross. She'd been worried, she told him. Kept her eye out. Was about to come over when she saw I'd got a book out and was reading.

I scowled. 'I'm not a *child*,' I retorted. 'I can do what I like. I don't have to *sail*.' I deliberately made it sound like a crime.

'I just want you to be...happy.'

'*Happy?*' Another crime.

'No, of course you couldn't be – we couldn't be happy. But...give yourself some ease, Ol.'

'I want to read. What's wrong with that?'

'Oh – nothing. Of course. But one can't read all the time.'

I said nothing. I saw no earthly reason why one couldn't read all the time. It was the only thing I wanted to do.

*

As he blossomed, so did the cherry tree. By the time the petals were falling at the end of the following spring, he had replaced my first mother with a second. A more opulent woman altogether, ample of bosom and hips, less well-endowed with grey matter. She was touchingly eager to please me and spent a great deal of wasted time attempting to coax a morose and boorish teenager out of hiding. The more she tried, the more baleful I became, pretending to have forgotten her name, which was Jean. At first I taunted and tormented her by addressing her by a range of different names, whatever came to mind, tacking the name on to the end of my malicious and chiefly monosyllabic replies. Later, I simply called her by no name at all. After all, the usurper could have been anyone. It cut my father to the quick. His pleasure in Jean, so bonny and uncomplicated, was contaminated by the guilt I wished on him. No doubt they could both have done with a break from my ungracious, and occasionally vicious, presence.

The poor man looked hexed. He and Jean must have felt that they were victims of the evil eye. For although I had brushed aside his well-meant offers of comradeship, it had mattered that he offered and needed it. I might with time have relaxed into a life of companionable chat and outings, good food and enjoyment of the present moment. Instead I made it my business to sabotage his skin-deep pleasures, hoping to get her evicted.

However, my father could not conceal his sensual delight. His gratification seemed to swathe the house in garish concupiscence, like fluorescent light. The oranges in the bowl on the sideboard glowed as if irradiated; the acid-yellow of the lemons bit the eye. Simple objects penetrated me with unheard-of edges and extensions.

Oh God, she rasped gratingly from my mother's half of the bed, *Oh God*.

He could do that for a woman at last; he could give her that. He bounced from room to room, ecstatic, as if he'd acquired those new trainers with the air-filled soles. He could make a woman's voice abandon control; sate and beach her on the shore of his desire. He looked younger; their mouths appeared swollen in the mornings and her chin, lips and cheeks raw and scraped by his bristly kisses. I studied their red faces with loathing.

I refused to speak to Jean after these nocturnal episodes. I refrained from looking her in the eyes and was deaf to her nervously cooing blandishments.

Jean was a wonderful cook: even to my jaded nostrils, the breakfast pancakes smelt golden, oozing with syrup. We had never been offered such food. Loyalty forbade me to share it.

'Aren't you hungry, angel? Do try them. My son Will' (she'd been married before) 'adored these. Just a weeny bite. Do.'

'Tell her,' I said to my father, 'I'll make do with the funeral baked meats.'

'Uh?'

'Nothing.'

'I didn't catch...?'

'There was nothing to catch,' I muttered. I watched their dance of courtship and envied their passion, even in the midst of my soul-sickened contempt. They were disgustingly old. How was it they seemed so much younger than myself? Only the past was real to me, and called: yet my focus was blurred, as if I had not yet selected the right optical lens, and its voices were a mutant form of the silence I entered like a house within a house, shutting my door on the fullness of their satisfaction.

✳

Six foot deep in the earth, my mother decayed. Her dear eyes melted into jelly and the beautiful, tapering hands became slime. Her mind was eaten by creatures, from bacteria to gross albino maggots consummating their harvest.

I awoke, bellowing 'My *mother!*'

It would be necessary to stamp the earth down over her or she'd burst up forever, appalling me with the vile matter she'd become.

There's no forgetting. There's only replacement.

But how do you replace the one-and-only? The only face you crave to see has been erased. I literally looked round for her every stillborn day: under the Anglepoise in her study, blondish wisps of hair straying on her forehead, pen-in-hand. I wanted to ask her now how I should go about navigating this vast ocean of her absence. How?

A year passed. I was sixteen. If I went to her now, I'd find a skull pouring out its contents in the generosity of endless recyclement. If I wished to love her now, I'd have to love her in earth and air, trees, rivers, birds and creeping things, and in my fellow men – a love as vast and impersonal as hers, which I was as reluctant as I was impotent to yield.

At Meeting, they were kindness itself. There we sat, in the silence which was God-in-us, eleven middle-aged and elderly Friends and two young persons. We were a remnant of families some of whom could trace their descent from the earliest Hesketh Quakers. An air of restraint and respectability prevailed; our inspirations matched our clothing, shabby-genteel and orderly.

I was surrounded by sympathy and understanding. Mute, I sat and sifted through the layers of silence for the Light.

The Light snapped on. It shone in the darkness. It burned at my furnace-heart with roaring like an incinerator and spoke in words that forked at these gentle people with lightning malice:

'There is no God. Nothing. Or if there is, he's evil. Your God is a lie.'

＊

Of the wedding-day I shall not speak.

What gave my father's wife the odd idea that somehow she'd also married me and acquired a licence to take my life into her control?

One of the first things she pointed out as we sat *en famille* round the table was that of my sexuality. Linked to this, my cropped head. My mannish gait. The absence of a single skirt or dress in my wardrobe, which had apparently been exhaustively examined.

My settled air of aggressive misery.

My tallness.

My stunted speech-acts, grunting or keeping silent.

My lack of friends and my mania for reading.

These topics were introduced in a light-hearted way, but with a serious agenda. Was it possible, Jean seemed to speculate, that I could be melted down, poured into a new mould and remade as a biddable, winning, feminine being?

'So when are we going to see a boyfriend brought home?' she asked coyly. What kind of boys did I like?

'What kind of boys are there?' I asked.

Taking a bite of toast, I rose from the table, ready to escape.

'Goodness, Jack, look at her looming. Doesn't she loom? How tall *are* you now, Olivia?'

'Five foot eight.' I was half way to the door.

'Goodness, I hope she's stopped growing. How will she fit under a man's arm if she gets any taller?'

17

I stopped, fascinated, despite myself. 'Why would I want to do that?'

'Why would you...?' she laughed. Her pretty blue eyes twinkled in the plump face. 'Well, men do like you to be petite, of course. But don't worry, I'll show you how to disguise your height.' She was able to pass on various cunning knee-bending postures which would cut off excess inches and permit me to nestle, as custom required. Failing that, she advised me to sit with the man rather than stand; and always wear flat shoes.

There was no man. In a flash of inspiration, it dawned that there would never be a man. Consequently no need to acquire nestling skills. The relief of it. Standing to my full height, I towered exultantly; but also with the vertiginous sense of a cliff-edge at my feet.

Leaving, I loitered at the door.

'I worry about her hair, you know, Jack,' she confided.

'Isn't that the style?' he enquired vaguely.

'I'm sure she could have really pretty hair if she bothered with it. It's a lovely red-chestnut colour. And, in general, her slovenliness. When I saw her in the street yesterday, I thought before I recognised her, she was a lad. Truly. You don't think she's a...?'

'Gay?' He hooted. 'Surely not. I think she's just one of the modern generation, sort-of unisex, and of course she's still grieving...it takes a while. Give her time.'

'A word of motherly advice,' Jean whispered, cornering me at the door. 'You can get terribly good falsies these days, Olivia. Nobody can tell them from real. Made of silicone and you just slip them in your bra; they joggle around nice as anything and nobody knows they're there. Here, just take a look at this.' She slipped me a catalogue for a firm called *Innovations*, which specialised in unnecessary but ingenious gadgets.

Before: a lugubrious female sorrowing over a bosom that had never been.

After: the same female, feline, purring over a pair of colossal inflations.

'We know you are an Intellectual, Olivia. We respect that.

Your father and I are proud of you. But we would like you to develop in all ways.'

'Except upwards.'

'Well, of course, you can't help your height.' She seemed to forgive my preposterous height as an inherited defect shared after all by Princess Diana, who had overcome it by making the best of her other features. But my hair, face and figure were another matter. There was a duty – a sacredly profane duty of improving one's few talents.

'Thanks for the idea about the falsies,' I said. 'I could become a sort of Frankenstein's Barbie doll. I suppose yours are implants then, are they?' And I poked at the spongy protuberances with my index finger. She winced with real pain.

Stepped back, gasping, ethically shocked. 'Certainly not. Mine are the real thing.'

A cluster of bottles and tubes appeared on my desk. I was being supplied by an invisible hand with cosmetics. In painting my face, I would somehow normalise it.

I could not bear to have my mother's photograph on the wall or standing on a shelf. Few likenesses of her survived, since she had more often taken pictures than posed for them; but those that were extant brought a burning ache to my breastbone which I could not easily endure for more than a few days at a time. They convinced me I had lost her rather than reassuring me that she had existed.

Neither could I often bear to look at myself in the mirror. Never vain, now I was, by choice, faceless. For in my own eyes I saw her looking at me, as plain as daylight. I was a living photograph of her. And an immortal reminder of her loss, in solution with my own grief. For my eyes, picturing hers, were puzzled and baffled where her gaze had been serenely certain.

Now I took the clobber of cosmetics into the bathroom and addressed my own image in the glass. I was being asked to put a new face on. Like a mask.

My mother at once appeared in the glass, her piercing eyes raying out through my watery ones. But the longer I stared, the more my anatomising stare seemed to see through the skin, through subcutaneous layers of soft tissue, criss-cross of muscles, to the skull beneath. This was what she was; and what she was, I was.

I powdered the face into lustreless pallor and, daubing the lips violent red, I surrounded the mascara-ed eyes with a charcoal line of eye-shadow. Like the effigy of an Egyptian queen, I stared at myself, my own *memento mori*.

Over my father's wife's lacy and bridal pillow, I poured the vermilion nail-varnish she had purchased with such care, like sacrificial life's-blood, or the hymeneal blood I had not shed. I have no clear memory of their return, to find the bloodied bed; only a muffled hubbub in the next room and my father, ratty and tired, saying, 'Look, woman, just leave her be and she'll let us alone.'

I was jubilant. He called her 'Woman', in that contempt-uous way husbands do when they wish to emphasise that wives are a lower species of whom rationality cannot be expected. I was winning. I foresaw a time when there would be no Jean in our house. Next morning, however, her puffy eyes and inoffensive kindliness of manner threw me off balance; the way she passed me the marmalade without any fuss unnerved me. But I wasn't about to cave in and recognise that she was an ordinary, decent sort of person.

※

Alex Sagarra and his family moved into the Victorian manor house near Bramhall Park. When I bumped into him at Kwiksave, he was loading a trolley with baby food and disposable nappies.

'I noticed you,' he said. 'Wasn't quite sure where I'd seen you before but now I've twigged. You were the person who made the seventeenth-century find in your back garden, aren't you – that lovely old farmhouse with the fabulous pots: are you still living there?'

I preened myself on being thought of as 'the person who made the seventeenth-century find' and beamed gratefully into his eyes.

'Oh yes, we've always been there – my mother's family.'

'We've just moved. Do you know the manor? Not really a manor in the original sense, of course, but a Victorian businessman's dream of grandeur. We've got half and it still feels immense. My wife, Eleanor, lately had our fourth – and we need the space. Come round, I wish you would.'

I helped him load tiny cans of infant food on to the conveyer belt. How could one infant get through all these cans? Alex scarcely looked old enough to have four children. Though his blond hair had now been cropped, he still looked ridiculously boyish.

'What happened ... about the bones?' I asked.

'Your find?' His response endeared him yet further. 'Well, she's been examined by all and sundry and put away in a box, labelled "Hesketh Maiden". I want to get round to having a good look at her myself, actually – but what with one thing and another, it keeps getting put off. Tell you what, I'll ring you when things quieten down and you can watch me try to put a face to her. What's your number?'

We bagged his purchases and I pushed the trolley to the car, from which a baby could be heard screaming and a mother shushing. A toddler was visible, waving his feet in the air on the back seat. I wondered, as we heaved the bags into the boot, when he expected things to quieten down.

'Really,' he said, fastening the boot-door, 'I can't thank you enough.'

'What do you mean about putting a face to her?' I asked breathlessly.

'Well, I'm a medical artist,' he explained. 'I make faces. That's my specialism. There are scientific procedures, you see, Olivia, whereby one can reconstruct a face – a real face, not a portrait, from the remains of a skull. A branch of pathology. I've used it with my colleague to useful effect in identifying murder victims: you remember the Hong Kong businessman whose severed head was found smashed in by a meat cleaver back in 1986 – our reconstruction identified him. But – hey, Tom, put your head back in the car this minute, I said, get back in, yes, I'm coming – we also do the Ancient Dead. Look in at the museum some time. There's a waxwork of Rostherne Man, you know, the bog-man. He was actually found not far from here. Eleanor, get him to put his head back in, he'll fall out.'

Cars backed out and inched in around us; bottles clinked

21

as they were posted into the bottlebank, and Alex's young son, yanked in by the legs, squirmed on to the back seat and pressed his nose against the rear window, puffing on the pane and licking with his tongue in bored circles. The child's exertions seemed to deride any ambition on the part of his encumbered father to cater for faces other than those belonging to the living babes he'd called into being.

'What are your plans?' he asked.

'I want to study history.'

'Ancient or modern?'

'Not sure yet. But would you really let me know when you decide to look at our woman? And, when you perform all these . . . processes . . . can you genuinely get a likeness?'

'Sure. Yes, really, far-fetched as it must seem. When we reconstruct your Maiden,' (he had said *when*, not *if*), 'I guarantee we'll get a likeness her own mother would have recognised.'

'You're on safe ground there,' I observed. 'Her mum not being around to be consulted.'

He laughed. 'We've done blind trials of living people: the results are eery. Look, I'd best be off. Eleanor'll be getting pissed off waiting. Come round and see our unstately home. We've got a load of heads I've done scattered around, Eleanor used to find it quite spooky but now they're old friends. All *right*, Tom.'

As I cycled away, a dreamy remembrance arose of the time we raised my woman from the earth, not so much the process as my evening of vigil, in which I had sat with the bones of the woman, all on my own, our own. The bridle had not been there, I realised. They'd taken it away to catalogue and exhibit somewhere. Her poor tongue. I dismounted at the corner by the dentist's, the customary flashback of fear causing me to patrol with my own tongue the soft interior of my mouth. I winced at the mere thought of the drill. There were so many nerve-endings in there, so much tender flesh with the power to be hurt. I remembered the skull's shattered teeth and her unholy pain seemed to gush into the cavity of my mouth.

Who was she and what had she done to invite such

barbarous usage? Why had she been buried at Pinfold, in unconsecrated ground? Quakers, I knew, were often buried in unmarked spots in their own gardens, but this woman had presumably been condemned as a witch. *Her poor tongue*, I thought again. My own seemed, as I explored my teeth with its tip, swollen, and there was a mouth-ulcer coming on my gum. Probably she had been one of those women who are constantly ill-wishing others, a mass of grudges and spite. I judged from my own infirmities.

✳

Jean's charms gradually seemed to pall on my father, or so she complained, and I did my best to reinforce her fears. Perhaps she had whetted an appetite she, at her age, could not hope to allay, I suggested. Dad undertook a fitness regime, perhaps to escape the bilious atmosphere of the household, and made regular visits to the gym, where he did punishing workouts, played squash, soaked up a tan on the sunbed and canoodled (I suggested to Jean) with female fitness fanatics, of which it appeared there was a limitless supply in Cheadle and Gatley.

Dense as she was on many subjects, Jean rose to the bait. She'd mortify herself by lying in wait at the pool, and ringing up any phone numbers she could detect in his pockets. The fact that these investigations never yielded any fruit could not allay her suspicions. She began to comfort-eat on chips and chocolate, and, forgetting her campaign to bring me within the range of normality, attempted to enlist my support in routing her husband's manoeuvres. I shed no hypocritical tears for her but quoted the bible to the effect that as ye sow, so shall ye reap.

My father, who remained guiltily grateful for release from years of austerity, shrugged off her complaints as the whimsy of a menopausal female and did his best to give her the slip, for her whinging, as he complained to Dan, gave him the pip. He looked for means to enjoy weekends away from the bosom of his family. He joined the National Trust, a fencing group, and the local branch of a group still existing which called itself 'The Sealed Knot'. Based in Preston, the club is a royalist society which annually re-enacts the battles of the Civil War. My cousin Michael had long been a passionate member of this dotty institution, fighting, as they all wanted to, on the side of Good King Charles.

'I'll be away next weekend,' he told Jean. 'The Knot is fighting the Battle of Naseby.'

'But Jack, do you have to go?' she asked, woebegone.

'Well, no, I don't absolutely have to but Michael asked me to come along, and it will be an experience,' he said.

'But I thought we could have a nice cosy time at home?' she whined. He looked depressed.

'We can have a nice cosy time any weekend, can't we?'

'You shouldn't inhibit men wanting to play their infantile games,' I informed my stepmother. 'They're testosterone-crazed and if they don't do one thing, they'll do another. It's in their genes, they can't help it.'

'What do you mean, do another?' she asked, exasperated. Jean never cottoned on to how her whining exponentially increased my father's urge to bolt.

'Well, football hooliganism or womanising,' I said. 'They're programmed to go haywire. It's to do with evolution, you see. They have to attack as many males and deposit their sperm into as many containers as possible, to put it crudely. For the strength of the race. Natural selection, survival of the fittest. Even the most civilised of them ... I mean, look at Mozart.'

'Mozart?'

'Randy as hell.'

'Oh,' she said, pained. 'Not Mozart too.'

'Don't take any notice, Jeannie love,' said my father and leant over her from behind the chair, engulfing her in a hug. 'She's a mischief maker. Hormone-crazed adolescent. You don't really begrudge me a weekend away, do you? You know there's no one in the world for me but you?'

Her watery eyes smiled. She let him cuddle her into acquiescence.

Michael and my father pageanted about in the garden in their royalist togs. The neighbours at their bedroom windows craned at the two gallants with long curly wigs, floppy hats with plumes, scarlet coats and flounces of lace. They stood by the fish-pond and conversed in a cinematic version of seventeenth-century dialect, theeing and thouing indiscriminately.

'Hast thou the time, fair Pimpernel?' asked Michael. 'I hath no watch yet as it hath not been invented.' He executed a flourishing bow.

'It hath been invented, actually,' I said. 'Lots of people had watches in the mid-century.'

'Did they now?'

'Isn't she useful?' said my father, fiddling with the oiled ends of his specially grown pencil moustache. I had secured a place to read History at New College, Oxford, and was venerated as a mine of information on odd details of interest to the two Cavaliers, constantly appealed to on matters of authenticity. Michael, now swaggering around drawing and sheathing his sword, was, when not engaged in archaic activities, a shaven-headed engineer, who I had always considered a bit of a lout. In his dark, curly wig, his face was transformed to an arresting beauty.

'Is that real hair?' I asked curiously.

'Shouldn't think so.'

'The periwig-makers used to cut the hair off corpses, did you know that, to make the wigs? And they were all full of nits.'

'It is a bit itchy in here. Why don't you come along, Olivia? It'll be a laugh. And you could fight on the other side. There are never enough Roundheads. Not the glamour in it.'

My father squirmed; shook his head in covert remonstrance behind my silent stepmother's back. He didn't want me along. The next thing he knew she'd be wanting to come as a premature manifestation of Nell Gwynne.

'Yes. Yes, all right,' I said, to spite him. 'I'll be a plain russet-coated captain. I'll come at you singing psalms. It's a boy's game, isn't it? You're all just playing soldiers.'

'Oh no,' said Michael, earnestly. 'Girls can come too. And fight if they like. We don't discriminate.'

'You wouldn't like it. It's not your kind of thing, Ol,' pleaded my father.

'I think she should go,' said Jean. 'After all, she's got the height.'

Mostly it rained. I remained in the camp of the godly with the small band of the elect, while hordes of lecherous fops sheltered in tents with beer and camp-followers, who paraded their cleavages and shouted colourful filth at our pikemen. When we issued on to the field of battle, the rain had turned to drizzle. Moving forward through smoke, explosions and shrieks with my comrades, toward an obscure enemy, a shiver went down my spine. I was scared, despite all the fatuous make-believe. I could get spiked by some idiot getting carried away with himself. How appalling for the men who had fought. To stick this blade into another human being's guts; to blow his head off with this musket: no, I couldn't. Never could. Surely? I shrank, but behind me they were roaring, 'For the Lord God of Israel!' A cause. A true cause. I fired the blank in my musket at the first red coat that came into my ken. I fired; he fell.

Then he got up again and fired; I fell.

As we regrouped, our elderly and infirm General, veteran of the Second World War and a not very persuasive Cromwell lookalike, reminded us that we were fighting not only for peace, justice, etc, and against oppression, tyranny and sex-mad atheists, but to establish the millennium. King Christ rode, he said, at the head of our army, and we'd be the saints who reigned for the next thousand years.

'I thought that was Hitler and the Nazis,' objected the chap next to me.

'They came later,' said Cromwell, patiently. 'They picked up on the same idea. The thousand year *Reich*. No, but we invented it. Out of the bible, do you see. As there aren't very many of us, and some of our number have sloped off to the pub, I am counting on the rest to really show the enemy what's what.'

Yes, I could imagine. The fear the night before; fear that churned in the viscera and turned to diarrhoea, that cabled men together in the solidarity of male bonding and an invincible creed. We were the elect and they the reprobate.

Some, of course, more elect than others. On the second day of battle the women actors were ordered to fight back in the rear, with the result that murmurs of 'Sexism' undercut

Roundhead morale; and several of us deserted.

'So,' said my second mother. 'How was the Battle of Waterloo?'

'Naseby. Ridiculous. Puerile. Regressive.' I felt disgusted with myself for going and playing along. All my childhood, my mother had shown me the power of her quietism; the importance of refusing all violence, even in game. When I came galloping home with the boy-next-door's gun, she physically shivered.

'Do you truly want to play with that?'

I did, actually. I wanted to charge round the block, neighing and popping off the caps. I wanted to take cold-blooded aim from my bedroom window at the pensioner over the way who objected to my ball in his garden, and blast him into hell.

She showed me pictures of Vietnam, Northern Ireland. Split heads, spilt viscera. The mask-like face of the helmeted American soldier, the barrel of his gun against the temple of the Vietnamese civilian. The moment before the world ended for him.

Aggrieved, I flung the toy gun on the ground and sulked off.

'I wasn't going to do anything like *that*. I just wanted to play.'

'Play with it if you want to. Just know what you're playing with.'

She had leeched the fun from it. And she cost me my only childhood friend: playing with boys, I felt more myself than with the doll-brigade. Robbed of my gun, I was a loner.

But then, so was she: with the courage to stand alone, should this be required. Now her face seemed to rise up at the breakfast table in reproach: not visually, but as a remorseful area of silence between the amber jug and the window. She seemed so vital a presence that I felt the room must be brimming with it so that even strangers might sense her there in our midst. I looked over at my stepmother, the quintessential stranger. Took note of her brooding listless-ness as she lit up a cigarette. Had she used to smoke? Her fingers were nicotine-stained and pudgy. Her whole person drooped, heavily. He had made her feel like a queen, perhaps

27

for the first time in her life. Then, with my malicious help, he had apologetically sidled off. Much of the vitality had seeped out of her. And I saw, too late, that the life had been vivid and sweet-tasting, to her, while it lasted. She was, after all, past her prime. It would be much easier for my father in middle age to find and attract women than for her to locate a new mate.

'Did he enjoy it?' she asked me, in a small voice, looking past me through the picture window.

'He was not seen on the battlefield,' I said, and returned to my book.

Every time I spoke, I fully intended to hurt her.

'When is he coming home?'

'Haven't a clue. Didn't see him.'

She had seen herself as his final, destined woman, towards whom his whole history tended. Now she feared she was only one in a possible series of displacements, replacements, in which she had no chance of competing, since she could never renew her novelty. I knew, without looking up, that she was weeping.

'What'll I do?' she sobbed. 'You don't care. You resent me. You never liked me. You came between us.'

'It's always handy to have someone to blame. Never mind, I'm going off to university soon,' I said coldly. 'Then you'll have him all to yourself.'

'I'm sorry,' she sniffled. 'I should have known better than to think you could accept me and I could be a mother to you. Stupid. I know you think I'm a stupid, uneducated woman. I did want to give you... something. Olivia...'

'What?' I didn't raise my head from the book.

'Could you... stop reading for a moment? Look at me?'

Sullenly, I said nothing. Squirmed on my seat. Mumbled.

'You never actually look at me.'

It was true. I didn't. Now, when she's dead, pondering her photograph, I still find it difficult to look her squarely in the eyes. It's too much of a threat to see she's human, and take the pressure of that, the demand it makes. A face is ethical, if you let it be. I preferred her bullying or mithering tongue to her imploring eyes. So, I'm sure, did my father.

28

We were made of the same weak putty, alarmed at the imprint made by the needs and deserts of others.

'What is there to look at?' I asked, unforgivably. And struck my chair out from under me, lurching it backwards as I left the room, book-in-hand.

Three

It was the day before I left for Oxford. My father and I basked in the lees of pale September warmth, with glasses of wine. Jean could be seen through the open casement of the kitchen window, part of her multiplied into irregular diamonds by the glazing, which was the original workmanship of a local crafts-man, crazily botched and prized by ourselves for the charm of its errors. The other half of Jean's figure was clear, its rounded-ness emphasised by a soft velvet tunic of a peculiarly beautiful shade between pink and red. She was frying onions and mush-rooms, and humming to herself: her hand waved a spatula to and fro, as if conducting the sizzling music of the meal. A lozenge of low sunlight evoked the muted brilliance of the red across her breast and shoulder, and one pearl earring swung, tipped with light. She looked the picture of contentment, as well she might, since I had abandoned my campaign and settled for cool toleration; and, so that her cup might run over, I was about to remove myself to a distance of several hundred miles. She would have him to herself; I had seen the two of them drawing closer together as she saw the end of her sentence.

Our mood in the garden was mellow and gentle. In leaving I could cede my tenderness to my father, shot through, as it still was, with streaks of pained contempt. He would be relieved when my eyes could no longer bear witness against his devotion to the here-and-now.

'So – from tomorrow you'll be a student.'

'Yes. But I've always been a student really. So are you, in a way.'

'Not me,' he said. 'I'm just an ordinary fellow. I'm interested, of course, if you tell me things. But it's in one ear and out the other with me.'

'We just study different things,' I said, without elaborating.

'If you say so. You're the intellectual.'

I could not focus it in words he would have grasped. But I saw him exploring the world of the kindled senses, drinking it in through nerve and pore, sampling pleasures in the plainest experiences.

'Well, grass, for instance, you are a student of grass. When I came home from the chemist, there you were flat on your stomach studying the light through the grass.'

He laughed and shook his head. 'I was just loafing around. Fruits of early retirement.' The tissue and texture of common grass or the leaves of beech were absorbingly beautiful to him, seen in early or late light when the sunlight makes the green translucent. When I came upon him that afternoon, he'd been lolling on his stomach in the back garden, humming, adrift in the pleasure of surfaces; then scrambled up embarrassed, as if caught in some act of private intimacy.

'Well, you can hardly call that hard work. I suppose now you'll say I'm a student of wine.' He swirled the drowsy liquid in his glass, holding it up to dissolve the sunlight in its depths.

'Well, yes, your tastebuds are studying it and your eyes are studying the light in it.'

'Must be a cushy life, then, the student's life. Think I should sign up for a course?'

'You don't need to.'

'I'm a natural?'

'Something like that.'

'Ol – thanks.' He leant forward and patted my arm. I had seen it coming and resolved not to blench from the contact. My body-space was the most important thing I could command, and it was only because I was about to extend it that I could relax into fellow-feeling.

'I don't know what for.'

'For...I know it hurt you, my marrying again so soon. And so on.'

31

'You needed to.' I turned my head away: the conversation needed to stop before it soured in undue warmth. 'Anyway, it doesn't matter now. It's all in the past. Look, I know I've been a pain with Jean and so on, but...'

'Olivia...'

'What?'

'I do remember your mother, I do think of her, I do... love...'

Sentimentality I did not need. Let him apologise to her ghost if he felt he needed to or she extorted it. Leave me out of it.

'Leave it, dad. It's all in the past.'

But the past was where I was bound. I did not tell him this.

✻

Whereas his hedonist's paradise was at hand, in the hand, mine lay always just over the hill, deliciously out of sight. I walked forwards facing perversely backwards, eyes straining for vision of the invisible, or cruising the endless terrain of text in the Bodleian. Antiquarian volumes became my passion. Their persons erupted from innards of books as the spines creaked open; and the dead spoke to me, with such vehement voices that when I looked up, my contemporaries seemed blurred and dull.

As my father travelled into the hinterland of my mind, so my mother relinquished hold and withdrew. She troubled me faintly in dreams, at decreasing intervals, a vaporous hand that tapped on the glazed window of awareness with scarcely any impact: a wave that broke as a particle of memory in the microsecond of awakening. But the woman we'd dug down to beneath the earth besieged me in dreams of towering reality. She came up like the shriek fabled of the mandrake root. Assumed her perishable garment of skin, flesh, hair, in a thousand teasing manifestations, exciting in me an untenable variation on the carnality I saw driving my fellow-students towards and into one another.

'God, I need a good shag,' said a fellow-student, rumpling up her short-cropped hair.

A hot quiver in my guts as if an arrow lodged there: I physically stepped back. She laughed; there was obviously a small buzz in shocking a creature anaesthetised from the waist down.

A *damn good shag*.

My mother would have carefully pointed out that this was men's language for sex; exploitative, therefore hurtful to women, who could rise to something better. Sex, she had explained to me, was a language. Not a thing to be had for itself. You didn't score, get laid, have a damn good shag.

The shag-girl was being helped to egg and bacon at the common table. I said nothing, turned away with my vegan plate. They all wanted a good shag. I wanted more. It was knowledge I craved.

Carnal knowledge: I understood that biblical use of the verb *to know*. Yes, the dry bones lived, in my mind, as if I could re-conceive and deliver her into a new lease of life.

I rang the curator at the Manchester Museum. The Hesketh Maiden's body still lay unexamined in a cardboard box, where I knew they'd dated her remains to the mid-seventeenth century. Alex had never got round to modelling her head and the museum continued to hang on to her, postponing analysis and re-interment until certain Egyptian Pharaohs and Macedonian luminaries had been investigated: after all, in the great sweep of archaeological time, my *entfernte Geliebte* was young and insignificant.

Except to myself. While I walked through the honey-warm antiquity of the Oxford streets, as if I owned them, the latest in an immense line of callow juveniles swanning along in privileged emulation of the gentry style, I fed more richly on the past than on quail and trout by candle-light, in the wood-panelled and raftered hall. Seated at a trestle where thousands of us had clustered, communed and dissolved away over seven hundred years, I'd lean back suddenly silent in the hubbub of young voices and squint into shadowy depths from which portraits of the ironic dead mocked us as transients. Somewhere, over there, out there, phantasmal selves sauntered. Dead eminences, old lost causes, vagrant persons as aberrant and untimely as myself, tongue-tied amid loose tongues that occasionally paused to request me to pass salt or sauce.

In this atmosphere of all-pervasive past, the Hesketh Maiden could seem neither archaic nor a mismate. I started secret burrowings for the writings of women in the mid-seventeenth century, which allured me with the kind of thrill most people of twenty keep for sexual discovery.

Woe upon thee, town of Oxford, wrote an incendiary Quaker, Esther Bradshaw, in a fiery pamphlet existing in only one copy, or rather half a copy, for it had been ripped in two and binned, and only the opening portion rescued.

Woe upon thee town of scoffers and whoremasters, I the LORD
GOD warn thee thy DAY *approaches, when the daughters of*
Lancashire shall tread thee under their feet. We came to thee,
my dear friend Sarah Hough and Esther Bradshaw, to tell
thee TRUTH, *& the ruffians of Sidney Sussex College stripped*
us and laughing thrust us under the pump with violent ill-
usage. And know, O depraved young men, you have abused
the LORDS APOSTLES *that had tenderness to you to come south*
many miles, from the LORDS WITNESS *that is in Manchester*
Hannah Emanuel & the spirits there, the Seed, but remember
the WRATH

I copied the message with a tremulous hand: here was a voice from my natal place, witnessing to a period of history from which I felt like an exile. Esther seemed unaccountably like kin. In the ironic light of retrospect, I am wryly amused that I battened on the wrong name to espouse. Esther's name glowed centrally in my consciousness, while the Hannah named just above the callous rip that rubbished the page, and whose surname endured part of that tear, was just another secondary character.

I hadn't world enough and time to devour my fill of the Revolution, the Interregnum, the Restoration. This was neither curiosity nor conscientious dedication to study: it was the ferocity of passion, secret and intimate. The Hesketh Maiden led me to my chosen profession as historian, and to what I feared as madness. They had silenced her, I now hypothesised, for political reasons. She had been a threat of some kind; no mere rustic scold bad-mouthing her neighbours, against whom the community bore a grudge, but a threat to order and hierarchy. I thought of her now as 'Esther Bradshaw': why not? Local name, Manchester origin, advertising herself as the 'LORDS APOSTLE'. Radical women, I found out, were roving the area tearing up bibles, claiming to be pregnant with the Messiah, announcing the millennium, prophesying, attacking clergy and magistrates. Now that I had a name for my ghost, she devoured my consciousness with questions. I'd awaken exhausted in the morning, as though the night had been spent wrestling with demons.

I learned that, as you can travel light, so you can live light. I ate sparingly: my bony ribcage would have indicated to any moderately competent doctor the presence of an eating problem. But I remained outwardly healthy. Inwardly, the rich feasts of vision that accompanied starvation rations and sensory deprivation afforded compensation for an avoided life.

When the voices began to speak to me, I was unsurprised. They leapt out of books with rhythms that were there on the page for all to read. They often had a northern accent.

'Don't you hear them?' I asked my tutor.

'Hear what?'

'The dead. Speaking. From the pages of books.'

'Oh.' She grinned, with a certain ambivalence. She knew I was a crackpot, but in her experience, the students straining vast-eyed through concave specs, with the obsessed intensity on their faces, were often the brainy ones. She had me down for a First. 'Metaphorically.'

But I believed in them the way others believe in God, and are not psychoanalysed.

*

Since then I've been Jungianised, Freudianised; I've been counselled by a dear little girl with baby-blonde hair and a cute way of saying over and over again, 'I see'; I've been treated to Ordeal by Silence at the hands of a fellow who raked in fifty quid an hour for saying nothing and hearing nothing. My relationships with mother and father have been trawled over. My past has been rendered lacklustre by repeated scrutiny: as I'd had my head in a book from the age of four, there was little but the gleanings of literacy to offer, and this held no interest for them.

'I have been a student of history all my adult life,' I said.

'But history...is the past.'

'No. The bones speak.'

'But surely you know the difference – a woman of your education...you've three degrees...between Reality and what you read in books.'

'"I can call spirits from the vasty deep...",' I informed the quack.

'Ah! Can you indeed? You do hear voices then?' He steepled his fingers and looked at me over the spire. His pen-hand seemed itching to pick up the Parker on his desk and write out a prescription for Venlaxafin.

'Quoting Shakespeare,' I said.

'Lost on me,' he smirked.

'Quite.'

'Sorry?'

'Are you?'

'Do go on.'

'Well, it's a quotation from *Henry IV*. It's made by a wild Welshman, Owen Glendower.'

'Yes?'

'And answered by Harry Hotspur: "Ay, so can I, and so can any man./ But will they come when you do call to them?" I thought you might recognise it. Voice of reason. Scepticism. You want to label me schizophrenic or something – you think I hear voices that you call Not Real.'

'And?'

'I don't.'

'So your voices are real?'

'Yes. Totally.'

'And you hear them through reading books?'

'No – not hear. I *am* there, in that world, when I read.'

'In imagination?'

'*No*. There. Truly there.'

'So...' The steeple gradually opened out, revealing the pudgy palm of a well-fed hand. 'You experience visions.'

'No. I don't have *visions*,' I flared. It is a word I abominate.

36

'Tony Blair has *visions*. Ezekiel had *visions*. I just see what's there. Books have been my life – as they have been yours.'

I refuse to be overawed by this elite, costly man in sleek middle age, his hair combed from a side parting and creamed to his head. I strive to equalise us by pointing out that his professional identity was born from between paper covers just as my supposedly pathological one was. I fear that he reads me; runs his eyes over my surface and anatomises what's within. And to his public school suavety I return the brittle arrogance of an educated grammar.

'Are you happy with your...experiences?'

'Is one happy with life? It just is.'

'So why, may I ask, are you here?'

'It's people...'

'I have noticed one thing. Since you have been in this room, you have never once looked me in the eye.'

*

The hard thing: human faces.

I first recognised my trouble when I went to the Rembrandt exhibition in the National Gallery. By this time I had my Research Fellowship in the History Department at Manchester and was living in my old family home, my father and Jean having retired to the lodge of a Brittany château.

I'd got my father to sign Pinfold over to me.

'The house is my maternal inheritance,' I told him brusquely.

'Well, of course, and I've willed it to you.' He was surprised at my uncharacteristic cupidity and perhaps ruffled by my ability to contemplate his decease and its financial consequences. 'You'll get it in due course, never fear.'

'That's not good enough. It should be mine now.'

'Olivia.'

'Sorry, but that's the way it is. If that woman gets her hands on it, I'll have been dispossessed. Look at the way she's travestied it already.' I'd returned to rose-pink walls, and fake warming pans hanging picturesquely at either side of the great fireplace, which she had blocked up and replaced by a gas fire with coal-effect. But these changes were a mere skin, which could and would be stripped away when she'd been ousted. 'And,' I said, 'my mother's buried out there. My mother. In *my* mother's garden.'

'OK, OK,' he bleated nervously. He turned his back on the window, as if she spied from the camouflage of the mound. 'Whatever you want. I just, well, think you might have a little more trust. And couldn't you even bring yourself to call the poor woman by her name? Look at her when she speaks to you? Such a small concession on your part would mean so much to her.'

'I'll see,' I said. 'When the deeds for Pinfold are in my hands.'

Pinfold was mine.

'Goodbye, Jean. Be happy. Thanks for putting up with me,' I muttered, suffering her beseeching kiss, rubbing the spot in case she'd left a lipstick-print. Pinfold was mine. I grinned at her, meeting her gaze as she clambered into the taxi, her slip showing as she tucked in her legs. *'Bon voyage,'* I yelled. And, 'Don't come back!' I added, as the taxi pulled out from the kerb and I tossed the keys of Pinfold high in the air and snatched them with a yelp of triumph. Threw the bolt over my fastness.

But wherever you are, human eyes home in on you. Travelling to London by train, I held up my newspaper against the threatening closeness of my own kind.

·The young woman opposite was yacking into her mobile. It seemed she was the buyer for a fashion department of a Manchester store and must keep a staff of minions informed of her constantly unfolding thoughts on colours and textures of crucial fabrics. She looked about eighteen, a bottle-blonde doll, who brought to mind the phrase *painted idol*, much favoured by one of the quainter members of Hesketh Meeting. I was haunted by mannequins sashaying down catwalks in midnight blue blouses. Blouses that altered with each new inspiration that darted into the mind of the buyer; inspirations that became dispensations as soon as the tongue delivered them to the waiting world.

Bodices, swags, scooped necklines, boob-tubes. Whoops, coming into Watford.

Catching my stare, she delivered me a look of calm appraisal. Her eyes took in an unmade-up face, spiky hair, a fraying Oxfam jersey. *Bull-dyke*, signalled her gaze.

Bull-dyke? My antennae caught the phrase that flashed in the air between us. With a sharp intake of breath, I averted my face to the window. Was that it?

I was a woman of Sparta, I told myself, lean and muscular; scholar and thinker, belonging to a higher culture. I accounted myself a citizen of another world. My alienation billowed like a tainted and tainting substance that smeared the faces of the friendly but garrulous woman over the way; the larking lads, blowing up a crisp bag; the chap with the laptop and a beercan. I saw them through the brew of my own corruption and fear, as people with whom I could have nothing in common. I was not the freak: they were. It was a relief to disembark, beat the long-striding businessmen to the Euston forecourt; then vanish into the back of a taxi whose driver did me the kindness of abstaining from conversation.

At the Rembrandt exhibition, the pictures had been hung in a gallery too small to contain both them and us. I resented the press of eager viewers whose heads bobbed into view just as you had stationed yourself in front of one of the great portraits.

The quietness of Rembrandt's faces impressed. Layer upon layer of varnished paint built those faces, pale and concentrated in the brown obscurity that surrounded them; their inwardness was expressed by a paintbrush that thought on the canvas, and respected each one in his or her own private truth. External beauty or harmony of features was not the important thing. For these were studies of ordinary people, often elderly persons whose faces were bunched and wrinkled, their hands gnarled. In the light of his looking, Rembrandt had brought forth the inner light assigned by Dutch Protestantism to each one. Isolated on the canvas each person was reverenced.

The gallery seemed to writhe as we strove for space. Several languages commended the dead Dutchman. As I moved in the squeeze from a portrait of Rembrandt's son, Titus, to the gripping face of an aged woman, in a gauzy ruff so delicate you felt you could reach out and touch it, I was rammed from behind by someone's elbow.

I felt quite desperate. Angry and cheated. Here was all this beauty, and here was the human race blocking it out. They shouldn't issue so many tickets. It was a bloody disgrace.

Imagine being here alone, completely alone, the room silent, with nobody but yourself to experience this once-in-a-lifetime vision.

A gap cleared: I entered it. For a while, I had my body-space and could half forget the mass of shouldering, avid folk. There she existed, the unknown woman, the artist's light reverencing her inner light.

Then the transient miracle happened: with a sigh I turned, and saw what I had been missing all the while. We were all part of the picture. Each eye-witness of the exhibition appear-ed to me now as an individual, bathed in the clarity of the painterly vision. Not a mindless crowd of supernumeraries but each a living person, stilled to gaze at a portrait; each an individual who might easily have modelled for Rembrandt.

As I made my calmed way around, the faces both of watchers and watched, flesh and paint, solicited the same attention. We had all been painted by Rembrandt; all were seen in an austerely forgiving light. I walked out into the street, testing my newly awakened eyesight on everyone I met. I knew it was mortal and perishable but how long would it last? I could eke and cherish it, like a candle. The blare of traffic in Trafalgar Square invaded but failed to destroy my apprehension of the inner light of each face I met; yet perhaps it was becoming frailer under the strain. I placed a hand around the flame. The ability to see with the empathy of those eyes was lessening as I joined the crowd sucked into the underground at Charing Cross.

It must have been in the fluorescence of the Manchester Pullman that faces eventually lost their tempered quiet. A garish light, confiding no shadows, threw over their features a livid pallor that exposed all and did justice to none. The hostile light discharged itself upon us in a modernistic art-form, ironic, edgy and disorderly.

But I had seen not only with my external eyes: with the eyes of the spirit. Turning in the gallery from the portrait of the elderly woman, I had understood how to look into the eyes of another person need not require very much courage at all.

✳

Is it possible to grow the courage to love, like cress in the jamjars we brought home from school and tended daily with the solemn-eyed diligence of childhood, little comprehending that the pillulous black seeds would have thriven with or without our supervision?

How, at twenty-six, could I have felt at the end of my life, a vestige of a remnant, to whom the marrying and giving-in-marriage of my contemporaries was as alien as if I had skipped two generations and was living on long after my time?

I can't answer. I hadn't the courage to love one single person in the way first my mother and now the painter had taught me to love; let alone the sea of faces floating by me as I stepped from the train at Oxford Road. How did I know I was even there at all? At times, eyes looked through me as if to read a notice on the wall behind. Head-down, I walked in camouflage down the station steps, past the beggar and his dog in the drizzling rain. I locked the door behind me when I arrived in the department and began to read and make notes before taking off my coat. My eyes were panes of glass, and she was the imperious face at the window, calling me back where I belonged.

Undress, she said, *undress. Lie down with me.*

✳

My students no doubt considered me the weirdest of the weird. From babbling in the corridor outside my room, they passed to queasy silence when I admitted them. To their shyness, I replied with my own taciturnity.

Shifting in their seats, they slewed their eyes and maybe winked as I sorted books and papers on the desk. I scared them with my cold dedication to the work in hand; my contempt for their casualness. But my students weren't casual: they didn't dare to be.

41

When they first arrived, it disconcerted them to be asked to *imagine*. Imagination is a Mickey Mouse talent appropriate to wishy-washy subjects like English and Art. They hadn't come here to imagine, they'd come...for what? To learn dates? To assess the bias of this and that document in order to show that the past is as inscrutable as the present?

Without imagination, I informed them, *you will never be historians*. This heresy was not approved by the department, but as my students, impelled perhaps by sheer panic, tended to be high-achievers, no one had yet denounced my methods.

'So how do you think it felt at the beginning of the Civil Wars in Manchester?'

Silence.

'Scary?' volunteered one young woman. 'You'd be in a Parliamentarian town surrounded by royalists. You'd have nowhere to run to.'

'Yes, but you'd have faith,' said another. 'And anger. They were mostly Puritans. And tradesmen. They'd been suppressed. And taxed. The Lord God of Jacob was their refuge. If you're fighting for your home, you just go all out. It's like Bosnia today.'

'Let's go and see,' I suggested. Fazed looks. Someone peered out of the window as if for clues. A snigger was stifled. 'Yes, we'll catch a bus and go and look for the seventeenth century in Manchester. We've got plenty of time. A two-hour session. You'll easily be back for lunch.'

'Excuse me – go and look for *what*?'

'For vestiges. There are always remains. There's always...litter. Leavings. Traces.'

It wasn't a warm day and nobody shared my proclivity for living with one foot in the grave, but perhaps a stroll down Deansgate, imagining the church-bells tolling backwards that Sunday in 1642 to warn of Strange and his army's advance from Warrington, was preferable to two mortal hours in my study.

As shoppers and office-workers mill around Kendal's, I point out that we have no walls and only one gun, which we position at Deansgate. No walls: so we spent all of yesterday throwing up mud-walls and laying chains to trip the horses at all approaches. No defences: God's arm round Manchester is an invisible barricade, which we will man.

And we've got a handy German engineer, Captain Rosworm. He defends us on Salford Bridge.

Captain Bradshaw holds Deansgate; Captain Radcliffe Market Street.

My students enter into the spirit of the thing with smirking solemnity by agreeing to imagine soldiers charging in and out of the traffic jam at Marks & Spencer's. They note the rain, which emulates God's timely downpour, mocking Strange's attempt to fire our buildings. Sodden timbers; soaked soldiers, with nothing to sustain them. Our men's psalms and prayers are heard rising above the Old Church, and Strange's cannon is no match for that. Battle straggles up and down for a week. Then the attackers, sick of the deluge, hunger, thirst, bog-eyed with sleeplessness, plunge back into the country-side towards Lathom, giving up and clearing off.

Students are referring pointedly to their watches as we reach the end of our war, at Long Millgate: one week of bloody fighting for Parliament, and another nine years acting as Parliament's garrison for the North West. We get an MP. We get the plague and are quarantined; our market closed; dearth and want; rise of Cromwell; beheading of Charles while the country runs with blood like the floor of a butcher's shop; Quaker radicals storming the churches, refusing tithes, defying the élite.

'Look where you're going.'

'Oh, sorry. I didn't see you there.' I had cannoned into a woman with a toddler tugging one hand, dragging a heavy bag with the other.

'Well you damnwell wouldn't, would you, jabbering on like that in the middle of the pavement. God almighty.'

Mortified, I led my remnant back to the bus-stop at the Royal Exchange. To cover my embarrassment, I told them about the ducking stool they used to keep at Pool Fold, 'down there behind Boots', later transferred to the clay pit pools at Daub Holes, the present Piccadilly. 'For women who talked too much, or cursed, or spoke their minds,' I explained. 'As well as female bakers of adulterated bread and prostitutes. The thing was an open-bottomed chair at the end

43

of a see-saw contraption, and it ended up being dismantled around the end of the eighteenth century. The chair was recycled and used in the Infirmary.'

This seemed to catch their imaginations as nothing in our Civil War campaign had so far. My mind flashed back to the Hesketh Maiden in her brank. I had to look into that. I mustn't let her be silenced.

In the premature twilight of a rainy midday, the commercial buildings towered in stone as if they had stood vigil for all time and would invincibly remain. The Exchange loomed, formidable and massive. Standing hunched outside Boots in drizzle, I gave up trying to talk to the students: the massive Exchange loured. Yet even that monumentality was a frail facade for transience, a site of change: where the cotton barons had held court now a marble space housed a scaffolding theatre. And wasn't the Exchange bombed in the war? I seemed to remember so, though nothing could look more imperishable at this moment.

'Thanks for the trip, Dr Holderness,' sleeked the caressive student who aimed to please, in the cause of grades. 'It's been interesting to go back.'

'This was the Roman road,' I blurted. 'Here, where we're standing now.' Everybody looked down at the puddled pavement. Cigarette ends and a greasy swirl of chip paper. No one could think of anything to say. No one believed me.

✳

'It's just been one of those days,' said Faith. She smiled wryly. I could stand Faith. I could even look her in the eyes, now that I'd noticed she existed.

Faith was the kind of person people rely on but take no particular notice of. Their opinion on sophisticated matters of judgment is not solicited. But if there was anything necessary and burdensome to be done, it was assumed Faith would be there to do it.

As the only two women in the department, it had been suggested that we save space by sharing a room. Faith was tranquil about it; I bucked and reared. If they wanted me, I'd have a room to myself, thank you.

'Oh – it was more for your own convenience. We assumed you might like to . . . powder your noses together.'

What century was the old buffoon living in?

'I've never *powdered my nose* in my life. I'm a professional person.'

From his less than compendious experience of women (that seemed to be, his mother, his wife and Faith), the old buffoon had evidently assumed I'd be compliant. I got my own room. Faith shared with the new boy.

'Do you powder your nose, Faith?' I'd asked her indignantly.

'Well, I do. But it's not my chief preoccupation.'

'Do you mind sharing?'

'No, not really.'

'How obligingly *space-saving* of you.'

If she was jolted by my tart dig, she said nothing.

The old professor was pensioned off and we became high-powered, management-driven, as if we were a company of tycoons rather than a community devoted to the study of history. Stresssed-out, hyperactive, our management now suggested that we women should power-dress. We had to look good if we were to exhibit excellence. I selected my best Oxfam male suit, and bought a shirt and tie. Strutted about, a walking parody of the team, disdainful and ever more costive with words.

My noticing Faith occurred when she told me she'd been taken to task by Our Leader. It was the end of a long Friday, and she and I lingered over coffee. The men were in the staff bar or had gone home to their wives and children.

'What did he say?'

'He said, could I dress up a bit? He meant, not as in dressing up for dinner, but dressing up as in upward mobility.'

'What did you say?'

'I said, I was terribly sorry but I couldn't change how I look. How I look is me.'

How did she look? I hadn't particularly noticed. Short and slender. Carrying a handbag. Her skirts were longish and flared; silky blouses; earrings like delicate butterflies. I ran my eyes over her.

She raised her cup to her lips. I noted the slight tremor of her hand and swerved my eyes away.

I allowed myself to look again. She was wearing a green corduroy jacket, a strong and striking colour. As my eyes rose to Faith's, I realised that they too were grey-green. Amazingly beautiful. Why had I neglected to see this? And her hair was not mousy but fair; it curled round her face, short and natural.

'The man is off his trolley,' I said, in my customary grating way, unable to think of the sensitive and sensible way to express solidarity. 'You are lovely. I'm going to speak to that fucking fraud.'

'No...Olivia, don't. I've spoken myself. Really.' She grinned. 'But thanks.'

Now whenever Faith was in the room, I was aware of her. A light, fluey sensation would raise the hairs on my arms. A feeling of comfort in her presence, which was always benign and listening, accompanied by a shimmer of anxiety, for which I could not precisely account.

So this was friendship then...a private closeness, so quiet and unremarkable a bonding, but whereas Faith had many such relationships, it was new to me. And if you had it, you could lose it.

I began to notice some odd things about Faith. She seemed so gentle and biddable but, beyond a certain point, she wouldn't be driven; you could hear it in her voice on the telephone. An abrasive clarity showed how carefully she had measured her response.

'See you at the Exchange tomorrow, Olivia. I'll be there at ten thirty: if you're late, don't worry, I'll be inside having coffee at one of those green metal tables. I look forward to seeing you.'

I replayed these simple, business-like words over and over on the answerphone. Hearing her voice in isolation from all visual signs called to my notice the iron in her soul: or rather, the tempered steel.

See you...Olivia.

The promise of seeing her again. She'd not let me down. She'd come if she said she would.

I'll be there . . . I look forward . . .

Desire and distress beset me, like the wings of twin creatures tangling and beating. I'd never faced forward. Never, since my mother went. And now that this simple cliché was put to me, *I look forward to seeing you*, I read into it volumes of future possibility, such as were never for one moment intended. I turned to the window, looking out to the mound with the flowering cherry. Did Faith know or guess how open I am to be hurt?

What right did I have to load Faith with my abnormalities? To take her simply offered, mundane friendship as if she had passed me some precious jewel? The sense of transgression grew upon me. It swelled with dreams of Faith, in which she and I embraced, simply touching lips, in some vista by the sea. I woke bathed in sensations of love and comfort.

I rang Faith, leaving on her answerphone a gruff message: 'I'm sorry, I can't make it, Faith. Something's cropped up. Another time.' Bereft and relieved, I put down the receiver; began to mark essays, scratching scathing comments down the margins.

The phone rang: 'When can we meet then, Olivia? I'd been looking forward to it so much.'

'I don't know.'

'What's the matter?'

'I don't . . . think I have it in me, to . . .'

'Listen, I'll be there, Olivia, and if you can come, please do.'

∗

The next day, while I was on the bus from Cheadle Hulme and Faith was somewhere in transit on the Metro from Altrincham or already arrived at our meeting place, the IRA bomb went off outside Marks & Spencer's. We never got our cup of coffee at the green metal table in the marble Exchange, beside the steel-girdered theatre. From the double decker I felt rather than heard the thudding reverberation as the city-centre exploded in a rain of glass and steel. Traffic was at a standstill. Dozens of burglar alarms raised their voices in a symphony of apocalyptic dolour. For days they keened in pointless, maddening lamentation, as police and firemen combed the wreckage.

47

Where Faith and I would have been sitting, the Victorian palace of commerce, built to last a thousand years, buckled on its foundations, and every single pane of glass smashed. The plays stopped. Meetings stopped. Business stopped.

'There's been a bomb,' the driver told us. 'At St Ann's Square.'

Faith, the soul of punctuality, would have arrived early at our destination – the epicentre of the blast. I shot to my feet gripping the rail. My heart juddered: be late, Faith, please, please have been late.

Shoppers were running, not in panic but as if some attraction had been advertised down Oxford Road; for they pelted in family groups, fathers carrying youngsters, women with bags marked NEXT, and one girl who ran, I noticed, wearing only one sandal, crying silently, her calves a mass of lacerations. The sandal slapped against her bloodied sole. From the bus, it seemed they ran in silence, though I can't suppose they did.

Please, Faith, don't have come.

It seemed forever until I could get to a phone.

'Faith.'

'Olivia.' We were both sobbing.

＊

Weeks later, when they reopened parts of the city centre, we skirted a scene of devastation. Boards fenced off Marks & Spencer's and the mutilated Arndale Centre; roads were roped off. My nerves became aware as never before of the fragility of a city tossed on convulsions of time. It could be and had been unmade and made again. A cornfield once waved in St Ann's Square, beyond the black and white huddle of the market town. When the corn was cut, the annual fair was held here; stubble was trampled by feet and hooves. Now it was fenced off. The eerie aftermath teemed with wraiths, so that, in the new sacking of the city by an ancient Irish cause, throes of past and present turmoil met in the open.

Skirting the ruins of the cordoned centre, we picked our way toward Chetham's Music School and entered the great court.

'How peaceful,' Faith observed.

Out of the wreckage of modernity, the medieval architecture endured. Brilliant boys in black and white uniform, with cellists' hands and mouths mobile for flute and oboe, were playing football in the asphalted court, where cloister and college buildings stood stately and quiet. Though they seemed immune to time, Strange's cannon once blew the roof off; in Cromwell's time, royalist prisoners immured here lived in pigsty squalor.

The librarian told us that not a window of Chetham's broke in the bomb-blast. Nor of the John Rylands Library. The old books, precious in the dimness of these sanctuaries, maintained their pacific time-travel, rocked by no explosion, though when you opened their pages, the seared, schismatic voices raged with passion always fresh and raw.

∗

I study her reading across the oval table: being the only readers today we have the beautiful old reading room all to ourselves. Faith has not my driven need to possess the books, as if sucking pith from a reed. She muses, touches with tender fingers the rust-brown covers of her book, browses, allows her mind to dream on the surface of the pages.

In the alcove of the window, Marx and Engels read and took notes, murmuring a seismic dialogue that would change continents.

Watching Faith read, quiet vision comes unbidden. A bent head silvered with light as if she'd aged; her hand flat to the table beside the book. She preserves a breathing stillness. It is possible to slow my own breathing to the measure of hers. I don't ask what she's reading, thinking, those greedy questions. I reflect upon the inner light glowing in her, I reverence the person and let her be.

She turns a page.

Her features, how still.

Her eyes now move to the left-hand page, and when I shut my own, I can still see her, face now fractionally turned toward the window, less qualified by shadow.

'Tired, Olivia? Want to go?'

'No. Please let's carry on.'

'Sure?'

'Sure.'

As a child at Meeting, I used to wriggle and sigh in the silence, thinking up all sorts of diversions, from worms to catapults. The hour of silence was the quintessence of dullness: it seemed to encompass in its longevity a Black Hole, into which was sucked all the colourful and loud life I could have been living outside, and wasn't. Sometimes you'd hear the children in the garden next door to the Meeting House squealing in their play: on hot days they'd be hosing each other down while I sat coated in listless sweat, in winter they might elect to climb a tree and inspect us through the window.

In that mocking heaven, they inhabited a sabbath I could only dream of. I fixed upon my mother a martyred look, which would sometimes cause her to shake her head in gentle admonition. My father didn't have to go; why did I, I demanded in the course of the grand sulk home. *You don't have to go if you don't want to,* my mother assured me. But each Sunday she drew me on the invisible twine that dragged you in, with all the semblance of playing you out.

Later, I learned the value and the meaning of the silence. I felt solidarity with the peace-ideal and social concern. I liked to stand with them on vigils with my candle, or march with CND, and welcomed wars and bombs with all the callow corruption of a young heart, in order to enjoy the carnival of protest. The earnest respectability of the majority of the members of our group, however, jaded me. From our vividly rebellious roots, we had allowed ourselves to petrify in the eighteenth century into a disciplined order, blinkering and muting women with Quaker bonnets and grey uniform; acquiring gentility and, through business probity, wealth. In my eyes, we were a come-down.

Later again, I sat and heard in the silence a void. An empty hole at the centre. Where God had been, now there was vacuity. Night, nothing, no one.

The purpose of our meetings together for worship was to declare thoughts God aroused in the silence of our individual hearts. My impromptu that unforgettable last Sunday in which I attended Meeting was to state, 'There is no God. God is an illusion. A fossil. The Spirit is a dodo.'

I said this in a spirit of savagery, with open eyes to see how they took it. That gentle but stoical flock took it quietly. They had fifteen generations of Friends behind them, fortifying them against assault. They waited for light to dawn; the due and meet response to rise to the lips of one of their number.

'I sense a sadness here, in dear Olivia,' said John Hale. I choked on an inappropriate giggle. He made Sadness into a looming spectral form such as mediums might conjure at a seance. My outburst had not been made in a spirit of loss but as an act of teenagerly rebellion, protesting against the middle-class niceness of it all, the years of keeping my mouth buttoned up while prayerful things were said by nice people.

'In our moments of doubt, let us wait upon the Spirit,' prayed Loveday Grant, and carried rambling on in words to the same effect, as she had been rambling for decades. Friends had never quite resolved the problem of what measures to take if the Spirit encouraged some dear old thing to longwinded exposition of her inspirations.

'We thank Loveday,' put in John Hale, aiming to cut in without offence at the end of one of her prodigious sentences. Loveday stopped in mid-word, as if struck dumb. 'In our moments of doubt, from which none of us is exempt, give us patience to wait till the light shines more clearly in our hearts.'

The light was shining clearly in mine. Painfully ebullient, I shot off on my bike whistling shrilly. I felt like a whole football crowd when its team has won away. It was all I could do do not to punch the air and shout 'Rah!' Only in the years to come did the extent of my loss become known to me, like the gradual unfolding of a scroll over time, blank and meaningless. A scroll from which my name, together with the matrix of that name, had been expunged to leave me an amnesiac wanderer in a world of veneers and mirrors. Historyless and abortive. Modern.

Later, individuals from the group would phone or visit just to see how I was. Like voices from the past, they affected me strangely. I cared to hear them but wished they would go away.

John Hale came. He said I was still one of the Meeting, as far as he was concerned. He held the liberal opinion that disbelieving was simply a dark form of faith. If that was how the spirit came to me, that was my truth. If ever I wanted to attend, he hoped I would. Jane had baked me a lemon cake, which he bestowed and I received, with more grace and chagrin than I could have managed at the time of my apostasy.

I'd known my loss for years by now. The mild vision, bathed in limpid certainty.

As my friend read, the light was in her for as long as I cared to look. I gazed at her with a sense that, just for once, I was seeing someone outside myself. I'd listened to her. She'd listened to me. Whenever we greeted or said goodbye, we kissed lightly.

She looked at her watch: 'Should we make tracks?'

Yawned and stretched, as if awakening from refreshing sleep.

Arm-in-arm, we made our way back through the bombed city. I was waiting for the kiss.

Four

The Egyptian mummies slept in open coffins, behind glass, swags of hair still attached to their scalps, exposed hands laid over a swaddling of decaying bandages. Their sarcophagi were flimsy boats, which, directed toward the Egyptian afterlife, had fetched up in Manchester. Well might Queen Nefertari stare at the ceiling through her hollow eye-cases, addled with astonishment at a detention so far from home and destination. Disembowelled, heart-free, mindless, they were sailors through time whose odyssey was encumbered by none of the mortifying lumber of heart and mind with which we are freighted.

Look at me, their exhibited nakedness invited. *Then look at yourself. What are you if I am this?*

I dawdled by the addled queen, half fascinated, half disgusted, idly asking myself what quirk made Egyptologists like Rosalie David devote their lives to the forensic investigation of this feast of matter. Well, yes, much is gleaned from such study. But my discovery of 'Esther' was over a decade past; the voices had receded. Friendship with Faith had quelled the dreams and brought me into closer companionship with the world of the living. My viscera revolted against the refusal of invisibility we made to these fellow creatures. It was an unhallowed spectacle.

The feet seemed, for some reason, especially piteous. From some well of memory, the recall arose of my mother taking both my feet in her hands during some fierce distress of early childhood; she held them in her palms, until I was completely steady. Perhaps her own mother had done the same for her; and her mother's mother. My mind murmured those haunting lines from the biblical Song of Songs: 'How beautiful are thy feet with shoes, O prince's daughter...' Once the soles of those bone-naked feet had met the earth, the tender instep with its thin skin webbed by pale blue veins.

As I idled my lunch hour away, a class of primary school children cascaded through the door and mobbed the glass cases: 'Ugh! Mummies! Look at her mouth! Ugh!'

I moved away smartly, nourishing distaste akin to fear of children. Far too messily and noisily truthful.

'Ugh! Toenails! Look at her toenails. Sir, she's got toenails.' Voraciously, their eyes gobbled mortality. I left the room with long strides.

It was then that I met up with Alex Sagarra for the first time in years. He was surveying his workmanship in the form of the reconstructed head of Rostherne Man, in waxwork.

'Olivia! I haven't seen you for ages. Heard you joined the staff. You've caught me in a moment of narcissism, eyeballing my creation. Well, actually, I'm just seeing how the old boy is getting on. Waxwork degrades, and I have to keep touching it up. Have you seen the original?'

I shook my head. 'Meet Rostherne Man,' he said, drawing me over to another case, in which lay a pitiable envelope of flesh, a torso tanned by two centuries of peat to red-brown leather, his crushed head tucked into his left shoulder like a sleeping bird. I blenched away. 'Not the original original, actually,' said Alex. 'An exact replica. See his beard stubble, his eyelashes even, fingernails, wrinkles. Marvellous, isn't it, how the chemical solution of tannin did its job: the bog's a preservative, an acid bath. He was ritually murdered: see the rope around his neck?'

I had no wish to meet Rostherne Man. I shrank from this leather bag of flesh, which no kindly oxidation had been able to dissolve into its molecules and hand back to the larger earth. Alex's cheerfulness over his ghoulish workmanship troubled me, perhaps because it struck a chord with something that jarred in myself. He seemed genuinely fond

54

of 'old Pete Marsh' as the team had nicknamed him. The reproduction held such a reality that the head, childishly tucked in under the wing of the shoulder, bore the look of a sleeper, whose eyelids with their rust-red lashes might at any moment flutter open. I stepped back, making it clear that I had seen my fill.

'So we're colleagues now, Olivia. How about a drink some time?'

'How are you, how are the babies?' I sought to return him to the here-and-now of the faces of the Sagarra young.

'What babies? Hooligans! No, they're lovely, but I come in to work for a bit of peace and quiet. Dead heads don't keep wittering on about crisps and Alton Towers. There's a lot to be said for them. Old Rostherne Man is getting quite famous, did you know that? He and I are going on TV together. By the way, we're getting round to thinking about those remains that were found in your garden all those years ago. Interested?'

'In?'

'A reconstruction?'

'Of?'

'The Hesketh Maiden's face. Phil and I are thinking in terms of a local exhibition of finds from the area – Rostherne Man and the Lindow Moss bog girl would be there. Your Maiden might be another? Think about it.'

My first intuition was to say, *No, for pity's sake bury her.* I'd not thought of her for months. The siege of dreams and voices had drawn off, as friendship balanced me in the present tense. But I didn't say no to Alex. His boyish face was full of goodwill and eagerness. There seemed a perturbing innocence about him.

*

Faith was fascinated by the story of how the Hesketh Maiden had been found. I was aware of her stasis, examining me carefully as together we uncovered the Maiden from burial in my memory. I allowed her to pick away skein after skein of swaddling bandages, as she delicately anatomised these deep remembrances, with the formidably precise scalpel of the acutely sensitive. Knowing I was conveying to her something of great moment and mystery, she wasn't going to comment until she could gauge more exactly the nature of my feeling.

'And you were burying your mother at that time. Oh, Olivia, how...what are the words?...shattering, macabre. Did it upset you? It would me.'

'I don't know. I don't think so. I was...I think, quite numb. I was interested. As if she diverted me from the present griefs. Like a message to be decoded. I kept track of her too, for years. It's only recently I've let her go.'

Faith lifted her sandwich to her lips, failed to take a bite and returned it to her plate.

'And does that feel better to you? Is that a relief?'

'I *think* it has been. But now there's a possibility of learning more about her, I'm intrigued.'

'What I love about you, Olivia...'

She said: *love*.

'...is the intensity of your...'

Jim Owen was hovering. Cut in. 'Mind if I join you, ladies?'

I did mind. I glowered but he wasn't looking at me.

'Of course,' said Faith hesitantly. 'Do join us...'

He had anyway.

'Don't call me a lady though,' I said.

'Meaning you're not a lady?'

'No. I'm not.' I muttered.

'Whoops, not PC, sorry.' He shot Faith a mock-crestfallen look. In his forties, greying, tall and stooped, he was an established scholar of the old school whom the new men had not been able to budge. I often saw him with Faith. As they chatted, I maintained dumb vigil, trying to construe her unfinished sentence. What did she love about me? The intensity of my what? Something she did not have. The word *love* burned in my brain like a dying ember. For the longer it was examined and the less it was fed, the more it cooled.

I glanced toward Faith. She was listening; making monosyllabic responses in all the right places. Didn't look bored. Might never reveal what it was she loved. Probably wouldn't remember that she started the sentence.

No: didn't look bored at all. I realised that they were

gazing straight into one another's eyes, with a smile more tremulous than colleague-like.

He was married already, and not the kind of man...

'Well, I'll be off,' he said. 'See you later, Faith. Sorry if I interrupted a heart-to-heart, ladies.'

'Jesus,' I said.

'Oh,' said Faith, flushed, and fished in her handbag for something which she didn't find. 'Jim's a rather sensitive man, Olivia, when you get to know him. Mary and he are going through quite a bad patch at present. What were we saying? Oh, about the remains in your garden...'

'I'll have to go, I'm afraid.'

'But what we were saying was important, Olivia. I'm so sorry we were interrupted. Where did we get to?'

She didn't remember.

'Oh, it will keep,' I said, standing feet apart, jingling the change in my jacket pocket, in a manner I knew would be identified by Faith as mannish. 'After all, she's been around for three and a half centuries at the nearest estimate: she won't go away, will she?'

Standing at my office window, I reproached myself for making such a fragile thing as a friendship matter so deeply. It was too much to load on the shoulders of one as well-meaning and multiply committed as Faith. In the depths of my mind, there was a flickering recognition that my love for Faith belonged to another order than her concern for me. Intensity. Deep affection, the marrying impulse.

Wilt thou take... keeping thee only unto her?

My love was therefore transgressive; beyond the limits of what Faith would ever be able to imagine or society sanction.

I was bereft at the flinch of distaste I knew my passionate attachment would inspire, not least because Faith would feel so wrung at having to reject me. She would know, with her antennae, how her rueful turning-away would lacerate me.

Hence anger goaded me; I felt aggrieved with Faith, for being who she was, the person I had grown to love and trust. But more chastened at my latterday discovery of the obvious in myself. How ridiculous to have kept the right half of my mind from communicating with the left into my late twenties: in a century when gay love is an acknowledged fact of life, the Pink Pound sways markets and there's even a Gay Village in Manchester, with its own Mardi Gras.

But while I was not part of the straight world, I felt no community with the gay one. There was nothing obviously sexy in my feeling for Faith. It was more the diaphanously sensational wonder one might feel for a Botticellian angel who has dropped out of a picture and fluttered into one's own sphere. Perhaps this image was lifted from the photograph I cadged of Faith in Florence, standing before the statue of some minor god, looking half her thirty-four years.

'I hate having my picture taken,' she had said, as if theft were involved, the threatened stripping of a layer of skin. Looking closely, I saw the sun in her pale hair, her fingers bunched into fists of embarrassment.

Who took that photo? I never asked.

I awakened the following morning with a headache that helmeted my skull and seemed bolted on by persons unknown who had bridled, ridden and taunted me in my sleep. She was here again, the Maiden, whom I had wished to bury without trace. As I turned from an abortive intimacy (*freak*, said Jim Owen's eyes, I was sure they'd said *freak*), she came rushing in to commandeer the space in my mind.

For lack of anything better to do, I picked up the phone and rang Alex Sagarra.

✻

'So, I'm ready,' he said, and tied on his apron, while I glanced round at the fascinating clutter of his studio in the Medical Faculty. Heads everywhere, both works of art and scientific reconstructions, photographs, oil-paintings, models in terracotta and wax, a row of skulls, yellowish to ivory. It reminded me of Pinfold in my grandparents' day, a mess of clay, tools and half-finished pottery.

'Are you ready?'

I nodded, perching on a stool.

'You sound like the dentist,' I said nervously.

'Not too far wide of the truth. Anyhow just to recap on

what we already know about your Maiden,' Alex said, removing the portions of her skull from a box. 'She died around the age of thirty-five in the mid-seventeenth century; dental condition not wonderful through, presumably, poor diet. Five foot two or three. Mild arthritis in the back and knees; injury to the pelvis at some stage meant she probably walked a fraction lop-sidedly. Pubic pitting might or might not indicate she'd borne a child. Strong and wiry build, we would guess, and not a lot of fat on her.'

Curiosity aroused like an appetite: an ambivalent appetite, however, as when saliva runs in the mouth of a vegetarian at the smell of roast lamb, somewhere between nausea and desire. A tainted relish.

'Cause of death hanging?'

'Certainly. The brank contraption was probably on until shortly before her death: sign of the scold, as you know, but also suggests some more serious deviation – witchcraft, heretic. Your field rather than mine. I'm happier amongst the bodies.'

'Christ.'

'I know. It's a shock, isn't it, human barbarity,' he observed lightly. 'There's a ligature mark around the neck – and the vertebrae broke there.'

'I hope to God she died quickly.'

'It was not a quick or easy death. Could take ten or fifteen minutes for the victim to asphixiate. Her jaw, as you know, was shattered by the brank. Anyway, to work.'

He smiled and then seemed to forget me. I watched his face as he worked, brooding on its dispassionate concentration. His face; her face; my face. Echoes and reflections played upon the screen of my inner eye. I felt the impersonal dignity of a person at work, all that you are and know brought into play. Inside the mask-like stillness of Alex's concentrating face, what scintillations of electrical connection must have been sparking.

First he glued the shattered parts of the skull and teeth together with soft dental wax; then covered it in aluminium foil, burnished on to the skull with a cloth.

'Now,' he explained softly, 'we puddle her in dental

alginate. So. To make a soft mould.'

Soon we had twin white moulds, covered in plaster, which were left to cure, and laid before me, like the halves of a walnut. We filled one half with plaster and, rotating them on a wheel, came up with a hollow cast. Now bone had been converted to plaster. Mounted, it was fitted out with glass eyes and stuck full of pegs, to indicate the varying thickness of the soft tissues.

'Now the fun begins,' he said. 'We'll find her here.'

My breathing was slow and shallow, as if suspended in sleep or lost in a book.

'But this is science,' he kept insisting, as if this were a sensitive issue. 'Science, not art. What we shall see is not a portrait, remember that, Olivia. A portrait's always a dialogue between the artist and the sitter. This will be how she really looked. And I don't know any more than you what she will look like. There are some archaeologists who tell you they know exactly what a face will look like the moment they clap eyes on the skull. Don't believe a word of it. The face grows, from the skull out, according to scientific laws. I am always amazed. But first we'll build on the muscle bundles. Can't do that today, I'm afraid. You'll have to live in suspense.'

Alex grinned, as he might do at one of his children, teasing them with paternal omnipotence.

'Fun, isn't it?' he said. 'Are you enjoying it?'

'You must be pretty used to this kind of thing.'

Was I accusing him of hardness of heart? The making of a living on the backs of the final agonies of suffering people? How calm their sleep appears, those Aztec child-sacrifices found on the frozen mountain-tops: and how the final image lies. I recalled a TV programme centring on a little parcel of exhumed girlhood, cradled in the rust-red mantle in which she had died: *I like to think she died without pain, and not knowing she was dying,* the museum-keeper crooned. *She crossed over to the other world without a sigh.* On came a doctor to point out that the red tint was the product of the child's shitting herself in terror, coating her garments in the red dye their priests had forced her to eat in some ceremonious rite of passage.

'You don't get used to it,' said Alex. 'You live with it. And, as with any discipline, you enjoy it. I don't have qualms or soul-searchings. I take things more matter-of-factly, perhaps, than you, Olivia. You scare me.' He untied his green, smeary apron and hung it behind the door.

'I scare *you?*'

'A touch. The intellectual passion. You seem to be looking for something . . . off the map. You don't take time off.'

I said nothing, trying not to show offence. 'And what are you looking for?'

'What's there, I suppose. How what's inside dictates what's outside. I used to like taking things apart when I was a child – putting them together again.'

'So did I. But what if it's all like an onion: you keep peeling and there's precisely nothing at the centre?'

'Come and have a beer with me and Phil. Of course you've got time.' As he shepherded me through the door, Alex's hand briefly caressed my back. I startled and wondered. 'No, I don't take my re-creations lightly, actually, Olivia,' he said. 'What we have is the remains of an individual, that person's beliefs and qualities. The brank, for instance. They meant to silence your woman, didn't they? Why would they feel the need to do that? What threat did she pose to the established order? It may be that to some degree we can restore her power of speech. She might tell us what they gagged because they were pathologically afraid to hear it.'

∗

Wide strips of clay are laid on to indicate the temporalis muscle. The masseter. Buccinator. The orbicularis oris which forms the lips. The levator anguli oris...on and on until he surrounds the eye with the orbicularis oculi.

Orbicularis oculi: the skull-simulacrum gives out its secrets and puts on its humanity. As Alex recites the names of muscles, my school Latin comes to mind, then the sacramental Roman Catholic Latin, medical Latin, the universal language, at once mysterious and precise.

Hermione in *The Winter's Tale* is the semblance of a statue brought to life by the wonder-working Paulina. I always soak a handkerchief with tears in that final act. The emotion I feel as Alex builds the Hesketh Maiden is awe beyond tears.

Yet how quickly she rushes to deliver herself into his hands. When he calls, she willingly answers.

Her nose, measuring from the aperture, is short but slightly wide, perhaps snub, he speculates, as he considers the profile at a tangent to the lower nasal bone.

'But the cartilage is never certain,' he admits. 'We have to make an educated guess. And the mouth – the width is dictated by the filtrum – the fullness by the prognathism of the upper and lower jaws – but you can't be totally sure about the exact shape of the lips.'

All the while, his hands are working, almost, it seems, of their own volition. His fingers know what to do. They listen, hover, smooth, braille-read, dream and scheme on her supple surface. The clay takes life.

'Now,' he says, standing back.

She is with us. A heart-shaped face, strongly developed eyebrow ridges, a high forehead. Her hair, he thinks, would be long: he decides to let it hang loosely, and to give her skin the creases and wrinkles you would expect of a thirty-five year old who spent much time out of doors, tanning and ageing the skin and screwing up her eyes slightly against the sun. In his mind's eye, he can see a lean woman, probably underfed though very active, since her skeleton bears marks of osteoporosis and thence anaemia, mild arthritis but well-developed sites for muscle attachments: 'more common in a male'. A wiry, athletic woman, who became (he speculates) emaciated in the latter years of her life.

I am grateful for the calm he has attributed to her face. She gazes straight forward without joy or pain, through and beyond us. That calm stills me as I gaze.

'Now – what about a waxwork?' Alex asks, with some eagerness.

'Oh, Alex, no, really not. I'd hate it. Please, no waxwork.'

'Why not? It would make her more life-like.' He turns sharply, intrigued by my strong recoil.

But as I am objecting, stumblingly, 'No – it would demean

her – Madame Tussaud's...Chamber of Horrors', he seems to startle.

'Good God.'

'What?'

'Oh, nothing. Just a whimsy. I get a bit spooked sometimes.'

'According to you, you're the empirical, feet-on-the-ground guy; I'm the ecstatic,' I crow, and my amusement at Alex's expense deflects me from enquiring further.

'Do you know what, I'd like to do a portrait of you some time. Or a life-mask.'

What is he saying? I have a nervous sense that Alex nourishes some tender feeling for me that disquiets him. I flush. He's a nice-looking, easy-going man, whom I like all the more for his disinterested willingness both to take me seriously and to add a pinch of salt.

'We forgot something,' I put in hastily.

'What?'

'The brank.'

'And?'

'What do you think about doing a copy, wearing the thing? It will memorialise...'

'What?'

Horror, injustice, fear and hatred of women.

'Her silence. Her silenced life.'

'Yes, OK, no problem. We can use a plaster cast to clone the Hesketh Maiden now that we've got a model – scores of her, as many as you like. By the way, Olivia, there's one other funny little thing I meant to tell you.'

'Yes?'

'She probably suffered from a runny nose.'

'A *runny nose?*'

'Brings us down to earth, doesn't it? There's some deflection of the nasal septum to the right which may well have led to a blocked nose, if she had a cold, say, or even all the year round.'

Somehow the runny nose is one shock too many. It brings us so close to everyday reality: the low-grade distempers to which flesh is heir. It carries the one-time reality of her impossibly near. And, paradoxically, it bears down heavily on the questionable authenticity of that or any reconstruction.

The immutable stillness of her clay cast.

Not only can it not snivel but it will shed no tears. It stares from unblinking eyes into a void as empty as the hollow within its own cranium.

How can I revivify that mask in the crucible of my imagination, so as to picture the lissom mobility of a human face, its openness to the process of change, as if weather streamed across its many expressions? What evasions or passions did that face wear when it was free to move? She would sniff, wipe her nose, give it a good blow. Ordinary details. The reconstruction failed dramatically in ordinariness.

Alex Sagarra did a waxwork copy wearing the scold's bridle: for several years it was on public view in the Museum, under the caption, 'Silenced Woman'.

Five

My love, my Faith, I wrote, behind a locked door. My hand sped across the page.

> When we sat at Chetham's reading together I was so at peace. I didn't pay any attention to the books, I just sat and read your face. It had more integrity than any face I've ever seen bar one and yet (which makes your goodness bearable) a living warmth too: I'm scared of truth, it's always seemed too lacking in – I was going to say – motherlove. But motherlove in my limited experience is also lacking in motherlove. Too abstract and theoretical by half. You are not like that. I came so close to you, I thought I did, it felt so tender but it was all in my mind wasn't it? Don't say so. I don't know, I can't read you any more, I thought I could but I've remembered all sorts of things about you and Jim, & they seem to whisper in my mind a kind of unbearable gossip – snatched glances, brief conclaves I'd glimpsed between you (or have I made it up? tell me I've made it up?) – and I think you and he, he and you . . . I want to ask you to put me out of my misery, but it will seem a mortal blow. Faith you are the most beautiful person I

The pen that had been hurrying along the page faltered and gave up the ghost. I willed it to say more but what was there to say?

I screwed up the page and threw it into the waste paper basket. But someone might find it. The cleaner when she came round might sit down at my desk and have a little read, or it might be dropped by accident. My private hoard of dreams, still precious though unrequited, would be out in the open betraying me. I rescued the document, thinking to tear it up but instead held it a moment suspended and then smoothed it out on the desk. I read it over. The person who had written this was able to open herself to another person. Her testament should not be discarded. Even if it were never sent, this was a genuine love-letter, the first I'd written in my life. I'd lived in self-imposed silence, behind a wall. What did they call those nuns who walled themselves up? Anchoresses, that was it. In closed orders. My whole life to date had been anchoritic. I thought of the sarcasm and irony with which I'd protected myself. The image of poor Jean blenching flashed across my mind. I folded the unfinished letter and laid it within the pages of a book in my drawer.

I thought again of Jean. She wasn't well apparently. My father didn't say what was the matter with her. He tried to hide his concern, expressing it casually, probably thinking I'd be glad. I winced. What kind of person did they think I was? What kind of person had I been? I began a new letter.

Dear Jean,
Dad says you're not at all well which I'm so sorry to hear. I hope you soon feel a lot better & I'll be thinking of you. Did Will come to see you as you hoped? He would do you good. I hope you forgave my adolescent craziness long ago – I must have been a bloody pain, excuse my French. Thanks for trying with me & take care of yourself.
Love, Olivia.

I posted that one on the way to Chester; the other is still unsent in the book in my desk.

❊

I hounded her down, through all the sources of information open to me, from parish registers to probate and criminal records. At Chester Public Records Office, I asked for Quarter Sessions rolls of the mid-seventeenth century.

'Looking for anything in particular?' asked the assistant.

'Scolds and witches.'

'Oh, we've plenty of those. Help yourself.'

Despite knowing very well that records for the period of the Revolution and its aftermath are scanty, full of holes, I felt sure of finding her. Whereas Alex had modelled a face from the skull, it fell to me to breathe life into the static clay. The hallucinatory strangeness of the model bodied her forth as an existence, begetting the conviction that the real person could, did, must exist to be discovered. And how safe such time-travelling passion seemed, beside the insecure bondings of the present tense. Should I find vestiges of this woman, she could not refuse my reading of her. Deep in the shadow world, she was subject to my light or none at all. Silent unless I voiced her, she would be impotent to reject me.

I trawled tome after tome. Starting from 1620, I found sundry scolds and a promising witch, Mary Tanner. Mary, having performed penance before the congregation in Chester Cathedral Church in a white sheet, with bare head, feet and legs, holding a white rod an ell long, had been several times punished as a scold. Her witchcraft trial appeared to involve the grudge of neighbours she had loudly aspersed, and was referred to the Assize. But no. For Mary had obviously got off. In the 1630s, Mary Tanner appeared again, accused of stealing a cup worth two shilling, and was given a prison sentence.

Suddenly a name appeared which brought a rush of blood to my ears: 'Hannah Jones, *blasphemously calling herself Emanuel.*'

Arrested in Bramhall manor, 1665, a known heretic and scold, presented at the Quarter Sessions accused of witchcraft, blasphemy, disowned by the Quakers, condemned as a witch at the Assizes of 1665 by Justice Mather and sentenced to be branked and hanged in the borough. Named as of Chedle-Holme, twin manor to Chedle, comprising the manor house, Hulme Hall, the Hesketh Arms where the Court Baron was held, a scatter of hamlets and a market square, surrounded by farm land and heath. Yes, I knew. I knew all that. The Hesketh is my local pub. Pinfold stands toward the centre of this manor. That's why the museum had called her the Hesketh Maiden.

I drove home from Chester, the name ringing in my ears. Where had I read that name before: *Hannah Emanuel?*

Pinfold lay dark, all its curtains open, my breakfast dishes still on the table where I'd left them that morning. I cut myself a hunk of bread and brewed a pot of tea. Here, among the notes I kept in my mother's old *escritoire*, was my pencilled copy of the ripped document I'd unearthed in the Bodleian. Esther Bradshaw's forceful 'I' had tricked me into scooping out the wrong woman. The name I'd wanted lay low to the page, adjacent to the rip in the extant half-sheet.

Woe upon thee, town of Oxford...We came to thee, my dear friend Sarah Hough and Esther Bradshaw...And know, O depraved young men, you have abused the LORDS APOSTLES *that had tenderness to you to come south many miles from the* LORDS WITNESS *that is in Manchester Hannah Emanuel & the spirits there, the Seed, but remember the* WRATH

Hannah – my Hannah – must have been the leading light of some renegade splinter group here. I longed to share the news with people: to pick up the phone as you did with a birth and say, with jubilation – 'She's here. She's with us at last.'

'Emanuel' means 'God-with-us'. *And they shall call his name Emanuel.* I was the means by which Hannah would be delivered from her long silence. I actually reached out for the phone, to call...who? I sat listening to the dialling tone, ready to break into some family's routine, as they sat over their evening meal or watching TV, and gabble the gospel news. The ancient news, today recovered. Should I ring Alex or Faith?

But she was mine: my find, my secret. I put down the receiver, with a jealous pang. *I've got you, I'll keep you. To have and to hold.*

*

The Assize records for that and the following two years were destroyed by a fire in the eighteenth century.

It was a blow. I kept bleating, 'Are you sure?'

'Madam, let me assure you we are not in the business of giving out false information.'

'No, of course not, but would you mind just checking. Are you sure you've got the right years? There are no copies? Everything was burnt for those years?'

'I am looking at the catalogue at this very minute,' came the nasal voice down the phone, officialdom keeping its temper just about. 'You will be making a wasted journey if you come looking for what I am telling you does not exist.'

I went anyway and trawled through the Assize record for three years either side of the given date, impelled by the familiar and infantile delusion that what we absolutely desire cannot be denied.

'You're right,' I told the nasal chap, in leaving, as if his sanity rather than my own had come into question. 'Those years are missing.' He was speechless.

*

I would try from the other end, with the Hesketh Quakers from whom Hannah had seceded. My Meeting: the one I'd left, but no born Friend ever truly sloughs her origins, any more than a cradle Catholic. Since I knew how assiduous Friends are about keeping records, I felt on firm ground. Everything was documented from the beginning, at Swarthmoor, by Margaret Fell and her secretary, William Caton. Whenever a new group was set up, it began to document its own activities. To the young movement, this written record was crucial: in journals, diaries, testimonies, records, minutes, a living witness was assembled. The Quaker memory is long, corporate and detailed. It belongs not to individuals but to a persecuted, inward-looking group. A memory bank waiting for me to tap into it.

In the event, Hannah was not so accessible. John Hale was, I thought, surprisingly costive with the Hesketh records.

'I thought you'd deserted us,' he said. There was neither overtone nor undertone of reproach but I seemed to register the hurt: *you blithely quit us, only to come back when your selfish ends want something of the system you abandoned with such contumely.*

'Well,' I said. 'I did. I'm sorry. But I thought you

understood. And I hope you'll help me with something that is important to me.'

'Of course.' John was grey and frail-looking; he wore a lamb's wool jumper with patches at the elbows. 'If we can.'

'I'm interested in a woman of the First Generation Friends, from Hesketh Meeting. A woman I think they must have cast out, who somehow or other put herself beyond the pale. Could I see the earliest records?'

'Well, the originals are at Friends House Library in London.'

'But we hold copies?' He looked up sharply: I had said *we*.

'We do. May I ask the name?'

'Hannah Emanuel.'

'Ah.'

'You know the name?'

He paused. 'I'm not sure that I do.' What was it that gave me the idea he was, not precisely lying (for John Hale was the soul of probity, a banker whose yea was yea and whose nay was nay), but indulging a certain equivocation, which he would be forced to abdicate if I hit on the key question?

A brainwave: 'May I ask if you have heard of her by any other name?'

I studied his face as he flushed. Why after so much time – centuries – would the name of a woman who was born and died in the movement's childhood have power to sway a sober Quaker banker to emotion?

Again, my mind fluttered against that sweep of the communal Quaker memory, outlasting the memory of individuals as families, intermarrying, riding the tempests of centuries. Resisting religious intolerance; campaigning against slavery, injustice, poverty, war; reforming the prison system, education, treatment of the mentally ill. It was my history too; and I could not easily shrug off its inheritance.

'You may have in mind Hannah Jones, the unstable woman who was supposed to have run amok and was, I believe, executed.'

'But why would she be known as Emanuel?'

'The tradition went that she assumed a false name, under the influence of delusions. I daresay she would be cared for nowadays as a schizophrenic. But I doubt if you will find anything in the records.'

'But could I have a look?'

'Certainly.'

I saw what he meant: pages were missing for various years, including 1663-5.

'When did the pages go missing?' I asked John .

'I've no idea. Generations ago, I imagine. They've never been there in my lifetime. Hannah Jones is only mentioned once – look here, as an early member who "*is in the Power*". Have a cup of tea, Olivia. I'm sorry you've been disappointed.'

Was he sorry? He inwardly queried my motives for raiding the proud lists of the heroic early years: fined and imprisoned; imprisoned and fined under the Restoration. Rent by schisms that somehow they rode: schisms often caused by women 'out of control', who would later be relegated to Women's Meetings, good works and poor relief. I knew, of course, of the campaign Fox waged for women, and the way he effectively subdued them through censorship and sidelining. Radical fire became pietism and good works.

'So they muzzled her. She was "in the Power", that means she had visions and trances, and told them things they didn't want to hear, and they muzzled her.'

'There was certainly some regrettable controversy. Some lack of mutual charity perhaps. It is always difficult to reconcile the individual with the communal voice. Are you sure you won't have some tea?'

I ignored the palliative and diversionary cup of tea. The image of a Quaker bonnet rose in my frustrated mind. I had tried one on at Swarthmoor, during a visit. The eighteenth-century headgear was produced by our guide from a Jacobean chest and passed round the visitors, who all smilingly tried it on, exclaiming about how 'focused' it made you feel, how calm and contained. As the black bonnet approached me, I shifted from foot to foot, mortified at the thought of fitting my near-shaven head into this quaint gear. 'Go on, do try it,' said my neighbour. I gave in. Its stiff forward cone had a peculiar blinkering effect and it pinched my ears, muffling the sound of voices. Nobody claimed it suited me. My cousin guffawed. A male hat that did the rounds of the menfolk increased their height by about a foot.

'She was a threat and they cut her out of the record,' I repeated.

'I hardly think so,' said John equably. 'Probably nothing to do with the poor woman. Records from that period do tend to be fragmentary.'

'Yes, but I would not expect whole pages to be missing, and look, the photocopier has picked out a tear-line from the original page. So it didn't just drop out.'

'I can't help you, I'm afraid, Olivia. Why not ask at Friends House?'

'I'll do that.'

✳

Odd that women's subjection should be defined by headgear. I went to see the Stockport bridle, on show in the museum. It was a shock, sickening me to my stomach, though less so than the card explaining its unique qualities and their function. It contained a blithe quotation from a Victorian local history, a work which found the whole thing a bit of a joke:

> The special characteristic of the Stockport brank, so ingeniously adjustable to any head-size, is the peculiar construction of the tongue-plate and gag. The three-inch bit has a bulb at the end, carrying nine pins: three facing up, three down and three to the back. This could not fail to fix the tongue and effectually silence the noisiest brawler.

The Court Leet had had the barbarous thing hung on a door on market days as a deterrent to any women inclined to scold or swear, entrusting a market official with summary powers to bridle offenders on the spot, 'in urgent cases'. This torture implement was given a carnival air, by its decorative topknot, a curlicue of iron.

Her poor mouth: it would have been running blood.

The brank was a prime attraction in the exhibition. I observed people bend to examine it. Amusement swiftly turned to thoughtfulness, and thoughtfulness to pain. Both men and women were silent. They visibly flinched and their foreheads creased. They turned away.

I went out and sat on the steps of the Museum where, in the Gulf War, we had assembled with home-made placards and candles in jamjars, a cluster of Greens, Friends, CND, a Communist and miscellaneous larking lads. We had done no good. Scarcely visible in the sleety darkness, we had protested against the use of 'smart weapons'. Commuters' cars rushed by, occasionally hooting in support or contempt; bus-passengers pausing at the lights looked out; we were accused by a few passers-by of supporting Hitler. We spoke and nobody listened.

But nobody had gagged us. Nobody came to remove the women and elderly men, to bang us up and cage our heads for bearing witness against our government. Nobody subjected us to ritual humiliation, shoving in our mouths that iron bit with nine pointed nails to bloody our dissident mouths.

My insides churned at the recognition of Hannah's agony. Who she had been and what she had done became a settled question that took root in me like a seed. The seed grew a little with every day, at a steady rate. It flourished in the dark soil of empathy. As I unconsciously nourished the seed with every night, so also I was fed by it. Small and secret, its presence reminded me of the Friends' sense of being 'one in the Seed'. I was one with her, across time.

✳

'About that life-mask,' said Alex. He had put the final touches to the Hesketh Maiden, including a wig. Her long hair, around my colour, fell down over her shoulders. Alex kept taking little dabs at it with a comb, like a hairdresser.

'What life-mask? For goodness' sake, stop prinking that effigy!'

'The one you promised I could make of you.'

'Did I? I don't recall promising any such thing.' I did indeed remember, and the memory made me flush hotly. I didn't want those designing hands playing over my features, taking away a reproduction of my face, making me his in a way that disturbed me. Again, I was visited by the suspicion that Alex had got himself emotionally involved with me. This was his way of cadging the elaborate equivalent of a photograph and mooning over it.

'Well, you did.'

'I'm sure I didn't. Anyhow, why would you want to...?'

'If you just let me do it, you'll see.'

'Look, Alex,' I said, and cleared my throat, hands stuffed in my jacket-pockets. 'No offence or anything, but as far as I'm concerned, we're just good friends.'

He exploded with an astonished hilarity so unfeigned that, if I hadn't been so relieved, I might have felt mortified.

'Rest assured, Olivia, I've no designs on your virtue. No, there's ... let's call it ... a whim of mine I'd like to test out by taking a cast and making a head of you. Similar procedure to the one you've seen except your real head gets to stay on your shoulders.'

He went to work, first taking a plaster mould of my face, then building on the muscles and flesh, using the same Cornish pot-clay, with its fine grog, as he had used for Hannah. I left him to it.

'Come and see.'

I looked long and steadily upon the red clay head his hands had composed.

'She's beautiful,' he said quietly.

'Yes. I suppose everyone is really.'

Under his hands I had, in my own absence, come to life. It was the quietude of the head that impressed. Turbulence was foreign to its calmly inward reflectiveness. Perhaps, I thought, if I gaze long and deeply upon the completeness of this likeness, I can take into myself some of its qualities. Like Alex's gifted hands, I too could render of my swirling human clay an essential composure. Next to my reconstruction he placed Hannah.

'So – Olivia – what do you notice?'

'I don't need to say, do I? It's obvious.'

I felt very calm. I had known all along. Alex and I had dreamed awake, and dreamed the same experience, collusively. I felt strangely close to him. The faces were, though in many respects incapable of comparison, twinned. We both studied that likeness in silence.

'But it must be – I don't mean any aspersion on your professionalism but it must be the likeness has come...from your subconscious or something. With me being here alongside. Do you think it may?'

'This is truly how she looked; just as this is how you look. I didn't design either of you. A portraitist sees the sitter in the light of all he is and knows and feels. You saw how I got the image of you. By purely mechanical means. Just as with her. If I were to sculpt a portrait of you, Olivia, believe me, it would be quite different. There'd be a tempest in that face.'

I stared, my lips apart. I looked from the simulacrum of Hannah to the likeness of Olivia, from Olivia to Hannah. I dreaded and yet longed to believe; wanted it too much.

'You don't think you might have...unconsciously...?' I pleaded.

It was the first time I'd seen him lose that hail-fellow equanimity. 'No,' he replied abruptly. The youthful features took on the expression of one whose enemies had gathered at close quarters. 'Murder victims – with their skulls smashed in or burnt – have been identified from my reconstructions. Am I likely to botch a simple job just because an interested party's been sitting in?'

'Please do forgive me. It's the shock.'

'No, no, it's OK, Olivia. Sorry. It's just...oh, all so bloody unscientific, that's what's making me ratty. I bawled Tom out this morning about eating his boiled egg. He was amazed; he said "Dad, it's just an egg!" I heard myself yelling, "No! No, it's not the egg, it's the principle!" I *mean*. No, Olivia, what bugs me is, the messy feelings, it's so...unscientific. I don't mean the reconstructions. They're standard, bona fide. But remember when I said I felt spooked? I looked from the Maiden to your face, and immediately saw her in you. Now I can't get rid of you. You keep on haunting me, following me about. But it's not...a sexual thing. Sorry to have laughed like that before, not very flattering, but Olivia, it's something much more profound.'

He had never once looked at me during this monologue, fixing his pale blue eyes on the clayey tools of his trade that lay scattered on his work-table. Now he darted a shy, bothered look at me. 'Actually, I think it's all your fault, I'm catching some weird brain-fever from you. Your kind of intellectuality scares me, Olivia: I want my feet squarely on the earth. Wife, kids, boiled eggs, plaster and clay.'

Now that he had met my eyes, our gazes caught and held. His told me, *You're beautiful. You mesmerise me.* I salvaged us both by retreating into practicalities.

'Could I be related to her, Alex? I mean a lineal descendant? Would the features last all that time – how many? Fifteen generations?'

'Well . . . I'm not sure. I'll have a word with the genetics guy who helps us with heredity.' He sighed and sat down on a stool, then casually spun the plinths that held the two heads. The return of his levity sabotaged the emotion arresting us. He worked to disperse the strangeness that lingered in the air.

'Probably just fortuitous,' he said offhandedly. 'When you look at the faces in some lights, there seems no resemblance at all.'

Six

As lovers are said by Donne to die with each life-shortening act of sex, so books are ravaged by readers. Each opening brings an embrittlement; our caressive fingers deposit snail-trails of moisture along margins and text. The reader's love for the book is a wanton outpouring of acid upon its surfaces. Rot ruddies the leather binding, which dries, porous and powdered. Molecules of the original cow, slaughtered and tanned centuries ago to make the binding, pass out into the street on the reader's hands, to be deposited on newspapers and ingested in a sandwich eaten on the hop at the station buffet.

Granted, the oldest books, made of rags, are sturdier. But even the seventeenth-century, rag-born book the Chetham's librarian passed to me was disturbed in its transit from hand to hand. Alum-stiffened pages met humidity in the air in a prompt rapture of acid dissolution. Brittle and discoloured, its leaves creaked as I turned them, and it received my warm breath as the exhalation of a fever. The bondings between its fibres broke down minutely under the stress of my search for the likeness of lost kin.

Books, I thought, have their own physical stories, and all proceed exponentially toward the one apocalypse. In that respect they are no different from ourselves: the more we tell our story, the further it is consumed.

This volume, David Lyngard's diary, appeared to have contracted mortal sickness early in its career, for the pages, tawny with time at the margins, were speckled with mildew.

While the print had turned rust-brown and begun to break up, the pages had crinkled from the spine, to lie wavy as a sea-shore when the tide is out. They smelt of ongoing decomposition.

Lyngard was one of the foremost Presbyterian ministers in the Manchester classis during the Interregnum: a vitriolic antagonist of 'erroneous, pragmatical' belief and all women regardless of religious persuasion. You naturally came to Lyngard if you were interested in picking up information about heresies in Lancashire and Cheshire. He had been vociferating in a sacred cause from, it seemed, cradle-days, and was especially antagonistic to the Quakers in the 1650s. Author of *The Ulcerous Pox of the Quaker Plague Displayed*, he was also a splenetic diarist, whose work I had come upon by chance, for the one copy in Chetham's was not listed in the Wing catalogue.

If books make faces at you, Lyngard's was wicked. I took delight in his naive pomposity, anxious vanity and sheer viciousness in what he had no doubt was a good cause. In his diary, we learned how he grew up under the care of a pious Scottish mother who educated him as a Calvinist detector of abominations in other people. She and his father died of plague, and Lyngard, surviving solitary quarantine in a stricken house, attended the Free School, to scrape an education. His diary reflects not only the turbulence of Manchester in the throes of Civil War and its aftermath, but also a hectic, riven self-justifier in an age of uncertainty. Half the time he hardly knew what he was saying: history pumped him high on the currents of its own agendas.

How candid he was. Everything must be shown. Each mole and blemish, every small profane action better forgotten, was bared to the reader's eye. For Lyngard was a dunghill, as he often insisted with something of Pauline vainglory, one of the worst excrements in God's Creation – but look at the Glory of God in saving such a one. Wet dreams, swearing-fits, bearing false witness, Lyngard had done it all.

When I was 13 & 14 years of age, residing in the house of Mr Shaw the minister, my body so clamoured night & day that I had no rest but performed the sin of Onan countless times, foully sinning against God & Mr Shaw & the temple of the Holy Spirit. I have fallen to my knees trembling in the heat of my lust & begged: O MOUNTAINS & HILLS FALL UPON ME, HIDE ME FROM THE WRATH OF THE ALMIGHTY. *Still I went on to perform the act of darkness, having no candle lit, as if in the dark God might be deceived & not see me furiously lechering. Afterwards I would hear* GOD *laugh in derision as I cowered naked beneath the clothes, believing the room to be full of devils & tempted to make away with myself. I took knives to bed but in the night a Voice said:*

'Thou art the Chosen of God and if thou wilt but keep thine eyes averted from the SINFUL WOMAN *thou shalt be saved for Great Things.'*

I stood up beside my pallet & asked, 'Yea Lord but who is the SINFUL WOMAN?'

'She of whom thou dreamest, she is the SINFUL WOMAN.'

However, in my lascivious imaginings I would dream of all & any women, even the minister's wife, Mrs Shaw, with her bulbous nose & few teeth, & in imagination would lie with her, wallowing in the filth of my heart. I would dream of the two maidservants, Betty & Sarah, & the cook-maid, Ann.

So next day, having the Spirit of the Lord upon me, I came groping my way downstairs to breakfast with my eyelids closed, & thereby shut out the temptation of concupiscence. Mrs Shaw was much perplexed.

Yet still these impulses disturbed me for many years. I struggled with them in a mesh of horror and evil. Satan fought God for my soul but God promised, 'I Shall Prevail, for in the beginning I have elected thee, & the greater the sinner, the greater the victory.' When I think how I would watch the dogs rut in the street, & grow aching-hot, I wonder at the GREATNESS OF THE ALMIGHTY *who is able to save such a beastly one.*

As Lyngard made his way in the world, he left behind such corruptions, satisfying primitive instincts by smearing Independents and Anabaptists. He never married, hoarding his energies to cull vindictive biblical passages promising doom to facile Quakers and glory to sage Presbyters. He would inaugurate public debates such as the one on the heath at Moss Side in the mid-1650s, in which he trounced 'the unrighteous'.

Much of the diary consisted of excoriated wrestlings with biblical texts which held little interest for me. I'd look up and yawn, annoying the clerical scholar who was reading in the seat I thought of as Faith's. Noticing his disapproval, I was able to produce a whole sequence of uninhibited yawns, with a view to triggering off an attack. He flushed as he picked up his irritated pencil and readdressed his book. I settled down again to Lyngard.

25 August 1655 As I was preaching, a woman came in wearing sackcloth and ashes, & stood before the pulpit throughout the sermon, her hair plastered to her head. Now & again she reached her hand into a pot &, bringing out a mess of clayey ash and water, slapped it on her head. 'It is a sign' (I told my flock, seizing the moment) 'that we must turn from iniquity in this land of beastly madmen ruled by beastlier madwomen, & all be of one Presbyterian discipline & accord.'

The woman, covered with filth as she was, waited till I had finished my sermon & poured the whole pot of foulness over her head, crying, 'WOE WOE WOE TO THE HIRELING WOLF, HIS ACCURSED STEEPLEHOUSE, HE STEALS THE BREAD OUT OF THE MOUTH OF THE POOR ETCETERA.'

The congregation beat the whore & turned her out, but back she came & stood looking on without speaking but, oh, she spoke, she spoke from her witch eyes. Eyes which were blue-green, & I took it from her well-shaped body she was a young woman, voluptuous though thin & under-fed.

As I looked down upon her my loins kindled, I secretly shifted from foot to foot, her eyes possessed & fascinated me. I panted, hot & quick, until I cried aloud 'WITCH WITCH!'

'No witch, priest. I am the apostle, called of this world Hannah,' cried out this impudent slut.

It is said that George Fox, accursed leader of these Quaking madmen, has the pale blue eyes of a witch whose gaze maddens humans & tames wild beasts. How much more then may EVE's rebellious daughters be possessed by the Devil's

power? A more shrill, ear-offending voice I have never heard
from man nor woman than this.

'Christ!' I muttered aloud. 'It's you! I'm sure it's you!'
There she was, my Hannah, executing one of the more
bizarre and messy modes of prophetic protest practised by
Friends.

'For goodness' sake,' objected my fellow-reader, usurper
of Faith's chair, wincing at my blasphemy. 'This is a library.'

'What?'

'Shush. I have work to do.'

'So have I. I'm doing it.'

'Then could you do it more quietly?'

'What's the problem?' I asked him. 'You keep kind-of
snoring, in concentration presumably, and I occasionally
mutter. This isn't a church, is it?'

'It's hopeless, utterly hopeless,' he said, clapping his books
together. 'I shall have to come back another day.' He rose,
rasping his chair back.

'Look,' I said. 'Sit down, do. Sorry. I'll keep my trap shut.'

We tolerated one another across the table.

27 August   Although Mr Heyricke believes the Quaker
Whore to be Margaret Fell of Swarthmoor, a gentlewoman
run amok, I take her to belong to the hive of Stockport Quakers
who have several times buzzed at me in my own church.

3 October   The woman impudently bounced down the aisle
arm-in-arm with a friend during divine service & stood before
my pulpit, which I affected not to notice. They were neatly
dressed in waistcoats, cross handkerchiefs about their necks,
but with no covering upon their heads (a Woman's Head
Uncovered being an affront to God & man). In my sermon I
warned my flock against dozing in service, for God hears our
snores in Heaven, & O! how we should abhor the thought of
snoring in a holy place.

One of the whores shrilled, 'A church is not a holy place,
thou man, but only wood and stones.'

However, I proceeded to admonish my flock in gentle, loving
terms to watch over one another &, should they see their

neighbour drowse, administer a nudge, in Christian fellowship: not a poke or pinch, but all to be done lovingly in a spirit of brotherly fellowship.

From the corner of my eye I could see HJ's breast rise and fall . . .

'HJ!' I said. 'Yes! It's her!'

The clerical reader looked up, and unexpectedly smiled. 'I shall be going for my lunch now,' he said. 'You may rampage in peace.'

'Sorry,' I said. 'I've found something here.'

. . . HJ's bosom rise and fall in breathing, & light from the great window fall upon her immodest hair. Rich-tawny-red swathes of hair, like oaks in Tatton in gorgeous autumn . . .

Alex had got her hair bang-on. But the wig lacked the lustre that had kindled Lyngard's interest. The written account of Hannah utterly outdid our attempts to realise her in clay. My fellow scholar had departed, leaving his books neatly piled. I craned over, curious in the midst of my triumph: an abstruse work on the Thirty-Nine Articles. After all these centuries, still fighting the same battles. I returned to Lyngard, to whom these Articles had been anathema, but not as much of an anathema as the inner light:

Strange indeed to see these impudent women stand up, surrounded by the rubble of the old religion, stone saints with their faces smashed off; wingless plaster angels & the trunks of effigies torn from ancient pedestals, as if there were no end to the iconoclasm until the whole world is torn from its foundations. Just as it was woman who set us all awry, so now she calls our reformed Reformation from its path of moderation.

When I had finished my sermon, I addressed these two with mocking courtesy, thus: 'Why do you stand before the congregation, women? Have you some sin you wish to confess to the Lord's people?'

'Priest,' said HJ. 'Why does thou stand up on thy Papist tub

and tell the people lies? – come down, thou hireling.'

The other joined in: 'COME DOWN COME DOWN COME DOWN', enough to set the teeth in a shiver.

With a forbearing smile, I requested that they be placed in the Whores Box, dressed as penitents, thanking them for their 'learned observations'.

'Thou art the Whore, thou beast and harlot, who does the lewd will of Satan thy whoremaster in this steeplehouse.'

To this I replied (wittily), 'I cannot be a Whore – I am a MAN. A MAN cannot be a whore. I am God's minister and THOU art the WHORE, though commanded by the Apostle Paul to learn in silence and serve thy husband in all subjection, for through woman we lost Paradise.'

At this the woman cried, preposterously, 'THOU art the woman! I am an APOSTLE.'

'Madwoman, be silent.'

'Nay, thou art the madwoman.'

Yet all the while my eye thirsted at the sight of her flushed face & throat, where the handkerchief had fallen away to uncover her skin's softness. Her eyes were green, a colour God has allotted to leaves & grass, but not to human eyes, where it is unnatural. Because her habit was grey, modest & becoming (except where the kerchief strayed adrift), those green eyes struck me to the heart & the chestnut brightness of her hair.

'Remove the witch,' I thundered, 'and cover the slut's nakedness.' When the people had rushed them out to the open fields, I calmly continued with the service, smiling upon my flock, to show them I was not disturbed by these termagants.

December 1, 1655 Today I received a lusty goose-pie, from my parishioner, the wife of Mr Jollie the schoolmaster, which I ate with relish. It was a fine pie, cased in twig work, which I devoured with my fingers, the juices running between my fingers & down my chin, thanking my Maker all the while for his bounty to his unworthy servant. Blest be the God that created the goose for the pie of the Justified.

The pie and other gifts from his parishioners ministered to Lyngard's inner man but could never appease his ravening inner emptiness; the legitimate sexual needs he denied

83

consumed him. Hannah had begun by hunting him; by and by he turned about and began to track her. Lyngard's obsession was auspicious for mine. At the debate on the open heath at Shadow Moss, between Presbyterian clerics and dissidents from Openshaw, Chedle and Stockport, 'that wasp's nest of sectaries', Hannah was there again:

the Quaker with green eyes, with her Yoke-fellow as she calls her, namely a common labourer Isabel Clarke, who says she could neither read nor write before she took to Quaking, but now boasts that she has written books & letters to judges against hanging poor felons who steal to eat – all which troubles my heart beyond expression, apprehending that such wretches will overthrow the whole order.

Green Eyes was a bane to me, I dared not meet those eyes, they consumed me, & I turned away shuddering when the constable took her by the arm and tore open her dress, pushing her down in the heath, for scolding.

I asked the famous Richard Hubberthorne, a more rational and calm-spirited Quaker than any I have engaged with, why they allow such liberty to these light-minded females? He, in his sober manner, asked me, whether I did not believe that women possessed souls? I replied, 'Indeed, but their minds are weaker & must be led with dading-strings like infants.' His answer was: 'We are all Babes, & are released from our fallen natures by the Light.'

At this Green Eyes sprang up & said, 'Christ is in me. And Christ is me. I may speak as well as he' (scowling at Hubberthorne). Like a parrot at her back, the taller menial woman, with a thick accent, squawked as follows:

'Yea, tha MAN, CHROIST *be in* HER. *And int' meanest & poorest o't' beasts.'*

'Oh certainly,' I mocked, 'even in that . . . bilberry there, or the slug beneath it, I suppose: Christ is in those too?'

'Aye, int' attercob on his canny shoining web & t'wood good fer nowt but burning, there yer foinds CHROIST *– but not i'* THEE, *tha* TURKEYCOCK MINISTER O' SATAN.'*

(I have rendered this creature's speech precisely as I heard it, the English of The Pit.)

84

I deigned her – it – no answer, with her burly shoulders &
face like a segg, a gelded bullock. Human? Child of God? I
think not. Truly these people should be burnt or in Bedlam.
September 2 1656   Millenaries everywhere, labourers and
vagrants in the main, telling of imminent WAR, Jesu's final
battle, & the thousand year rule of the Saints, although, as Mr
Heyricke judiciously reminded me, 'Who are the Saints? Surely
you & I, Mr Lyngard, Mr Martindale & Mr Newcome,
together with the congregation of those who have taken the
Covenant.'

In the house of one Norton there was found a pile of muskets
& an arquebus from the reign of Queen Elizabeth. Mr
Martindale told me the rhyming prophetess (she-charlatan)
Hannah Trapnel of Hackney, meditates a visit to the North,
where I have no doubt the millenaries of Stockport will flock to
welcome the witch, as if we had not plentiful supplies of our own.

Green Eyes still haunts me like the ghost of my lost boyhood.
I took horse to Chedle Holme in hopes that I might happen
upon the wench along the way, but saw only homespun women
with their great scythes getting in the last of the hay. I marvel
at the women's muscles like massive cord as they sweep the
scythe, all in a line, & lay low the swathes of hay with a
rhythmic swish, which shows how God can turn to our use even
such low cattle as these females that jabber barbarous English,
& cannot write their own names. At Pinfold Farm Goodwife
Mather offered me a cup of milk fresh from the cow & I did
her the kindness to sit & drink, offering wholesome words of
edification. But, happening to ask: 'Do you know the green-
eyed Quaker, Hannah Jones, of this hamlet?' she was mute,
which I took ill.

'Goodwife Mather,' I exhorted her, 'silence is commanded &
commended by God to women, but when a man & minister
requires an answer, a woman not only may but must speak.'

Her lips were pursed tight, which is a kind of negative
scolding. This was proved when her husband returned from the
fields, for when I asked the yeoman the same question, she
slammed in, 'Hold thy clacking tongue, husband.'

Overturning, overturning, is all the tune. The world upside
down.

For I have seen women in men's hose, strutting up Cateaton Street. They ride horseback, legs astride stallions. Artisans & vile persons claim the Light, servants dictate to masters, the blood-soaked Army rules the usurped land, the pious clergy is despised, while roaming madmen preach the Latter Days & uppish women preach and prophesy. It may be that these Jezebels are sent in sign of the Last Things. We should strip them bare & hang them naked from the City Walls for dogs, vultures &c to tear. O LORD WHEN WILT THOU COME, WHEN, WHEN? City walls being intended figuratively, Manchester possessing none.

My ears rang as I stretched back in my seat, as if they had been roared into by the zealous Calvinist. But I must thank him with all my heart for his sex-obsessed scolding: for here she was: my Hannah Emanuel, his 'Green Eyes'. I had to let Alex know we'd guessed her eye-colour wrong when the glass eyes were inserted in the skull. Green, an astonishing green, enough to unnerve the celibate, unself-knowing minister, to make him feel he was being worked on by some force outside himself.

I'd take a break for my hands were quivering, my mouth dry. But how to leave the book? Paranoia kept me hovering, as if some jealous rival might swoop down in my absence on the precious tome, stroking it with his eyes, taking Hannah to himself. Tearing a page from my pad, I laid it over the book, as if making a bed.

At Victoria Station, nineteenth-century dream of the railway station as cathedral of material progress, workmen's hammers clanged. Under the dome of the buffet, a jukebox beat time. From here in Lyngard's time one would have smelt country air, manured pastures dotted with men toiling for twopence a day on heavy soil. At the next table sat a man who had stuck, apparently for all time, on page 3 of the *Sun*. Sipping coffee, I tried to read his face. It was expressionless: the eyes of a repetitious over-eater licking a salty snack that in the moment of tasting had lost its savour. A consumer's eyes.

So were we all: consumers. What would Lyngard and

Martindale, Lilburne the Leveller and Hannah Emanuel have felt, could they have glimpsed the secularity that would succeed their throes? The death of the sacred. Meaning now must be within and private. It must be whispered between friends or lovers like seditious secrets which, if overheard, would be exposed as delusion. I did not want to tell a soul about Hannah. If Hannah were to be published, she would be lost to me.

Our millennium was nearing, to usher in a new chapter in a degenerating memory. As we read on, the prologue fell away and, even when retrieved, appeared to be written in a foreign language whose exact meaning fled like a fugitive. My personal past shared in this abortiveness: it was written in a cipher whose key I had somehow hidden from myself. Hannah was more vivid to me than any of my own people. I had left mother and father to follow her.

But what did I know about Hannah? I tried to put it together under the fluorescent dome.

Quaker woman from Cheadle Hulme, in perhaps her late teens or early twenties in 1656. Went round with a woman-companion, whom she called her 'yoke-fellow', named as Isabel Clarke, a same-sex union not uncommon amongst the pioneers of the movement. The friend seems to have been an illiterate farm-labourer before her conversion. Hannah was obviously arrestingly beautiful, with chestnut-brown hair. And strange, with a magnetism exerted by her eyes, with a witchy (sexy?) quality. Aggressive and unruly. Liable to court notoriety and to put herself centre-stage. Unwomanly therefore, and a dangerous element to the establishment. A lashing tongue and shrill voice. Idealist. Single. Small of stature, since Lyngard makes the point about the comparative tallness of Isabel.

When Lyngard speaks of her 'fascinating' powers, he means a direct power exerted by a witch on her victim, emitting toxic rays from her eyes which 'possess' the victim – or can kill, or force him to behave in a way he would never do of his own accord. Reading this word, I'd flinched with anxiety for Hannah, loaded with the onus of the minister's sexual guilt. Evidently she looked you straight in the eye. And he felt hexed. For God's sake, he even went out looking for her in the fields and calling on the farmer's wife he thought might supply an address – at Pinfold, my Pinfold. And the farmer's wife covered up for her. Why? The anxiety that began to quicken made me wish to intervene in Hannah's story: I shook myself mentally, to remind myself that it was all over centuries ago. She chose her path and must have foreseen her end.

Heavily, I carried the partial knowledge of Hannah like some child that had been entrusted to me but squirmed in my arms, and might at any moment slip out of my grip, back to Chetham's.

10 December 1656   Heard details today of the blasphemy of James Nayler, Quaker, betrayed by corrupt power-hungry Eves. This man, having in the frantic folly of his mind ridden into Bristol on an ass, was greeted as Christ in his Second Coming by women hosannahing & strewing the miry path with palms & cloaks. The wild women are: Hannah Stranger, Dorcas Erbury, Judy Crouch, a woman called Mildred, & the lewd harlot, HJ of Chedle Holme, with her helpmeet, IC: at which I blush for Cheshire, that this godly shire should bear a daughter so vile as to bewitch a crazed man – she who in this very church has called for my downfall & is given to buzzing at the men leaders of her own sect, who now begin to discern where this liberty to women must lead.

Nayler is now condemned by Parliament to be whipped by the hangman from the pillory at Westminster to the Old Exchange (I calculate he should receive 350 lashes, till his back be skinless). His tongue to be bored through and his forehead branded 'B' for BLASPHEMER.

Then to be ridden backwards into Bristol, whipped again and placed in Bridewell. A merciful punishment when one considers the horror of his sin. But more heinous is the women's sin, vile creatures excommunicated even from the vile congregation of the Quakers. Were I a magistrate, I should brand 'em on the bare breasts 'W' for WHORE & stand 'em naked in the stocks at the town cross of every borough in England & all this is too good for these filthy harlots.

However, they are merely imprisoned and to be released. It is this pernicious false-clemency of ours that will ruin the commonwealth.

7 January 1657   The severest winter any man alive has known. The crows feet are frozen to their prey. Ducks are frozen into pools and ice-fish lie on the surface of the Irrwell. A sign, I believe, of God's coldness to the usurper and his Army.

21 Jan   Dismaying BOIL on my fundament, a divine judgment on my too sedate life, in which punishment God asks me to arise, arise from my backside & place my hand to the ploughshare with more zeal. It is black, but nothing issues.

2 Feb   Dreamed of Hannah the Quaker whore. In my dream she placed her hand upon my fundament & looked me in the eyes mockingly, saying, 'This is for thee, VILE PRIEST, thou shalt have plague-sores upon thine arse full seven years like the Egyptian Pharaoh.' I awoke in a lather of sweat & took the mirror to my fundament. Seeing there the gross enlargement of this BOIL or PILE, I took counsel with my soul, debating whether this dream has been sent me by God to point out my enemy.

3 Feb   Fundament still noxious.

4 Feb   Black fundament continues. TO THEE O LORD I CRY.

5 Feb   Clarke & Green Eyes are returned to Chedle, I hear on the authority of Old Mr Johnson of Stockport, telling me, to my revulsion, that the whore is with child, either that, or grown very fat. I divine from my distended fundament, together with the dream GOD vouchsafed me in which HJ tampered with my person, that God had warned me of her impending return. This gives me hope that I shall soon be rid of this Job-like affliction.

7 Feb   In viewing my fundament today, squatting at the window with a mirror, I gave thanks to God for the bursting of the BLISTER, & praised him for his infinite mercy in communicating through tribulation.

28 May   I hear HJ bore a bastard, said to be of monstrous birth, with several arms, and 3 legs, joined at the navel, with eyes on its stomach, the product of EVIL, such as pious Massachusetts saw in the 30 monstrous births of the Antinomian, Anne Hutchinson, herself torn to pieces as a judgment by wild Indians.

O Lord where shall we find wild Indians in this land of

England to tear in pieces these sacreligious harlots?

The monster, it is said, died. HJ & her co-strumpet having been driven from Chedle to wander on the wasteland of Chedle Heath.

'Oh my poor Hannah,' I thought, my heart bursting. As I looked up, it seemed I had broken out of a bad dream, into a waking world which was now informed with that dream. Hannah had given birth out there on Chedle Heath, to a stillborn child, *and I had not been there to befriend her*. But it was absurd to nourish this thought. Whatever was happening to me? The boards of the massive table were all aslant to one another, with gaps between the timbers: I fought to align them with my eye. The cleric looked up.

'It's the table,' I said, in explanation. 'Seems to be rocking.'

'*Trompe l'oeil*,' he observed placidly. 'I understand from the librarian that you are studying seventeenth-century heresies, Dr Holderness? I am in the business of defining the minutiae of the Church's doctrine during that interesting epoch. Perhaps we could compare notes? After all, to understand a controversy, one must grasp the fine detail of orthodox belief.'

A conversation in hell, I thought. *Picking nits*. Since he had learned from the librarian that I was a bona fide scholar, despite the criminal implications of my hairstyle, my fellow-reader was prepared to subject me to ordeal by credal monologue.

'Gracious,' he added, in an embarrassed pastoral tone. 'You're crying.'

'God, no, Christ, I'm not crying. Something in my eye.'

'Well. I think I'll call it a day. My advice to you, young woman, is: blink.'

'Blink?'

'Blink away the speck in your eye?'

'Oh. Right. Yes, it's gone now, thanks.'

I smiled as I spoke, for I recognised the sense of his advice. What did the bible call it: *the plank in thine own eye?* Self-infatuated whimsy blinded me to the humanity of others but

90

brought tears to my eyes for Hannah, delivered centuries ago of her stillborn child. I turned the page. To my dismay, I saw that Lyngard had only one more page to deliver. The Restoration was nearly upon us.

7 Sep 1658   She has gone across the seas where I shall never see her again, O Child, O my life.

Cromwell died, nobody much minding it. None cried but dogs, his body stank through the lead coffin & had to be buried swiftly.

[Nov] An effigy of the tyrant lay in state on a catafalque, people filing in to view this waxen idol pranked up in purple robe, orb·sceptre & imperial crown on a throne behind. Its eyes were shut, to signify death but people were much amazed one day to find the ruffian standing up, glass eyes wide open, which used to signify in the Papist religion the king's passage from Purgatory to Heaven. O infamy of the Stinking Whore of Rome, with their effigies & gewgaws, reliques & statues. All to the cost of £100,000.

Her form, shape, spirit is here in my chamber night & day besetting me & in my dreams I see not God but Hannah's demon.

July 1659   Mr Heyricke resolved to rouse Manchester to arms upon the score of the Quakers being in revolt: impostors that say they are for peace but we know what plotters that insolent faction are.

August 7   Earl of Derby came in to Manchester with a troop of horse, who shot off their pistols. I leapt in to the great chest with fright, & remained there, until Mary my maid lifted the lid to tell me they had withdrawn; I rising to my feet with some dignity and explaining to the silly, sniggering girl that I use the chest (my grandfather's, a stout country piece of workmanship) as a private sanctuary or Ark of the Covenant to pray for peace in our unhappy nation, stepped out.

August 19   Battle & rout of rebels at Northwich. Soldiers, soldiers everywhere, & our maid Mary said, 'Why not get in the great chest, sir, I won't tell,' for which she deserves flogging. Everywhere horses are pillaged, good men imprisoned, houses stripped of all goods. Citizens hide their plate & ornaments.

May 12   King Charles II proclaimed in Manchester! amid prayer, bonfires & churchbells not heard for twenty years. I was for the king ALL ALONG, *for a legal monarchy is always better than a giddy, hot-headed, bloody, Anabaptistical multitude. Under a legal monarch, the godly are persecuted more kindly.*

Shadows lengthen as I complete the last page of Lyngard's diary, and retrace my steps to see if I have missed a possible sighting. The librarian hazards the existence of a second volume because the loquacious Lyngard survived a further twenty years, evicted from his church in Manchester, to head a dissenting chapel at Altrincham. I have culled from the volume less than a tithe of the contents, omitting the theological argy-bargy, the stuff of Lyngard's daily consciousness irrelevant to my personal quest.

I stand at the window, stretching, looking out at the pinkish-ochre sandstone of the college buildings. A librarian trundles a trolley of books across the quadrangle; a stream of young men and women traipse between classrooms. All share a timeless, casual quality, as if no conflict could penetrate the serenity of this enduring relic of the archaic Manchester. Students pass, carrying violin and cello cases, the youth of their faces and hair burnished by sunlight: seraphic as they appear, I am tuned to awareness of their turbulent adolescence beneath the quiet surface. Mutinous hairstyles and warpaint remind me of their quarrel with the grown generation.

Hannah ... I see you now more clearly.

I can begin to comprehend. She was one of the rebel Quaker women, who shouted down the leaders and were ripe to fall under the spell of James Nayler's tender spirit, in all its charisma and unconscious power-hunger. Nayler's women were demonised by the movement as Eves debauching Adam's terrestrial paradise. Women who went into the wilderness, tore up bibles in the streets, attempted to raise the dead (as they had seen Nayler do in prison for Dorcas Erbury), women ministers who took the Quaker freedom to speak one's mind too literally.

If Lyngard was right, Hannah came home to Cheadle

pregnant and gave birth to...what sounded like siamese twins or a disabled singleton. And the baby died.

But was Lyngard right? I've read the infamous rant of the Presbyterian misogynist, Thomas Edwards, whose *Gangraena* gloats over divine judgment on dissidents, manifested in deformed offspring with thumbs on their knees and mouths on their stomachs, God signing the mother's guilt on the corpse of the child. I recall the fate of aggressive Quaker Mary Dyer, executed in New England in 1660, mother of a stillborn baby girl, a 'monster' according to the government, 'a woman, a fish, a bird, & beast all woven together': scientific proof of Mary's depravity and 'misshapen opinions'. Since women's imaginations were said to imprint themselves on the foetus at conception, whatever they bore, they had first thought up. So perhaps my Hannah was just tarred with slander. Lyngard would have been avidly ready to believe in her sexual depravity and its consequence. In fact he would have been more-or-less expecting it. But what about Lyngard's testimony that Hannah and Isabel were cast out of their community, to roam the wilds of Cheadle Heath? This certainly suggests that Hannah grossly offended her community.

Charged with a complex mingling of ruth and curiosity, I turn back to the last page of Lyngard's Diary, as if somehow my eyebeams can extort from the blank space of the flyleaf some further information.

I turn over: someone has constructed a sort of pocket by gluing two of the extra leaves together. Like an envelope.

In that moment of discovery, it seems impossible that the sealed envelope was not meant for me. Between those glued leaves, someone has deposited a letter, to be opened by the person most interested in those connected with the story. Who could be more passionately involved than myself?

No one is about. Only the faint whirr of the fan high in the roof outside the closed double doors of the reading room can be heard, mingled with the purring tick of the long-cased clock. I'll hear in good time if anyone approaches. With trembling fingers and lurching heart, I fumble out scissors from my briefcase and gently slit the vertical join with a blade. It opens readily.

Pausing, I listen. No one is stirring.

Out slides a double sheet of paper from the envelope. Covered in minuscule handwriting, on both sides; and as Lyngard's diary is mottled and blemished with speckles, as if to preserve for posterity his rash of rage, so this thin sheet of handwriting has caught the same contagion, though less virulently. It has travelled in its frail cocoon down centuries, and now, like some dun butterfly, unpacks tissue-thin wings and lies in my hand delivered at last.

∗

I did not think of my act as theft. The message simply belonged to me. I accepted receipt.

Placing it carefully at the centre of my notepad, I secured the notepad in my briefcase, which I locked.

'I wonder if you would kindly reserve Lyngard for me for the remainder of this week?' I asked the librarian.

'No problem. And by the way, we've come up with something else you might be interested in. You were asking about Anna Trapnel. We've an anonymous tract, dated 1656, you might care to glance at. Seems to have to do with the visit of a Fifth Monarchist or suchlike prophetess to Manchester. Looks to me like gibberish: I thought as soon as I saw it that it was your cup of tea.'

Whereas yesterday I'd have relished the unintended joke at my expense, and tingled at the prospect of getting my hands on some new material about Anna the Voice, today I felt only the resolute urgency to get home that accompanies the onset of some illness.

'Thanks. Would you put it aside for me?'

I was out and on the Metro, jealously hugging my briefcase. Faces passed by me unregistered, as the tram like some toy train gave out its soft 'Poop poop', cleaving a gentle but persistent path through the rush-hour crowds.

Nothing of this external spectacle was real. These massing people in the bombed-out city were spectres who dimmed and thinned before the arousal of the vehement dead.

Perhaps I was beginning to feel ill. My head seemed charged with electricity as if a storm loured in the offing, and

94

I staggered in negotiating the escalator at Piccadilly, and again in boarding the train for Cheadle Hulme. How unreal it all seemed, this engine-noise and precipitation of so many people in one direction, not with a sense of homeward-going but with uniformly deadpan faces and barely concealed jostling antipathy, impelled daily to repeat this flight from the condition to which we are inexorably condemned.

Just before I got in the door, one of my whirlwind-migraines broke. Though I cringe before their onset, I would say they are a small price to pay for love.

Seven

In pencil at the top of the first page, in educated handwriting, probably early eighteenth century, I read the single sentence:

I Venetia Drew, into whose hand this curious testament has come, offer it to Time for safe-keeping, being forbidden by my father to keep any of the letters &c left by my poor great-aunt Jones, & in the hope that her grandmother's persecutor David Lyngard may serve Providence as postmaster to deliver the same into sympathetic future hands:

There follows, in minute, crabbed and inelegant script, in ink whose gall has bitten through the page, making the obverse difficult to decode:

TESTAMENT OF I.C. OF CHEDLE BULKLEY

I was born the tenth child, seventh daughter of Luke and Elizabeth Clark, my father & mother keeping an ale-house, & cruel poor. As to my true name, I do not know it for I never saw it written down: it might be Isabel or Ishbel, but I was called plain Izzo by my family, or Dim, & Boggy Bo by my brother for he said my sour face, high-coloured as earthenware, would welly frighten the dead like a boggart. Likewise the date of my birth is dark to me, though I was talked of as born the year of the Irish Massacre. My brother Isaac and sister Rose and I being the only surviving children of our parents, he was bound apprentice to a tanner but was antiprunty as a reckless horse, & ran away to London, to my parents' grief. We two were put out in service at the age of ten or eleven, & neither could read or write, & clemmed & ran round barefoot for my father and mother spent all on drink, to snore away their lives like many poor folk.

How sunk in the mire of ignorance I was, let the reader judge. I was no better nor a clod of clay with a mouth in it, & more used to roar than speak, & cawper & cample back to my mother when she bothered to scold me, which was not often. Yet for all that, I grew up cant & lusty, & could give any of the lads a dab in the eye. 'Thy brother's a molly cot to thee, Izzo,' my father said. Yet all thought there was nowt up top & that I was little better than a noddy, big & slow, & would jest about & over me while I was there. They got to calling me DIM, from the Welsh DYM SASSNACH, I dunno, which Cheshire people use for a simpleton. I would get all the heavy work, emptying ashpit & cesspit, carrying coals, all which tasks I performed with grumbling-bad grace, chunner chunner chunner.

When I came to Pinfold Farm the mistress exclaimed that I was as strong as an ox & got the master to come & feel my arms & shoulders, saying I would do the work of a man at half the charge, so my master and mistress valued me highly. For that reason they fed me well, butter, milk, cheese, bread & bacon, sometimes beef, whereas I had rarely eaten flesh in my parents' home. My tasks at Pinfold were to yelve & spread manure, harrow, & dressing meadows, peat- & wood-cutting, working at hay, pulling hemp. Also I washed clothes & did all household tasks, which hard labour I performed not willingly but in sullen silence, as I have seen oxen do grinding round and round a mill. Goody Mather would have me work on the sabbath for there was work to be done, she regarded me as less than a human soul for I never spoke except to cuss quietly under my breath, no better nor one of the dogs in the yard.

One day Master Mather said he had an urge to feel my arm-strength & shoulder-strength once again, taking me to be a cow that would bear any ill-usage. Saying he wished to test the strength of my thighs, for he suspected I was the like of Herckles below-stairs, he thrust his hand under my heavy skirts & tossed them up when I was bending to the fire, whereupon he did feel the strength of my strong arm for I hoiked him up &

hurled him to the floor & kenched his arm so that it dangled limp at his side for some time. And all this done, I remember, without one word said, by him or by me, but I stood up and smoothed my skirts and went back to the logs, & then fell to spinning hemp for the sacks, & not one word said.

I expected, when he shuffled out of the chamber, to lose my place, for the nookshotten man would accuse me of attacking him. But nothing said, he being that afraid of my mistress, who was shrewd of her tongue & sniffed like a dog after him, for she knew his ways. Perhaps also it would have shamed him to confess a woman beat him. The cunning woman came in & set his arm, better nor a surgeon out of Manchester. After this, being a nesh babby of a fellow, he gave me a wide berth.

One of my first memories when I was a very little child is of an Irish girl at Chedle Bulkley, I cannot tell what year this was. When the regratress came peddling honey, I banged open the door of our tenement, &, begging for a lick of honey, ran out into the street after her. Seeing a crowd, I rushed up & saw the Irish girl, & was taken by the brightness of her hair, the colour of a copper pan our neighbour had that glowed in the firelight. The people of Chedle Bulkeley shouted 'Irish whore' & 'Papist whore', & they hustled her on, & yelled GIMBO, GIMBO, which is what us Cheshire folk call the natural child of a natural child. I saw she was great with child, & could hardly walk, her face pale, much pitted by the pox. And it seemed to me that, though nobody pushed her, they swept her away with invisible brooms, for she went staggering (heazing & coughing) along before them, saying 'I am a good Protestant, a Protestant as well as you'; whereupon a man all I covered in flour, said 'If the fremd lass be a Protestant, she must be given alms', but the constable threatened her with flogging & the House of Correction. I saw that her feet were bound with bloody cloths, covered with mud, & every step was a torture to her. But folk tricked her, by telling her the next parish, Didsbury, was rich & looked after strangers, & lay only a furlong on, over the river-bridge. This was a lie, for there is no ford over the Mersey at Chedle. At Gatley, there is a ford but not at Chedle. So she hobbled off, &, floundering into the commons, stumbled & fell into the hay.

Next day her body was fished out from among the bee-nettle, her half-born child between her legs. All these years (I being now 72) I have not been able to forget her burning flamy hair like copper, the honey on my fingers & the Christian cruelty. Later I thought, the Daughter of Woman has nowhere to lay her head.

When I had been at Pinfold three years or so, I was visited by the Spirit, as I shall tell below. When the people called Quakers arrived in Cheshire, I went to hear them in William Hulme's orchard, where apple blossom drifting from the boughs lay on our heads & shoulders as Jacob Wakefield spoke Truth. I wept, for the Spirit of Truth had come already into my heart. I went striding home and told the mistress straight-out, 'I will serve thee, Friend Mather, but I will not bow or curtsey to thee nor use any other profane outward form for we is all equal under the Lord.'

She said, her face a furious red, 'Dost thou THOU me, scum-of-the-earth?'

'Aye.'

Then she was dumb, as was my master, for they could not do without my work & feared to lose me. I laboured faithfully & well. But when the Lord blessed my union with my dear & tender yoke-fellow HANNAH EMANUEL, I must leave them whenever the Spirit bade me. But they saw I was still worth employment for they must pay a man tuppence a day for my work.

It was in the following manner that I first met with my only beloved HANNAH EMANUEL.

It was a day like any other, a dree morning of mist & drizzle, in which my pattens & skirts was dagged with mud before ever I reached the nether field with the tumbril of cowsharn to spread on the earth. I began to fork the stinking sluther with my wording hook, yelving it into the clogged soil with many curses & blasphemies against my Maker which themdays did satisfy my mind, as braying does the goaded mule. So there I was minding my own, or rather my master's business, yelving & cursing, when a lad in brown breeches & a stained leather coat came trapessing into view, round the cop – to whom I said nowt, nor did I trouble to notice him any further.

But when he hunkered down on his haunches, I told him to scat, & threatened him with the yelve if he would not whap away.

'I am no vagabond, friend, & no lad neither.'

I could hardly forbear to laugh at the tyke's singsong tongue, & said in scorn, 'Thart not neither, for thart a Welshie, get back home Welshie & let's be shot of thee, tha canna speak the king's English.'

'I am a maid,' she said then, 'I wear breeches for safety & ease of travel. And why dost thou curse & scold, dear heart, when God's love cloaks all around thee?'

At this I stared & saw that she was what we call in our country a WILL-JILL, neither man nor woman, fish nor fowl – a hermaphrodite, you would say. And a little person in stature, the rittling of the litter, a nobody, yet she came to me, as I saw afterwards, like Robinhood's Wind, the soft breeze that brings the thaw for outlaws & vagrants that bide in the open.

'Thart nowt but a scrat,' I taunted her. 'Get off, tha shakassing, shattery sucking pig, & leave me to shit this earth.'

At this, she drew nearer, asking if she could help me with my work, for it hurt her to see a human soul used as a beast in the field, while others smoked their pipes at the hearth.

'What can tha do, pitiful arsey-varsey tadpole?'

And I brushed her off like a fly, whereupon she perched on a hummock & watched me while I continued to bradow the lower field, giving it a good strong jacket of muck: which (being watched) angered me, & I fell to cursing her, God, master, mistress, field, the cow that shat & the dung I spread, until I was in a lather of sweat, & felt fit to baste her with my bare hands.

'Why curse thy mother the earth?' she asked me softly. 'Isabel, thou art the precious daughter of God & I am come to thee from God to call thee home from Egyptian bondage.'

'How dusta know my name, Will-Jill?' I quailed from her, & the green of her eyes fair snatched at my heart & squeezed it.

'I have always known thee,' she said, turning to go.

'Well, I dunna know thee, & I dunna want to neither.'

I brooded on this mystery as I traipsed back to Pinfold, & could not rid myself of the way she enticed me with her eyes, *till it occurred to me she were foxing, she must have picked up my name from my outburst of cursing. Her hair seemed to me like a vixen's brush, yet she had child-like gentleness, so that I half believed when I arrived home with the empty tumbril, that a Spirit had met me in the far field.*

I sat & golloped the coarse bread we called Brown George & determined not to tell of my visitor. I hilled her over in my mind, like a mound of bedclothes on a bed, devoting what must have been many hours of thought to who or what she might be.

There are breathings in the room. Though I have always slept alone, as far as I can remember, this must be how it feels to half-awaken in the night with a loved person breathing there beside you. Warmly intimate, the drowsy heaven of it. I have been reading propped on one arm on my bed at Pinfold, Isabel's Pinfold. Raising my head, I listen. Vague shushing noises and a train rumbling past.

I hilled her over in my mind, Isabel writes in that trenchant dialect of Cheshire, clay on its roots. *I hilled her over*. The words chasten and harrow. The double duvet lifts in a thick ruck beyond the nest I've built to read as if it buried some deep sleeper. Isabel's testament glows on my pillow, my sole companion. *Oh but Faith*, I think convulsively, *I want you now*.

But Hannah became my friend, my soul's joy; & in the orchard by the hives in the cool of evening we exchanged the kiss of peace.

The Lord called us to go throughout Lancashire & Cheshire, to witness against the priests & their steeplehouses, sometimes stripped naked to the waist to cry Woe upon the magistrates for their cruel taxes, imprisonments & hanging of poor souls that perish for want of bread. We was ducked as scolds at Pool Fold in Manchester & in the Bollin at Macclesfield, at Cocknstoole Hill, where the people infamously abused us, for Christ had come among them in the form of two women, & they knew her not. We laughed them all to scorn, my dear yoke-fellow & I.

In Salford House of Correction, my dear one taught me to read & write. When I first wrote my name in my unsteady script, it seemed the Power tingled in my arm & into my hand

& to my fingertips, from which day I have never ceased to write, penning letters to Oliver Cromwell & the King when he was restored, & to wanton judges & men of power, to command them to act in gentleness to all creatures, not only humans but all that can feel pain.

But they MOCK this, for, they say, 'A Horse is for our use, and not a Rational Creature.'

To which I answer: 'How many Men are rational creatures?'

Is there reason in cruelty? reason in pride? Have you never heard Men bray like Asses? I have. But if we sit in the grass where the creatures graze, we shall hear in that silence the beasts cry to God to hide them from the cruelty of man.

They shall rest with us in Heaven. There shall be no shambles nor no eating of flesh in Jerusalem.

Priest LYNGARD persecuted us furiously & came looking for Hannah where she preached in the meadows, the first man who called her Witch.

One day we visited the prophetess Anna Trapnel on her visit to Stockport, but my friend, having listened for the space of eight & a half hours (an unconscionable time, as she said, to sit still & listen to raucous ravings in rhyme) finally broke her silence & denounced her, saying, 'Anna is no true prophetess & not from God.'

One morning I said to my dear yoke-fellow, 'Let us arise, my dove, my undefiled, & go to Exeter, for I have dreamed in a dream of a work of love that we must do there.' So we went to Exeter, sleeping as we went in barns, pig-troughs & ditches. They told us we must submit to George Fox & Margaret Fell, the great woman of Swarthmoor in her black silks. But Hannah, dressed in simple array like the lilies of the field, retorted, 'Our Light is Our Own Light. Are we not freed from tyranny by the Light?' What befell in Exeter, Cornwall & Bristol with our beloved James Nayler she has told in her Testament.

Our dear child, Grace, was born when we returned to Cheshire. Now, we knew that, since Hannah had never been known carnally by man, this girl-child was the daughter conceived in the love between Hannah & myself, through the grace of God. For this reason we called her name Grace. Though she was said by the beastly-minded hireling harlot brothel-keeper Lyngard and his friend the subtle Heyricke to be both BASTARD & MONSTER, I testify that our child was perfect in every limb, with eyes of violet-blue when new to this world (but they changed to a shade of blue, more like mine than Hannah's, which are green), & black hair which soon fell out, leaving a fair thatch of curls. Seeing her, it came into Hannah's heart to call us all EMANUEL, God-with-us, for our babe was a sign of our Loving Saviour's Coming in these latter days, not in the form of prince or carpenter's son, but as a mother's daughter, the lowest-of-the-low as a lamp around the Light. And even as we have at home a tin lantern, in which wafer-thin sheets of bone do duty for costly glass, & give out the light & draw the gaze, so are we to our daughter, Grace. Frail sheets of bone sheltering the young body of the Ancient-of-Days.

We was chased out into the wilderness of Chedle Heath, where we wandered, drinking water from the stream & eating dark bread, & a handful of late whimberries which by God's Providence we found in a hollow of the moor. We was outcasts and wanderers upon the face of the earth: to fulfil the Scripture prophecy that the Saviour shall roam in the wilderness 40 days.

Winter came on, & the becks crisped, so that I must break the crust of ice to reach the water. But Friends came down from Lancaster to relieve us, as Hannah has told in her paper, & our babe was succoured by us both as our one ewe lamb.

My dearest yoke-fellow was in travail three days, & I sole midwife delivered the child in a barn in Chedle, a ministry in which I have some skill from delivering neighbours' children in Hesketh. I bound the child in a hipinch of rags. But though many enemies & some Friends spat upon us & turned their backs upon the Good News that Grace was come, & a scurrilous paper came out called 'The Ranters He-She-Bastard Delivered', we was taken in by tender Friends of Macclesfield. Hannah has told of our arrest, to be carried at dawn in the third month, 1658, to Liverpool, to a ship bound for Jamaica. We sang all the way 'Blest be the Lord, rejoice in the Lord', but Hannah & the babe was sick unto death, & the ship boarded by pirates & we taken to Turkey (but the Turks is humane souls beside the cruel English Christians). At Smyrna we saw Mary

Fisher, on her journey to convert the Great Turk, & enjoyed refreshing talk with her. Our dear babe was two years old when we took ship for Bristol. We spoke lovingly to the crew & Truth was over all. But when the crew knelt to our babe Grace, we said, 'Do not kneel, Friends, for Grace is born again in each one of us,' & they set us down safely in the port of Bristol. The land was full of bonfires & church bells, morris dancers & maypoles, 4000 Friends in prison, men strutting the streets with long hair curling & bolstered with hair-pieces, & the King restored, so we carried our babe to London, to warn & admonish the King.

In London, we stayed in the house of Rebecca Drury, & was told of the death of our dear James Nayler. My companion tore her hair in her grief & raged up & down, so that I was troubled & asked, 'My lamb, why grieve? For he that suffered has found his peace.'

But Hannah said, 'Thou knows not, thou knows nothing, Isabel, NOTHING,' with great bitterness of heart.

'Then tell me, sweet heart.'

When she would say nothing, I covered her with my body, like the hen brathering her brood. And if any man should object that our union was unnatural, or against God's law, shame on him & may he be struck dumb, for he sins against the only Law we recognise, which Law is LOVE. Otherwise there is no law at all & no sin except hardness of heart.

Sin is a bugaboo dreamed up by rich men to keep the poor in subjection & leave them the cheevings of the corn.

Sin is prisons, churches, wealth, priests, parliaments, courts, constables & men pockfretten with lust.

And the rich man's estate is stolen goods, built on violence, for he has creamed it into his hand in the dead of night.

My beloved was pure & spotless, she was a snow their trampling feet could never mark.

We went to see the King as he walked on St James' Park, with his gallants and Beauties. My yoke-fellow ran up to Charles with a letter, in which she reminded him of his promise made at Breda to honour liberty of conscience in all his subjects: at which the soldiers penned her like a ewe in a pound with their lowered pikes. But she, ducking under (being adroit *and strong), rushed up to the king & said 'Friend Charles, a word with thee.'*

'Does thou THOU the King, insolent slut?' said a courtier.

'Aye, I THOU the King, & am no slut neither, though I see around me whores painted red & white, with filthy black patches to cover their spots & pimples.'

The King, a towering-tall man, swarthy like a Spaniard, laughed aloud.

'Friend Charles, thou has cast thy true friends into dens unfit for beasts. And gives thy mind to false counsel. Friends do not refuse oaths & tithes & hat-honour for hatred of thee but for love of God. Here's a paper I have writ for thee. Will thou read it?'

The king smiled, amused, saying, 'I will read it over.'

We stood gazing as he strode away, the ladies snatching up their silk skirts, apricot, eggshell-blue, sea-green, scampering after. I was drunk with colour & luxury. When I told this to my yoke-fellow, she smiled & said, 'Will thou turn coat, Ishbel, & become a Cavalier?'

Though she jested, I could gladly have laid down my burden & surrendered to the delights of a world I (bred like an ox in the hask winds of the north) had never tasted. I welly fainted with desire. And still (at 72 years of age) I can see this sight.

My dear yoke-fellow comforted me, sadly saying, 'Ah, if thou knew all about me, Ishbel, thou'd cease to judge thyself.'

Returning to Cheshire, we found Priest Lyngard removed from the Old Church & the millenaries being risen, there was great persecution in . . .

My mother's elegant *escritoire* stands beneath the casement window in what used to be Pinfold's dairy. Weary and chilled, I sit in her place this morning with the manuscript, in a space that goes back to its writer. Isabel must have toiled in here, day after day, mixing the creamy afterings of the milk in the vat, churning and testing and skimming, cutting curd with a wire sieve, pressing the cheese and binding it with cloth. I drag a sweater down over my head, for the chill in here is old, musty-smelling, the window small to keep out flies from the cheese.

Days and nights of obsessive labour have been spent in the light of the Anglepoise, decoding the document with-magnifying glass, handbook and guesswork, for Isabel's letters scurry over the page on cryptic feet. The dialect words I can only guess. The excitement of the task glitters, darkened by complex awareness that everything salvaged lies upon a boundless hinterland of lost information. We skim in the light craft of one single matter-of-fact paragraph from Macclesfield toward Jamaica and back *via* Turkey (could it be Turkey? Yes, it was Turkey). A global journey spiritually less arresting than the manna of out-of-season bilberries on Chedle Heath.

As Isabel's glimpse of the court-beauties aroused the repressed sensuality in her, so my glimpse of Isabel and Hannah kindles a lust within me. I read and re-read, curtains closed. I correct words and whole phrases misread the first time, and then, doubling back, query my revision. Now I stretch and dizzily focus my eyes on the opaque asymmetry of the casement panes: shaky because I've been passionately overbreathing for hours, as if making love, or about to make love. My tantalised nerves sing and my right hand has gone to sleep. I shake it till the fingertips and palm prickle.

Where she has been once, here I am now. *Isabel*: the mirage of her nearness is so potent that, if I call, it seems, she must come again.

The casement is composed of individual leaded panes intended as diamonds, but things evidently went awry at some early stage of fabrication, and the diamonds ran out of true; they are what the Tudor glazier would have ruefully acknowledged as querks, a crazy paving which grids a botched view of the orchard. Some of these nookshotten panes are flawed with whorls and swirls, giving an impression of underwater strangeness to the world out there. This strangeness I have always taken as a norm. Isabel must have looked up from her hard graft, sweaty in the cold room, amid the urinous curdy smells of the cheeses, the tang of rennet and herb, and hazarded a view through these same aberrant panes.

Isabel wrings my heart in a complex of ways. Anger at the

way she was worked as a young woman shakes me. She tells it so matter-of-factly. It was like this. I was treated like an ox. These are the jobs I had to do. She must have slept above the byre, on a straw pallet. The huddled, breathing warmth and night-stirrings of her fellow creatures would have accompanied her sleep. Great-boned oxen with their liquid eyes and long horns; the cattle she would milk at dawn. Isabel at least, in an age of malnutrition for poor women, was well fed. And powerfully built – enough to strike back when her yeoman-master interfered with her.

Hannah and Isabel were yoke-fellows. What did that mean? They seem to have believed (and I shall have to think about this) they were the biological parents of a daughter, Grace (and what happened to Grace?) What was their relationship, then? Partners in the way, say, the Quaker apostles Katherine Evans and Susan Chevers were spiritual spouses, held together for two years by the Maltese Inquisition? But Katherine and Susan were married to husbands they left at home in England to mind the children: Hannah and Isabel were more.

My feeling toward Isabel and Hannah is the rush of the iron filing answering to the call of the magnet. How can that be? How can you fall in love with people dead hundreds of years? Plainly it's ridiculous. I see that with wry clarity. Still the call comes and I answer.

But books do exert that power, I remind myself. As I stand blearily at the window overlooking my mother's grave, I remind myself of how barren my life has been of intimacy, except that communion with books.

The cherry blossom has long fallen and summer's foliage gleams in its heyday on that well-established tree, whose roots have webbed their fibres in humus fed by the goodness of my mother's body. I let myself out into the pale, undecided air of morning. Traffic fumes have not yet built up, and, save for the occasional plane, there is enough quiet to allow me to imagine I can listen to the garden's introspective secrecy.

I crouch beside the mound, under the awning of leaves, carrying my questions to the earth that smells so fresh. The air on my unwashed face and arms drifts coolly temperate. I look for the presence of my mother, as I have seen folk do in graveyards, coming to chat with the dead-and-gone, filling them in on gossip. Daisies dot the turf; uneasy foliage shimmers in gusts of breeze. I wait.

Her tranquillity during her life made heads turn. She had such a quality of serenity: partly through her carriage, upright and still, and partly through the attention she vouchsafed to any human dealing. God, how it used to irk me: did other mothers, I wondered, pay the milkman on a Friday as if there were some special meaning in the exchange? She'd hold the eyes of the person to whom she gave her attention, suspending her self throughout that time, acknowledging their uniqueness. I'd envied the other children their mothers, some full of fun, others comfortingly stodgy and stolid, all free of the other-worldliness that haunted our household like the tiptoe footsteps of the dead.

So now her tranquillity has reached its logical extension: perfect indifference. I feel, as I crouch by the mound, both hands on its grass, that she lies at ease in non-entity, promiscuously sharing and recycling her being with all and sundry, permeated and permeating. I knew all along she'd never needed me. Peace was her one true love. She'd even named me after the olive of Peace: Olivia. Better, admittedly, than Honour or Verity, which might have incited to a career of dishonour and mendacity; or Faith, which my friend had borne through life with gritted teeth. But still, my mother was asking for it. Better have christened me Irony, or Riot, or Anomaly, and have done with it.

Hannah would never have been indifferent; Hannah, restless and burning and passionate, would not keep quiet. Tranquillity was as foreign to her as to myself, looking over the hedge to where next door's washing billows cheerfully on the line: a row of bathing costumes and beach towels, for they've evidently just come back from holiday in California, with sand in their shoes and a jetlag hangover. Confused between time-zones, I rub my eyes and wonder about the time.

Eight

Visitors to the chamber of Charles II were amazed, not only at its marble glory, and a paradox of puppies and prize spaniels tumbling on the sumptuous royal bed, warm and smelly as nature intended, but at the pandemonium of clocks. One magnificent and up-to-the-minute time-piece told not only the hours but the direction of the wind, a *bijou* example of classic Anglo-French modernity in polished walnut. In a world high on information technology, time was passed watching time pass.

Looking round the king's chamber, you would have counted no fewer than seven clocks, ticking and chiming away to their own tunes. Not one was synchronised with another. The bedlam of temporal dispute played on the nerves of skivvies and lackeys with monotonous insistence, and now and again broke out in a clamour as the foremost clock announced his quarter. Then all spoke up in a turbulent medley, a parliament of dissent, in which no one timepiece could ever permanently concede his opinion to another, for all the Royal Clock-winder's pains.

Had you asked the king how he knew what time it was, he would explain that he regularly checked his watch by the sun-dial in the Privy Garden; it was clocks he loved, not time, and would fondle the case of one curvaceous timepiece with a sensuous palm, much as one might stroke a breast. All gadgetry he loved, omnivorously curious.

The air was thick with the diseuphonious tut-tutting of the seven clocks, a disagreement he could not only tolerate but would have felt bereft without. At six o'clock on the last morning of his life, Charles woke up and asked as a matter of urgency that the eight-day clock in his chamber be wound.

✳

What was the time? I looked at my watch. Far too early to pay calls; but having been up all night, my internal clock was urgently counselling haste if I didn't want my visit to come too late.

The brick of Faith's house was auburn in the slant of early morning sun: a nineteenth-century railwayman's cottage, immaculately restored, free-standing at the end of a terrace. Humbler artisans once inhabited the terrace, their narrow strips of garden recalling the strip agriculture of a feudal age, while the detached cottage with the pear tree and high hedge reflected the status of their foreman. Now these vestiges of the railway age had been converted into unique residences, coveted by middle-class professionals. In an area of new housing, they had accrued the novelty value of the old.

I hovered by Faith's garden gate irresolutely, and with a sensation of twitchy transgressiveness, for we had never invited one another home. I was curious to see where she lived. But my presence seemed to violate a taboo. I realised with a pang the boundaries set on friendships: thus far and no further. I had already overstepped the mark in prowling unknown her personal space.

The four downstairs windows were framed by shutters, painted white; a trellis of clematis was fixed between them, so that the purple flowers curled their way up the auburn wall with a glowing contrast of violet against terracotta. Rambler roses trespassed the hedge and swarmed up the pear tree, with an effect of licit exuberance. When Faith had confided her passion for gardening, I had imagined a style more formal and decorous: which showed the paucity of conjecture, unable to conceive that what was denied by a person's clothes and manners might be given its freedom in her private garden.

What I love about you Olivia, is . . ., she had said in our last real conversation, but never completed the sentence.

Since then I seemed to have gone through some migraine-storm, in which my skull was perforated with holes through which the bright persons of the dead filed in and out. Faith had left two messages on my answerphone asking if I was unwell: no need to phone but, if I needed anything, to let her know. A note had arrived through the post this morning to the same effect. It slipped through almost into my hand, like some message from another time-zone. I sat with the envelope in my lap unopened, gleaning calm simply from the handwriting.

Dear Olivia,
This is just to let you know that I am thinking of you and concerned about you. If you are unwell, would you mind letting me know & I can always do shopping or whatever. I'm afraid we parted in a rather nervy way & I'm so sorry.
Love, Faith.

I could always say I'd come to deliver my reply in person.

There was a head in the downstairs window: the back of Faith's head, with sunlight catching the tips of her hair above a wedge of her left shoulder in its silver-grey blouse, picking it out like mother-of-pearl from the area in shadow. A photographic stillness; then she moved slightly. I decided she was eating: yes, having her breakfast. The slant sunlight caught the rim of a cup as she raised it to her lips.

How vulnerable the back of someone's head is. I felt ashamed of watching: it wasn't a fair thing to do, even if you loved the person. Nevertheless, I continued to gaze. Framed in the window, itself framed in shutters, Faith, familiar as she was, seemed remote and problematic. What, after all, did I know of her? What can you know?

I stole in closer. Nothing clarified except awe at the difficulty of imagining the reality of another person. Another person's life. How private she was, following the palimpsest of her own personal routines, unknown to me; cleaning her teeth, going to bed (nightgown or pyjamas?), reading for a while before she slept. Did she sleep on her left or right side? Did she dream and if so, of what? Under her sensible and

111

clement exterior, did Faith like me have a curdled, vindictive side?

The sense of trespass, of encroachment, had built to such an extent that I blushed hotly. A childish impulse to bolt contended with a somnambulistic compulsion to stay. Now that I stood so close, I could see that her head was in constant motion. She seemed to be murmuring or talking, and gesturing with her hand, for she bent forward and stretched. Perhaps talking to the cat. She did have a cat, didn't she? Or had I made up the cat, like the phantom formal garden stocked with neat rows of bedding plants?

Then she threw back her head and laughed.

I heard the laugh from where I stood behind the window, and her pale hair flopped back into the sunlight.

Someone else laughed too, a male voice.

I started back, the pane's glitter needling my voyeuristic eye, that abrupt duet of laughter imprinted upon my inner ear. Perhaps hearing the scrape of my sole on the paving, she turned, peered and caught me there, pinioned on embarrassment. There was a moment in which we locked eyes and her grey-green stare carried no welcome, only defensive alarm. Then she smiled, turned away and must have said something like 'There's someone outside.'

When, after a fractional pause, she opened the door, which gave straight into the living room, no man was evident.

'Olivia. Are you all right? I've been...concerned. Come in.'

'Well, no, I won't bother you, Faith. Really. I just came to say I'm OK, and thanks for the phone calls and note. I've...been away.'

'Please, Olivia, bother me.' She laid her hand on my sleeve.

'But you've got company. And anyhow, it's so early.'

She coloured up. Would she deny the man's presence? I was intrigued to know whether Faith would be prepared to lie if necessary. One did not associate her with lies – but cats, tidy borders, conscience. She hesitated as if she too wondered whether a lie might be in order. After all, the man might have been, or been made out to be, anyone: relative or neighbour or visiting colleague. Her hesitation confirmed my suspicion.

'Jim,' she called back, into the house. 'Olivia's here. Refusing to come in.'

I stepped in. The urge to enquire after his wife and three charming children was almost irresistible.

It would have been hard to decide which of the three of us was the most red-faced. Jim glowered beneath his smile, as he came in from the kitchen, tea-cloth in hand. He flourished it foolishly, as if having just snatched it up on a whim, to demonstrate ... what? That he had only run out of the room out of a passion for washing up? That he belonged here, as a domestic fixture?

'Olivia,' he said, with gritted teeth. 'What a pleasant surprise.'

'We were just finishing breakfast,' said Faith. 'Jim's staying for a few days. Have you had breakfast, Olivia?'

I shook my head; then nodded. I'd lost the sense of breakfast–lunch–supper that structures the day of those who inhabit normal time.

'I'll finish the washing up,' offered Jim, as a sacrifice to Hospitality. 'You girls have a nice tongue-wag; then perhaps we can have coffee.'

As he shut the door, Faith said, 'I'm sorry I didn't tell you, Olivia. I couldn't, you see. The divorce isn't through and it's such a sensitive subject.'

'Of course. I'm so sorry to barge in on you, Faith, in this intrusive way.'

'Not intrusive at all, please don't say that. In fact, if I think about it, it's a real relief. So many times I've wanted to tell you...'

'How long...?'

'Oh, around ten months,' she said. 'Ten months next Tuesday.'

So, all that time while my tenderness was growing, so delicate and uncertain, yet at the same time healing and intense, Faith had been oblivious. She swam in another element, the dreamy ocean of clandestine passion, fighting her own underwater demons of guilt and excitement, never touching my own experience, except through glass. On and on she swam, round and round the integrity of her own sealed world, blissful and finished. For she'd been gobbled up. He'd taken her. And so unworthy of her. As he must know. Him and his tea-towel. Him and his History of the Cistercian Monasteries.

'I hope you don't mind?' she pleaded.

Did she guess then? If she guessed what I had hardly articulated to myself, knowing myself so little, did it grate, offend, gratify her? Was she sorry for me? This thought was mortifying.

'I hope you're happy,' I said stiltedly.

'I am. Though happiness ... is rather a complex thing. I wish it didn't so often take the form of its own opposite. I'm troubled for his wife: she's so dependent. I've tried to renounce him – quaint word, isn't it? – but the trouble is, what you deny yourself you only end up wanting more.'

'Tell me something I don't know.' *I hilled her over in my mind*, Isabel had written of Hannah.

'Are you OK, Olivia? What's happened?'

What could I tell her now that she wouldn't pass on to him? They're a couple now. He's probably got his ear to the door, whilst making such a drama of clattering the crockery through there.

'Oh – just getting rather deep into some books I've turned up at Chetham's. And having what I've decided are migraines.'

'You drive yourself too hard. It's wonderful the way you live your work but I worry that you're so ruthless with yourself.'

'I'll go now. I won't keep you.'

She made no effort to detain me, perhaps seeing that at any moment the tears mounting from so deep inside would overflow. Maybe there flickered in her eyes an inkling of how much hope I had sacrificed by snatching this scathed peep into her private world. I wandered over to the towering spread of rambler roses, luxuriantly encroaching across every tree on the south-west-facing side of the garden. The scent was as pale as their faces, milky-mild. She stood at the door in her slippers, arms folded, an outward-facing smile on her lips, her eyes daunted, watching my dark figure in sweater and trousers, staining her garden with momentary black.

'See you soon,' I promised.

'You must come over when things have settled down,' she said. 'Let us give you dinner.'

It braced me that she said this, in that brittle way. The falling-back on the phoney culture of etiquette, inviting and being invited in return; the beast with two backs of 'we' released me from the fist that had reached inside my ribcage to squeeze my heart. I wrenched myself away, turning back only to enquire, in what must have seemed a wild manner, 'Where's the cat?'

'Cat?'

'I thought you had a cat?'

She shook her head, baffled.

*

Faith's house and the terrace of cottages was set back and screened from the main road. I walked steadily down the path to the road; then turned to look back. Faith had walked out to her front gate and stood where I'd been standing, in her slippers, arms folded, watching me disappear. Probably making sure I was off the premises, or still revolving in perplexity my half-baked interest in her non-existent cat.

I waved, in a mock-jaunty way, and started off down the road toward the bus-stop. I would get on any bus that presented itself, regardless of destination.

When I reached the bus-stop, I glanced round and saw that she had followed me out, still in her slippers, and was standing where I had stood to look back, where her path met the road. Arms hanging limp at her sides, she made no move in any direction.

There was something uncanny in this series of leaps, in which she took my place without my seeing her move: it made the hairs on the back of my neck shiver unpleasantly. If I were to advance further, would I turn back only to find Faith standing at the bus-stop?

What? I signalled, out of earshot, with a lifting of my shoulders and hands in what might have seemed an irascible gesture.

What is it?

Was this Faith's idea of seeing me off; making sure I went?

Yet that didn't ring true to Faith (what did, in the light of Jim?) and her stance expressed no wish to be shot of me. It expressed no wish at all, not even to be standing there. The long perspective contracted her into a remote smallness, centring itself in the pupil of my eye but trivial in the panorama of the road, houses, bellowing traffic.

And still she stood and still I looked, irresolute, for now a bus was coming, which in spirit I had already mounted.

But she held me.

I shook my head at the bus driver. There was no queue and he drove off, the bus almost empty.

Now I glanced back and she had moved again, a few metres toward me. It was like the childhood game of statues: but why would she be playing with me? A tremor shook me, as if I were dreaming awake. This was not, could not be, the real Faith, but some phantasmal wish-fulfilment figure my unconscious had dreamed up. Finally I was seeing things. For so many years, inch by inch, things had been slipping, and at last I'd lost hold. Palm over my eyes, I brought it sweeping down over my face, as if to drag off the mask of hallucination.

I would sort this out. There are no such things as ghosts. If I went to meet her halfway, she would shrink if unreal, under this broad daylight, and, if real, would probably turn tail and retreat home.

As I began to walk, she began to walk. Our paces quickened.

'What's all this?' I asked her breathlessly. 'It's like Orpheus and Eurydice. I keep turning round and you keep creeping up.'

Her eyes seemed oddly blurred, as if not properly focused, or – no, with a suffusion of tenderness.

'What?' I asked her. 'Whatever is it, Faith?'

She reached up both arms around my neck, raised her face to mine. I took hold of her around her waist, hands on the cool of her silk blouse, and hugged her hard. But when I let go, she seemed to spring in my hands, so that I had no choice but to catch her up; my mouth met her mouth in a kiss at once raw and tremulous. Our faces remained close and we gazed open-eyed into open eyes, and brushed our lips softly against one another, as if in blessing.

116

A thousand times I went over it on the bus home, with (each time) peaceful jubilation. There are no words for it, though something was said: a speech in fragments, brokenly, a crumbling of reverie into the falling-apart of language.

Whispering, something like: 'But what about...?'

'It's not – exactly – as you think. I can't...'

'You know I've felt...'

'I don't know anything.'

Probably it only lasted a few minutes, this epoch in my life, when the inner wall of partition came down between myself and the world; I saw face to face. But time seemed suspended in its entirety. It was set aside as inconsequent. In my joy, I could at last have the wealth to spare for generosity. We turned our eyes with one accord, and there he stood, precisely where she had been standing, at the junction of path and road, slack-mouthed. She turned back to me, still having hold of my hand.

'It's OK, go back,' I said. 'Tell him I got upset or something, and you were comforting me.'

'I don't really understand what made me...'

'You don't have to say anything, or understand anything. Just let it have *been*. Go back.'

She would not have grasped that the tears that overflowed as I walked away, fast, were not of loss but came from some deep spring in my nature that had never been allowed to flow, leaving me parched, black earth, whose every act had been fruitless. I was glad she could not see. She would inevitably have misconstrued such tears. She would have thought that, should the experience never be repeated, I'd be devastated; which would have grieved her. Nothing could have been farther from the truth. These tears were rain to my blight.

Over and over I relived that kiss. As the bus jolted its way through Timperley and Gatley, again I lifted her clean off her feet, and felt the power of her slight frame as she raised herself in my arms. Sole inmate of the bus, I looked down with a crazy incredulity at the curled-open palm of my hand in my lap, the hand that still seemed to take the pressure of Faith's. As we swayed round a corner, there was a dazzle in my eyes. The whole of the rest of my life lay ahead, with or without a repetition or development of this joy; but at last I had lived, I had come out of mourning.

*

It would be false to pretend that what fed me did not, by infinite recollection, consume itself. The kiss went on all day and I awoke in the early hours of the morning knowing that it had been prolonged in my dream. Next day my body was still kindled and my heart surcharged with emotion.

By evening I was famishing to see her again. If I went round...? That bright remembrance made the interior of Pinfold not only shadowy but tedious. What was she thinking? Was she thinking of me? Would she ring? I prayed to the telephone to ring.

More probably, Faith was trying to re-establish the routine that her sudden aberration had jolted her out of. I had to be satisfied with the gesture that had been given – certainly against her better judgment. I struggled to retain my belief that it was more than the light fare of a moment; that it could be sustained as the testament that I could be loved and recognised. Could a kiss be a witness or testament? Surely it could. If it meant enough to you.

The long summer vacation stretched ahead with a kind of finality. Nothing was in prospect but drought: for there had been no rain for a fortnight and temperatures were in the eighties. Next door had decamped again for the beach and I was quiet with my work, sitting in the shade beneath the copper beech at the far end of the garden with books and papers. The ground lay hard and parched, and the turf was blond with thirst.

Quiet had grown in me, child of that brimming moment of tenderness. It was not something I particularly examined or questioned, but lived in it from hour to hour relatively free of lonely introspection, my mind concentrated on my transcription of Isabel Clarke's testament. Already I had a sheaf of notes, mainly in the form of tentative exploration.

A note from Faith read only:

Dearest Olivia,
This is to tell you, in the midst of packing etc that we are

*going to Corinth for three weeks. I will be thinking of you,
and hope to write from there.
Take care, Love always, Faith*

*

In the medical faculty, my life-cast and Hannah's reconstructed head kept each other company in a corner of the
studio.

The pang again hit me when I had closed the door behind
me: *twins*, I thought. It was only gradually that you began to
dissociate the faces and to break loose from the eerie brain-
teaser their proximity posed as to which was the original and
which the reflection. I must tell Alex when he returned from
holiday what discoveries I had been able to make concerning
Hannah and her history. And he would listen humanely,
glancing from me to the clay head, ascribing her experience to
the likeness he had conjured, thinking up in the artistic part
of his mind a portrait instead of the scientist's replication.

*For this is not really you, I silently told the stillborn head.
This is a mere simulacrum.*

The information I had gleaned from Isabel's and Lyngard's
memories had enabled me to reconstruct what I believed to
be a more genuine likeness of Hannah. Her portrait was
being realised through the medium of me. I was the paint, I
held the brush, my warp and weft were the canvas, my
psyche the crucible in which she would come to live birth. A
portrait is inevitably a twin composition: the painter's gaze
falls on the face like light from a window. All portraits are
self-portraits.

Taking up the cool wax head from the litter on Alex's
bench, I placed it on the modelling plinth, and softly spun it.

She turned away, until I could only see her from behind.
The back of her head seemed for a moment no more
inscrutable and no less real than Faith's, seen through the
irregularities of the windowpane. Now she turned her head
around, into the orbit of my ken. Stared somewhat past me,
far-away-eyed, disengaged from my moment. I sat down on
one of Alex's stools and confronted her, giving my mind over
to imagining the life of which this cast stood as mnemonic.

Imagine, I'd perpetually instructed my classes, impervious to their squirms of embarrassment, as if I'd required them in the name of academic excellence to undress and exhibit their nudity. *Imagine what you think you know; show it like a film, checking back to the documents as you run the spool.* It had been in the nature of a dare, challenging them to plunge out beyond the stagnant history books into the winy waters of conjecture.

It was easy in the arrogance of my public role, on my high horse of publications, to pontificate about using your imagination, for my posture was that of equestrian among footsloggers. And besides I was a fraud: for imagination takes empathy, and more than a gift for the vivid collage of reconstruction. There were Facts Men, and there were Foucault's Men (there are no people, only discourses), and there were Doubt-your-Sources Men: Imagination had died and been interred with Keats, or walked like a ghost at Disney World.

What, for all my blether, had I actually imagined? How quiet had I been in listening to the past? Eye-to-eye with that silent head in Alex's studio, I was face-to-face with the reluctance of the dead to answer our questions, to take roles in our films, to come at our call.

She stared straight forward, her mouth slightly open, an archaic hinted smile on her pale lips.

I had read Isabel's testimony, or part of it, and felt I'd achieved some intimacy with her mind and life. But so far I'd read nothing directly written by Hannah. What I had was guesswork, not imagination. And my guess was that Hannah, being of a higher social status than Isabel (for she'd been in a position to teach her to read and write) had held her low-born friend in thrall, admitting her to the deepest intimacy and elevating her to the likeness of a peer, but unconsciously tyrannising over her. It is Hannah who takes centre stage, speaking up against Lyngard, while her henchwoman sets up a grating chorus of COME DOWN COME DOWN. It is Hannah that the constable beats on Shadow Moss, ripping open her bodice to the frenzied excitement of Lyngard. She too slams in against the eminent Hubberthorne: 'I may speak as well as he.' She gets pregnant, and is responsible for the group's change of name to 'Emanuel', herself both God and mother-tabernacle of God. She tests out Anna Trapnel. (On the other hand, when Isabel has the dream that they must go to Exeter, Hannah follows the leading without demur.) She approaches the king, breaking through the cordon of soldiers. And, finally, she gets herself executed, while Isabel lives till at least seventy-two.

But it's the detail of the eyes, green and audacious, that comes up most often in both Lyngard's and Isabel's accounts: a running theme. Something fey and strange in her face, then; a wild challenge to the norms and codes that are there to control her and her ilk.

It interests me that Lyngard associated her green eyes with something unnatural, *because* they were the colour of nature. God meant grass to be green: green grass conforms tautologously to the colour-code of the divine palette. Had Lyngard looked out one day and seen the grass bright purple, he'd have shaken in his shoes as he did at the eyes' witchy usurpation of the colour of grass. They stood in her face like statements of demonic intent.

This cannot be shown in Alex's head, where the expression of the eyes (which we guessed blue) is patient and pensive. I try to imagine them in motion, in a mobile face, full of attack and passion. Small, around five-foot-two. Lean and muscular.

A fury, a vixen, a termagant, then. Physically fearless and shrill of voice. A shrew.

You were really asking for it, I tell the silent face, which superciliously replies, *Think what you like. It means nothing to me.*

My hunch is she depended on Isabel more than she would have liked to admit. And the tenderness between them was such that they imagined they'd conceived a child.

Surely there must have been physical passion? How else did Isabel think 'their' child, Grace, had been conceived?

Their contempt for a merely human science meant that the facts of biology – no male to supply the seed – would have made this obstacle seem paltry. For lesbian love their culture had no names, save among the hyperlearned to whom the name Sappho meant something exotically Greek. Who could imagine that a woman could possibly prefer a woman to the superior sex? It was not even a crime, being simply unthinkable.

What were you hiding from Isabel? I ask Hannah. Whose was that baby? Isabel would have believed any story you spun her.

The Mona Lisa smile Alex has given her mocks any attempt to possess her secret. But if it takes the rest of my life, I shall hunt her story down.

Nine

Surely Chetham's would offer a cool refuge from the sweltering pool of polluted air through which we gasped our passage, like a nation of asthmatics. A building centuries old, with walls feet thick, would afford a sanctuary of cool at the heart of the city.

Wrong, of course. Whatever throes and vicissitudes we outside had to undergo, the book-world also suffered. High in the vault a fan billowed warm air about, without cooling anything. In the torrid reading room, only one small window could be opened, linking the inferno within to the inferno without. Two scholars were already seated at the oval table, men whose brain-pans might be cooled by baldness but whose outfits proclaimed a sensitive reluctance to display their braces: shirts, ties and elderly linen jackets carapaced them from the eyes of the living. In such humidity, they must suffer for knowledge's sake.

Up they looked as I came in, along with the cleaner who took to swiping with a duster at any object that came within her reach. Both of us were regarded with frigid suspicion, as interlopers into the tabernacle of learning; the cleaner for being a menial nuisance and myself as a representative of the T-shirted masses, who could not be conceived as doing the solemn work for which Chetham had set aside this fortress against ignorance: 'for scholars and well-disposed persons'. I in turn glowered, for their presence created a difficulty, should it come over me to steal anything precious.

The heat oppressed me so that my head swam. I elected to

remove trainers and socks, which involved surreptitious bending to untie my laces, and wriggling off my footwear with my toes. With a sigh of relief, I propped nude feet on a spar of the table. It was the kind of liberty your genteel scholar would not brook, however tempted.

My books arrived: Lyngard, and the volume of Anna Trapnel the librarian had thought would interest me, on account of its extreme barminess. Clearly, he had failed to detect my criminality in slitting open the joined leaves of Lyngard, extracting the precious wafer of communication.

If only it would rain.

I lolled my head down on my notepad, my eyesight reeling down the gap between the great oak boards that composed the table-top, at an angle to one another, to the wooden floor, like the sea seen through pier-slats. The table seemed to roll with the tides of heat. Solid and venerable, the oval table had travelled down the centuries like a galleon from the old world to the continent of the New World, its timbers hewn from giant trees, girded together by master-turners. Into our throwaway, mass-production age it sailed – all its planes askance to one another but congruent with the whole – and took the gossamer burden of our books, elbows and pencil-points with the same massive, durable indifference.

Round this table we cajoled the dead to reveal their innermost secrets from the stretched integument of cows rendered into vellum and sheep limed into parchment. We consulted the beaten, bleached rags of our ancestors, sized with glue culled from hooves, for intelligence of the dead. Tanned and tawed skins of beasts stripped by illiterates from animal carcases cradled the quires of pages on which we fed. Between the covers, moulds and funguses throve, foxing the pages; bookworms ate the delicious matter into a lace, binding pages together in indissoluble liaison. Thus I pondered, oozing sweat amongst my cerebrating fellow scholars, breathing in particles of powder, product of extinct slaughter-houses whose floors had once been slick with creatures' blood, questing among these mortal vestiges for a quickening of mental life.

John Dee, mathematician and magus, had been a Fellow at

Chetham's conjuring and exorcising here. I'd seen him labelled quack: but how much more potty had been the astrologer's conjurations than those of today's scholars round this elliptical table, stalking the departed in mutilated animal-hide and slivers of defunct tree: galloping millennially toward entropy? Humphrey Chetham, our cadaverous benefactor, looked down upon us from the wall, as my T-shirt, like saturated blotting paper, darkened under the armpits with sweat. How could I work in this simmering heat?

> At the round world's imagined corners blow
> Your trumpets, angels, and arise, arise,
> Ye numberless infinities . . .

Donne had imagined the bodily resurrection of the dead: a leg lost in Africa would remarry an arm lopped off in Asia. My project, having turned up a woman's skull in our back garden, was to whistle up a spirit from between the warped boards of a dying library.

*

I had long nourished curiosity about Anna Trapnel. Nobody really knew what had happened to the rhyming prophetess after her notorious journey from Whitehall to Cornwall, where, having denounced Cromwell and incited her fellow Fifth Monarchists, she was tried and imprisoned at Bridewell in London. After that, there are only scattered sightings and one vast volume of her rhyming rants in the Bodleian in Oxford, taken down in 1658. A few months ago, if I had been able to show that Anna had visited Manchester, it would have set my pulses racing: now my passion for Hannah overrode all other interest, including that of making spectacular discoveries to consolidate my reputation. But I'd glance through it.

The book, however, gripped my interest. Testament of Anna, it had been heavily annotated by some bystanding busybody, half-credulous, half-sceptical, who claimed to have attended Anna's sessions and was tickled by the experience of viewing Anna flat on her back, venting revolutionary prophecies at top speed and high volume. Oh for the earlier invention of tape-recorders! Had I only been able to listen in to that deafening incantation, the holy clamour to which Anna could rise in divine coma, so at odds with her coy lispings when awake. And unlike her auditors, I'd have been able to turn down the volume.

A TRUE REPORT OF ANNA TRAPNEL'S VISIT TO MANCHESTER, BETTER NAMED DEVILCHESTER & SODOM-SALFORD, 1656

I am Anna Trapnel, daughter of a pious shipwright in Poplar, respected, one that pays her taxes and obeys the Government IN ALL THINGS LAWFUL, a humble handmaid of the Lord.

One morning the Lord said to me 'ANNA'.

'LORD' says I.

'Go unto MANCHESTER.'

But I quailed, being of a timorous maidenly disposition, & begged, 'LORD, MANCHESTER is so far a journey, and there may be robbers & bandits upon the way to trouble thy hand-maiden.'

'Did I not protect PAUL on his journey to MACEDONIA?'

Though I answered, 'YEA LORD,' I was unwilling to ride to the dark northern town & there meet with ill-usage, so I asked the Lord, 'LORD, may I not go a shorter journey? Send me to WATFORD, LORD, or to AMERSHAM, where I may do thy work.'

But the Lord waxed wrath, saying, 'DOST THOU REFUSE, my beloved, to go to MANCHESTER? What if I should send thee to LEGHORN or CONSTANTINOPLE?'

I replied, promptly, 'LORD, I WILL GO TO MANCHESTER.'

I took coach at Westminster, & a government spy travelled in the carriage with me, which troubled me greatly. However, when I filled the coach with singing, he held his ears; for he was not able to hear the Lord's handmaiden without cringing.

On the fourth day I alighted at Captain Adshead's house at Stockport, on a hill overhanging the pretty river of Mersey, a peaceful rural place, full of birds singing, under the jurisdiction of Major-General Charles Worsley, right-arm of God's Enemy, the Usurper OLIVER. The Captain & I enjoyed sweet talk concerning the merciful Coming of GOD to Cheshire, with his armies. I shall be on the battlefield singing while my sweet CHRIST, THE LAMB smashes the priests & judges of the North.

This was indeed a tender thought for our weary spirits.

But warrants for my arrest had gone out, a tribulation to my peace-loving soul.

The Captain said, 'Have no fear, the End is Nigh, perhaps tonight, when we shall see HIM face-to-face.'

I lay down without tasting meat or beer or water six days. They told me that I was in a trance for five days, but I remember nothing. Magistrates came to view me, with constables & two ill-disposed priests, Lyngard & Sale, bad men fed fat upon the miseries of the poor, & left crying 'A MANIFEST WITCH!' but God stopped my ears to their clamour.

AND I SANG.

During that week, the saints of Manchester & Stockport came & went, to hear my revelations, & Quakers came to test me. Empty nothing people who believe that God has come already without an army in every man & woman, & that all are ministers who have the Light, whereas we know that Christ will come with muskets, pikes & cannons, & the elect few shall rule one thousand years.

There came two Quaker women, who sat in silence & stared at me. I being not in my trance, was seated before the fire, with my hands in my lap, contemplating with rapture the End of the World, sipping elderflower wine & nibbling morsels of seedcake.

Ralph the boy said, 'Two dirty women's at the door, come to see the prophetess.'

Mrs Adshead asked, 'What manner of dirty women?'

'Quakers, nasty things with mud all over their skirts & hair down their backs. One's the witch Jones what was flogged at Shadow Moss.'

'Send them away,' said Mrs Adshead.

But the Lord commanded, 'ANNA, See the Quakers. Teach them their FOLLY & VANITY & FALSE SPEAKING.'

'I will see the Quakers,' I said.

'Let them wipe their feet and wash their hands & come in decently to the prophetess,' ordered Mrs Adshead.

So they came in, one burly & brawny like a man, a servant or day-labourer, the other, Hannah Jones, a little woman, foxy-faced, with strange piercing eyes & sharp features. 'Pray sit down, sisters, at our hearth,' I said. 'And tell us what business you have with us.'

When they sat down, their skirts steamed in the fire-heat, for both were soaked with rain and mud. These are turbulent, brain-sick people who stand at the market cross whole days shouting WOE! & run about with no Christian garments to cover their nakedness, as if they lived in Eden before the fall.

Then the Green-Eyed one said, 'Friend, we do not come to speak but first to listen. We are here to test whether there is TRUTH in thee.'

'But,' said Mrs Adshead, 'Anna does not prophesy unless in a trance.'

'Not I, but the LORD through me,' I said modestly.

'Then we will wait,' said the Green-Eyed Quaker, & began to stare. In my unease at this rude staring, I presently fell into a trance, for (I was afterwards told) eight & a quarter hours, whence, waking, I saw that the big rough Quaker was gone & the foxy-faced said, simply, 'There is no truth at all in the prophetess. Thou babbles worse than babe, My yoke-fellow could not endure to sit and listen to thy noise.'

Mrs Adshead raised her hand to strike the foxy-faced devil's issue. But I said, with long-suffering, 'Be meek, my love. Let us walk through the paths of the unrighteous with humility like Two Doves.'

Anna was summoned to her trial, bawling, 'HE WENT AS A SHEEP, DUMB BEFORE THE SHEARERS!'

Manchester Sessions House was packed out. Several Justices, Lyngard and a dumpy little woman she was told was the witch-trier, sat round three sides of a table. At the sight of her, Anna panicked but crucially held her nerve.

The witch-trier stared at Anna; Anna stared at the witch-trier. Face-to-face they wrestled. Had Anna given in to this eyeballing and lowered her eyes, it would have implied her guilt as a witch. But if Anna glared too balefully, this would indicate that she was an instrument of Satan. Anna therefore essayed a middle course, and, gazing steadily into the witch-trier's eyes, though trembling with fright, murmured benedictions and beatitudes. The witch-trier blinked and sagged.

'You are accused of fomenting violent revolution in Stockport,' said the magistrate.

'I am innocent as a newborn lamb.'

'What has brought you to Manchester?'

'Why should I not come?'

'I understand you are not married?'

('No man would have the ugly sow!' bawled a yob from the body of the hall.)

'So,' said Anna, 'being, by choice, single, and not by lack of offers, I can go where I please, if the Lord so will.'

'You are a masterless woman – a vagrant,' the Justice probed her status.

'No, no, I have a Master. And his name is Jesu Christ and him I am bound to obey.'

At this dab hit, a disruption commenced in the court. A shrill female voice arose from the benches, on which a small woman in grey had climbed. Anna, put out by the hi-jacking of her Hour of Martyrdom, was also relieved at the deflection of judicial wrath.

We all turned to see the QUAKER *shrew on a bench, crying: 'Revile not the Spirit, thou Whore of Babylon, thou sot & idiot justice of No Peace. Revile not the Spirit, I say, or* SHE *will smite thee, yea, & crush thee into pulp.'*

The magistrate looked from me to her & from her to me: 'Bring this woman forward,' he ordered, and to me he said, 'I take this wildcat to be a disciple of yours, Mistress Trapnel?'

I earnestly denied it, gathering my skirts around me as the vagabond was brought forward by officers.

The Quaker Jones appears to have lived on the road & washed her clothes, if at all, in streams along the way. Her face is brown as a common wage-labourer's, & I saw the shameful point on her arm where the sunburn ends & the fair, soft skin begins. Her hair, worn loose & short in affront to Bible-teaching, is shorn jaggedly. My own hair, being comely & long, is covered beneath a white & pious hood.

The magistrate declared, 'I know thee, Hannah Jones, thou art the bad daughter of a good merchant, Master Jones of Wrexham. Where is thy hair, woman?'

'On my head, man. Where is thine?'

Justice Holdsworth being a bald man, this impertinent answer made the rascals in the hall hoot. But I stood sternly by, my eyes downcast.

'I'll have thee flogged naked in the market square,' said he.

'Man,' said she, 'leave off thy canting for Christ has come to silence thee in the person of a woman.'

'Indeed,' said Mr Holdsworth, jesting, glancing round the throng. 'Where is he? I do not see him in this company.'

'I am the Christ, man,' she said. 'Take care how thou use me.'

There was uproar in the sessions hall. Whereupon a Welshman burst out of the crowd & seized the Quaker by the wrists, wrenching her back & (his hat off to the Justices), said, 'I beg your worships' pardon, this is my wife, & she is mad. Give me leave to take her home.'

So he hurried her out, she fighting him, the crowds cuffing them & spitting in their rage: the Quaker crying, 'Let me alone, let me alone, I am the Christ.'

I saw the witch-trying woman crouch at the table like a spider on her web, gazing narrowly at the heretic. The cry went up, A WITCH! A WITCH! but she escaped, for that time.

This creature, Hannah Jones, is about 28 years of age, & very thin. She has been whipped at the market cross many times, also ducked as a scold. They say the skin of her back is so hardened by the whip that it is like leather, & she laughs at blows. She tells the people that God is a Mother Hen that takes her chicks beneath her wings & the Nursing Mother that cannot fail her babes; & foully misnames God (clean against Scripture) SHE. I told the Justices, the ministers and the people that the woman Jones is an ABOMINATION, with whom the saints have no fellowship.

When Anna returned to the Adshead household, she deplored the monstrous tongue of the Quaker witch, relieved no doubt that Hannah had deflected attention from herself. Exhausted, she fell into a trance and was conveyed to her bedchamber, where all followed to inspect the swooned saint. The shorthand-writer whipped out pen and paper.

'Ah see! Ah see! my Jesus comes!' Anna pointed up to the timbered roof. Everyone swivelled to stare.

> And Quakers, you may see
> The Spirit flying from his mouth
> On Hannah's tongue to be.
>
> And you may gape, and you may quake,
> But, Spirit, he will call
> HANNAH to sit upon his knee
> In the celestial hall.

On and on she rhymed. How the company bore to sit there a mortal two hours, gravely pondering Anna's doggerel, in solemn hermeneutic quandaries, taxes the modern imagination. They watched her like a television, time failing to register as tedium. Mrs Adshead and a band of female believers surrounded the bed, and the Captain looked in from time to time, as I might have done at home during the weather forecast, to ascertain whether anything of meteorological moment had been predicted, requiring the fetching in of washing or provision of raincoat.

Now comes Anna's account of her trial for witchcraft. Never did Anna Trapnel's eccentric combination of religious passion and theatrical adroitness stand her in better stead. I read with deep attention for surely my Hannah must have undergone some similar test and utterly lacked those instincts for self-preservation that served the Fifth Monarchist as the full armour of God. In my mind the terror of Hannah's eyeless skull broke from the earth with the bridle beside it. Like Christ crucified, my Hannah had courted a crown, but unlike Christ's, hers had gagged her. The jagged mouthpiece, with its rusted prongs to spike her tender tongue. No Old Testament predicted Hannah and no quaternity of gospels immortalised her, unless a later age could piece together the fragments of contradictory text that traced her journey. No pietà. No myrrh to anoint the wounds. No rock rolled away on the third day by angelic agency from the tomb's mouth. Only my broken, bitten fingernails scratching soil from around a bone tabernacle, defaced by the centuries.

Did Hannah forgive her enemies? I doubt it. Did she embrace her end? Or did she kneel to ask, at some wayside Cheshire Gethsemane, 'Father – no, *Mother, for God was mother to Hannah* – Mother, if it be thy will, let this cup pass from me.'

Anna made sure to avoid that cup by keeping her tongue sacredly wagging and her wits about her.

I was taken to the Sessions House to be sifted by the Witch-Trying Woman with her Great Pin. I was to stand blindfold before her and her matrons & be pricked by the pin, which, if it should hit a mole or patch of dead skin, I would not feel, & hence be adjudged a WITCH.

Sore afraid was I in the night & cried to My Lord, LORD, *what shall I do?*

And the Lord answered, and said, ANNA, MY HANDMAID, *be nothing afraid, but sing* PSALMS *unto the* LORD.

So upon entering the chamber, where I was to be searched by these ignorant women for a witch's mark or teat, from which they say a witch suckles her familiar spirit, I burst out into exultant songs of Praise to my LORD.

I sang Psalm 1, followed by Psalms 2, 3, 4 & 5. The witch-triers were astonished.

Then I sang Psalms 6, 7 & the first three verses of Psalm 8. All without book. Whereupon, pausing, I said to the witch-triers, 'Do you think the LORD'S ENEMY *could sing Holy words, without being struck dead?'*

Huddling together, they bickered among themselves, one saying, 'She is of God,' but another, 'She counterfeits.'

So I sang the remainder of Psalm 8, & the whole of 9 and 10, with much refreshment to myself. Now I was In Voice.

'Come, dear sisters,' I invited them freely, opening my arms to them. 'Won't you sing with me, the Psalms of David?'

So we all sang together, with such warbling that men peeping through the grille were amazed. But the Witch-Trying Woman was a sinister & deceitful spirit, who, when we were all singing, having reached the 41st Psalm: ('All that hate me whisper together against me: against me do they devise my hurt'), whipped out her pin & stuck it in my back. But I (being fore-warned by my Maker) shrieked out, 'Wherefore, O WOMAN OF SODOM, dost thou interrupt the holy Psalms of David by Pricking GOD'S HANDMAID in the small of the back with thy Pin?'

She quailed, & my innocence was presently reported to the Justices, who let me go. Never did God's daylight bless with such a sweet dazzle the eyes of his Beloved. I swooned when my friends conveyed me to the Captain's home, whence I left the next morning, after a dream in which God told me the people of Manchester, Salford, Stockport & Chedle (all but 49 named exceptions) were people of the Devil, Ranters & Presbyterian wolves, & Cromwell's beasts (for Lucifer raised his rebellion in the North) & so I took coach for the south into the kingdom of THE LAMB, singing meekly but not weakly all the way.

❋

Limp-leaved and withered as pot-plants unwatered, the inhabitants of the reading room had wilted. We wiped our hot, moist palms on our trousers before turning a page. My pencil stuck to my fingers and my mind swooped and swirled. The gent nearest the window gave up, scrambled together his books and donned an elderly panama hat before wading out of the choking airlessness of the room. That left Baldie and me, Daniels in the furnace.

Anna was marvellous but she wasn't a fan. All I really needed was a fan.

I blew on my fingers to cool the inflammation in my joints; then laid my head on my arms, letting her book float away over the sea of oak timbers. I beached, exhausted, on a tongue of my handwritten text, wondering if this was a migraine coming on.

When I came to, it was to music. Like Caliban upon his enchanted island, I sat gaping, as if I had awoken corporeally in an outpost of Heaven. For something elysian had broken my trance: sounds more enchanting than anything Chetham can have known, for he lived before its time. Flutes brought me back to myself – Gluck's 'Dance of the Blessed Spirits' wafted through the floorboards from where, in the chambers below, the adolescent flautists of Chetham's School of Music practised; and now a choir of students joined them. The music lifted into the suddenly enchanted reading room.

'Wow!' said an American voice. 'Wow and wow again! Like we've died and gone to Heaven!'

I rubbed my eyes. A sensation of wistful desire floated through me, inhabiting me like a misty ghost. I shivered in the heat.

'Didn't like to wake you,' said the scholar, a species of outgoing reader you meet in every library, keen to spice the occasion with comradely chat, to strip you of pith like bamboo in a few sentences. Who are you? Where from? What doing? Brief life history? 'You looked kind-of peaceful.'

'I had a migraine,' I muttered.

The admission was a mistake: my companion announced himself as an eminent *migraineur*, whose major episodes he was keen to narrate, to forestall which I slumped my head down on my book, as if concussed.

The 'Dance of the Blessed Spirits' was not unfolding without hiccups. The flutes would stop in mid-cadence. There would come a silence. Then they would recapitulate one phrase again, over and over. Young voices echoed through the floorboards, disciplined and pure. Their invisible master, like a magician, conjured them up and blew them out like a candle.

Tears rolled down my cheeks. The music, in its faltering perfection, recalled both Faith and Hannah.

'Kinda moving, ain't it?' commented my fellow-listener.

*

That night I suffered the kind of migraine that makes you wonder, in the spaces when words can be found between explosions, whether you are having a stroke. I called the night service and told them I'd got a naigrib but it might be a ghost, no, hang on, not a...coast, but stroke, not naigraib but gravedig, no...

The doctor arrived, Drew, the one I'd known since childhood, an eternally handsome man, doted upon by ladies as a medical bimbo. He perched on the edge of my bed, while I rooted around for words and struggled, through the pain lancing my right eye, to assemble them in order.

'You see, I've been in the seventeenth century,' I explained. 'Ouch, Jesus. My head. The past exists,' I went on. 'It's just the visibility problem. Too much light.'

'Are you hearing strange voices again?' he asked.

'Not at the moment. Only yours.'

He injected my backside. 'This should help. How's the visibility problem?'

'The storm is coming,' I said.

'Yes, it has been sultry.'

'That's not what I mean.'

I mumbled on about the clouds building in the west, the ozone hole, pollution, nuclear waste, why can't they see? 'It's not me that needs a doctor,' I said. 'It's you people, who can't see.'

A plane roared overhead and my right eye twinged as if skewered. Even the rustle of paper hurt. His briefcase hurt when he snapped the locks.

He stayed, as if he'd time. His loitering confused me: normally they're in and out like whirlwinds, and if you complain of being depressed, they scowl suicidally.

'What was that about the seventeenth century?' he asked.

'Oh – just reading.'

'Books,' he meditated.

'Well, not women's magazines, that's for sure.'

'Let me try out an idea on you,' he said. 'If you're up to it. You've been coming down with migraines since you were a young scrap of a thing! I've lately come across a migraine disorder called *mirror agnosia*. The symptoms are curious. The sufferer is persuaded that the phenomena in a mirror are the true reality. So that if, for instance, a victim had to choose between this pen, say, and the image of a pen, he'd choose the image. He'd try to *get into* the mirror. Lewis Carroll syndrome. What do you think?'

'I don't have a thing about mirrors. I hate mirrors.'

'No. In your case, for mirror, read – '

'*Book*.'

If so, he is just as text-bound as me. Our whole culture has been born between the covers of a book. Tumbling asleep on the miraculous power of the injection, I recognised that, though I could bear the thought of a world without people, the idea of a world bereft of books would be to me a living death. If I have what he thinks I have, I'll stick with it, thank you.

✱

The tumult within had redeemed the air, like storm after stifling heat. Anna Trapnel's eyes had allowed me a further glimpse of my Hannah, who stirred me more deeply than ever. Not that Anna was less than wonderful. I was more endeared to her than to anyone I'd met in the Revolution: the crafty way she hid her militant radicalism under a mask of femininity; her glorious freedom from the constraints placed upon us by a sense of humour; her attention-seeking neediness; those political swoons, in which her Tongue was delivered over to a divine garrulity. All this delighted me.

But my Hannah was a five-foot-two-inch blaze of candour, each of whose words was a spark struck to kindle establishment ire; confrontational, aggressive. I saw her leaping up on the bench to denounce the magistrate in her mud-spattered dress, and heard an unprecedented revolutionary language: her God was 'She', not 'He'. While other folk were denying church, episcopacy, heaven, hell, virtue, sin, Hannah Emanuel denied the masculinity of God.

She was a lamb for the slaughter. From the moment this heresy sprang from her mouth, she was destined for brank and gibbet. Anna was the male God's supine instrument; Hannah was the mind that hatched a goddess. Anyone could see that the fate deflected by Anna through her brainwave of singing the Psalms from memory must wreak its utmost revenge on Hannah.

And who was the man with the Welsh accent who plucked her out of the sessions-house, before she could condemn herself to death? Who was the man prepared to fight for Hannah against herself, saying (I looked it up): 'This is my

136

wife, and she is mad'? And where was Isabel while this uproar was going on? Of course she might have been there all the while, Anna not noting her presence, since after all, it was her own position that preoccupied her. Anna had not compiled her record for my benefit.

Rising from the table, walking steadily so as not to jostle my still delicate brain, I squinted at the screen of the word processor, and typed:

FATHER OF GRACE? HANNAH'S HUSBAND? NAYLER INCIDENT? WELSH ORIGIN?

There was an electrifying sense of being on the verge of a discovery. I'd been running along a line of retrospection, a leyline into the past, doubling back on my own life. It was as if I'd glimpsed a woman's figure in the distance: she'd turned a corner, but now through this time-travelling burst of speed, I'd nearly reached the vanishing-point. Round that corner, she'd come into range again, nearer now, and if I could maintain this marathon sprint, I'd overtake her, grasp her shoulder, spin her round, and see that one face.

Just as I'd softly spun the model of her head on Alex's plinth, until it turned to confront me, so I was about to stand face-to-face with Hannah.

My skin prickled, as if a lover had abandoned me for remote parts, out of range of telephone, fax or Internet, leaving everything between us in the air. She is suddenly seen to cross a road and disappear behind a building.

At exactly this point, when I was sure I was closing with Hannah, the light went out. The trail went dead.

*

Summer wore on, blistering and still, reservoir-levels dropping with every day. I tried Friends Library in London; chugged in the stopping train to the Chester Public Record Office, and visited Cardiff, Lancaster, Oxford. Nothing happened except that slowly she withdrew, a creature turning to diaphanous steam before my chronically straining eyes.

Reverting to Lyngard, I found his loquacity irksome and empty. The sense that there was something behind the pages, if only my tantalised eyes could X-ray them, faded. He manifested now as a desiccated old ideologue, his print lying flat to the page, row on row of turgid stuff, cobweb-heaped with theological abstractions. The light that had led me on went out.

Always the world has seemed like a theatre-set in which some manic-depressive electrician has appropriated the lighting system, and plays fantastic games with the dimmers, transfiguring some commonplace scene under voluptuous light, only to drain it arbitrarily to dull monochrome. I'd turn away listlessly, as now I did, though I could not give over.

At the John Rylands Rare Books Collection, the much-put-upon, bottle-green library assistant, aggressively flustered, gave me to understand that I did not exist.

'I rang in yesterday,' I said.

'There's no note.'

'But I did ring in.'

'Well, sorry, but there has to be a note. That's the rule.'

'You mean, if you forgot to make a note, I didn't ring.'

'But we always do make a note.'

'What if I go downstairs and ring you to say I'm coming, and you make a note, then I come back up – ?'

'Ah but you'd have to do it *yesterday* to get your books ordered up today, you see.'

'For fuck's sake, I did ring yesterday.'

The foggy gloom of the late-Victorian Gothic cathedral of scholarship extended into obscurity with an air of smug doom. *Give me strength*, I begged the smarmy white marble statue of Wisdom at the desk, who gazed down the dim aisle like a vigilant schoolmarm of limited IQ.

'Whoops. Here's the note. Wrong pile. I'm new,' she confided.

So was Rylands once. The builders had hurried to finish it for an opening on New Year's Day, 1900, a pseudo-medieval cathedral complete with clerestory. Vaulted in stone, carved with scrolls, glorified with stained glass, it had escaped the era of gaslight, bursting into the modernity of the electric revolution with its first moment. Yet already its time was past: such sandstone monumentality, with Gothic curlicues and dim magnificences of wasted space, was already archaic.

I had asked for Wing, the catalogue of seventeenth-century publications. But Wing had flown. It had cunningly nested in a sanctum of authority from which the nasal voice of an unseen male buzzed at the girl to be quick and take it. Carting the heavy volumes down the library, to dump them in a recess, I reflected on the conundrum of the note.

Absence of documentation was ocular proof that I had made no request.

Yesterday did not exist except on paper. No memo, no event. And without corroborating memory, everything depended on a written record.

There might be no more trace of Hannah extant in the world. If I searched for the rest of my life, I might find no further word of her.

The sun went in. The library, dim at its brightest, became a vault of emptiness. A few just-about-alive scholars sat hunched in niches under green-bonneted Art Deco lamps, spindling curiosities with wrought iron stems that hoarded rather than dispensed light. We were albino creatures in a cavern. Our blanched, weary, indefatigable faces pored over the pallid sheets of books and our bony fingers ferreted amongst the shards of a past world. Out on Deansgate, traffic snarled and sunburnt shoppers and office-workers hurried; babies squalled from pushchairs.

Out there was quick time; in here, time was disputed and imponderable. We grudged its passing and made effortful feints at retrieval, throwing a net back over our shoulders to see what could be trawled into the present. Our prey lay inert on our book-rests.

Meanwhile, we pored, jotted and clock-watched. We must be turfed out by five. Beyond the grimy windows, we heard the mob of the living and at day's end rejoined them, blinking at the glare and noise. Within this vault, you were not one of them, but a strange, envious form of troglodytic life, limpeted to the ancient rock of choice, with a limpet's pertinacity in monopolising the area on which it has elected to batten.

I say envious because we were all manifestly afraid of being pre-empted. Someone else might get there first if we failed to sit hugging our pile of books till closing time.

Get there *first* to the *past*?

This was our pathological anxiety. I recognised my own neurosis in a woman who snatched and cradled to her breast a pile of folios. Opening one on a charcoal-grey foam pad, she reverently laid a lead chain like prayer beads over the pages to prevent damage by live fingers. Everyone watched. The man across my desk exhibited a relentless nervous tic as he observed her rites.

He was thinking (I knew) what I was thinking: *is she on to the same thing as myself? Has she got there?* We were vultures fighting over carrion. If we could politely and inconspicuously do so, we would poke each other's eyes out. I sharpened my pencil; Nervous Tic still stared, his eyebrows working. As I squinted over to glimpse his book, he threw round it a defensive fortification, guarding territory with his arm, like a child in the schoolroom.

What if my luck was running out? I could not countenance this. It seemed more than curiosity: this was eros, the spiritual form of carnal passion, the compass needle's quivering insistence on homing to the remoteness of the Pole. The Rylands has an unequalled collection of Quaker and anti-Quaker tracts: I determined to trawl through them one by one, to see if anything had been missed.

The bottle-green girl began to thaw. Day by day, we became closer comrades, despite our enlistment on opposite sides of the internecine conflict: the one dedicated to appropriating what the other guarded. Each morning, her fraternising hand volunteered new trove, to which I bent my head under the lamp's blossom of light; each day my excitement rose and every evening I came away with nothing.

*

Sometimes you want to see someone so badly that you bestow their features or name on every look-alike. On my crazier days, all words have seemed like cryptic signs of Hannah's immanence. Language winks scornfully into my

140

obsessive stare and scatters alphabetical permutations like a riddle pregnant with children that cannot be delivered, but remain half in and half out of the maternal body, like the Irish girl's child in Isabel's Testament; like Isabel's Testament itself, only half-extant, concluding in mid-word.

Everything depends on the documents having been conserved. But what if they haven't been? And who would be motivated to keep them, given that Hannah disgraced the Quakers, making herself a byword for sexual laxity and spiritual vagrancy? Second generation Quakers had had to stifle such stories in order to survive the great persecution. Only the tiny and transient underground Hannah and Isabel had built up would have had reason to preserve their writings.

History, gagged and branked, struggles in the silences that are left when dissident voices have been discredited. How do you know which silences are the pregnant ones? All that tearing up, shredding and burning of paper...The ensuing silences brim with sadness for me; so too those muffled voices that survived the purge.

Isabel especially. Once the illiterate maid-of-all-work got that pen in her hand, she surged with hope and confidence; surely nothing could ever be the same again? I look back at her over the centuries through rueful eyes, in the knowledge that her ardent hopes will turn to ash. I look back at her standing at (I suppose) around the same height as me – women built on too massive a scale, independent, harshly spoken, odd – and silently ask her, *Where is your good old cause now?* To which she answers, in the words of Harrison being dragged to execution, *In my heart and I shall seal it with my blood*.

Still I am troubled by the determined ripping of paper in books no one wanted, or some wanted available to no one. In Hannah's recycling age, use was made of disbound books as toilet paper or to wrap pies from the fast food shops that mushroomed all over London in the Restoration. Or it might find a vocation in lining packing cases; and turn up a couple of centuries later in an attic. It might or it might not.

Books sometimes take a while to die: an aftermath of

spasmodic rustling in a waste-paper basket records their final throes, until they reach a final rigour.

*

Faith didn't write from Corinth. Each day was a further instance of her not writing.

Morning by morning, scooping up the mail, I thought, with desolate triumph, *There you are, she hasn't written.*

Not that I expected her to write. Nor, after a while, did I want a letter or a postcard, telling me, in that neat, careful handwriting, that such-and-such a view had been spectacular; that she wished I'd been around to see it. It was better that she kept her self to herself. What did we have to say to one another? She had kissed me goodbye, that was all.

Part II

One

All has changed, beyond imagination, in the year since I lost the trail leading from Hannah.

My stepmother's death was succeeded by my father's conspicuously rapid remarriage, to a French woman, Thérèse, hardly if at all my senior. My father, in glowing health, appeared to spend much of his sun-bronzed, sybaritic twilight swimming in the pool he'd had built in the grounds of the château lodge, watching Thérèse execute swallow-like dives off the side. 'We adore each other,' he crooned in his letters: 'she makes me feel (don't laugh) half my age. Like a king.'

And now he proposed a mini-Restoration, in the form of a visit in which he would show off his new bride to myself and his brother's family, which was disgustedly agog.

I shrank from the thought of this proposed idyll, and cooked up excuses for not putting them up at my house; for getting out of the country. I was afflicted with sensations of shamed rue for my stepmother, whose life with my father had not been improved by my vicious campaign to rid us of her presence. I vividly recalled her face, with its often forlorn and perplexed eyes. Though I had long outgrown my antipathy, it had been difficult to communicate my fellow-feeling. Jean had died a slow, stoical death, urging my father to marry again and be happy, and confiding to me her suspicion that a man, being fundamentally helpless, was unfitted to live without a wife to take care of him. To my notes and cards, she had replied with eager amity, as though there were nothing to forgive.

Pia said: 'Have them here, why not? On your own terms. She might be OK. Lay some ghosts.'

'You've laid the ghosts,' I said. 'I'm not bothered about ghosts.'

'Well then,' she said.

Pia at twenty-three is the incarnation of the laid-back yet hyperactive and searching youthfulness I never knew. She claims to be taking time out to consider a career in counselling or the ministry. She would be the wildest minister I could imagine; the most fey; the bonniest. Turning cartwheels in the garden one morning she circled round and round, until she fell in a lithe heap of slender limbs, panting like a cat.

'You'll be defrocked,' I said, 'if they ever take you.'

'Nonsense. They should be grateful for ministers with performing skills.'

Also, mystifyingly, she doesn't seem to believe in God: but she explains, with arguments savouring of casuistry, that dogma doesn't interest her. She catches on her antennae, she says, vague, numinous scintillations of the Mother-Spirit in the cosmos.

'You can call it God the Father if you like,' she explains. 'Words don't much matter.'

'But that makes a complete nonsense of language.'

Pia says, 'Well, language is a nonsense.' She's a post-modern, as well as a cartwheeler.

'What you really are, Pia, is a witch.'

That delighted her.

'And a sophist.'

'Sticks and stones,' she said. She likes it that I come from a Quaker family and once sat with me at my mother's mound, both palms flat to the turf, listening, it seemed, both to my stammering narrative and, through her nerve-endings, to the quiet beneath. Then she put her head in my lap and cried. We both cried, and felt much better. That way of losing herself in the other's emotion, without sermonical affectation of superior wisdom, is one of the things that makes me feel she'll be a brilliant (and at the same time hopeless) counsellor or pastor.

Also Pia is broad-minded: she doesn't mind that I need my space. Perhaps it relieves her of the weight of what I'm afraid would be worship. A bind. My sombre need for retreat leaves her free to lavish and nourish herself in many friendships, which are as important to her as any lover. She is always flitting out of the gate to visit some soul-mate, a whole collective of soul-mates, who will all hypnotise one another, cycle up a mountain or go skinny-dipping in some cold Derbyshire stream, there to amaze the shepherd or wool-hatted hikers striding down a mountainside.

I was doubtful: would this giddy dryad expect me to join them in their cold, nude Paradise? But she seemed to love and leave me as I was, amphibiously coming and going between unlikely worlds.

'I seem so middle-aged beside you.'

'No you don't. You're full of wonders.'

Our bed was full of wonders: my skin flowed silk, I'd cry for joy. Everything seemed to happen at once that autumn. The dammed desire of so many virginal years burst the banks and overflowed my barren soil.

Perhaps it was my father in me, I thought, as I underwent my inner revolution. Love of life and pleasure came welling up like a spring, or like the daffodil-spear piercing up above frost-impacted ground, a light from the underworld. That autumn I'd planted the mound with crocus and daffodil bulbs, turbulent swathes of colour which excited my eye to tears when they powered up before the season seemed clement enough to receive them.

Faith said nothing as she saw me branch and blossom, to my own extreme confusion. She was polite. Often her face appeared grey with sleeplessness and inner strife. As I went bounding along, I'd pass her and see her strained eyes which smiled carefully and asked no explicit questions. Their grey-green beauty still arrested me. But after all, what future could there have been for us?

I said nothing to Pia of how I minded about Faith. Not that Pia would have objected but Faith was my private knowledge, too intimate to share. *I've hilled her over in my mind*, was the way I put it to myself, scarcely recalling where

I'd cadged the phrase. Down there, hilled over, she could neither hurt me nor be heard.

*

Pia was in the shower, bubbling with song while the water splashed. I sat perched on the end of my parents' king-sized bed which we'd commandeered, with one sock on and one off, while the radio told me Princess Diana had died in the night.

'Pia!' I went and yelled outside the bathroom. 'Guess what?'

'What?'

'Diana's dead.'

'Diana who?'

'Princess Diana.'

I put on my second sock and a T-shirt. By the time I got downstairs and made breakfast, that face was all over the TV screen on every channel. The more they told us she was dead, and revealed the violent manner of her passing in the car-crash, chased by the paparazzi bikers who had fed our appetite for her matchless face, the more the haunting images of her in motion resurrected her.

My father rang: 'Olivia, I can't believe the news, I can't. It's just unbearable.' His voice broke. 'And here in France too, in Paris of all places. How awful it is.'

'Why? We didn't know her.' A childish sullenness broke over me: when had I known him shed tears? 'She wasn't related to us.'

'Oh. She was. In a way. And she was beautiful. Such beauty. And so caring. Thérèse says she's so glad she'll be seeing you next week. She feels we can comfort each other in our loss.'

'Our loss of . . . ?'

'Diana.'

'Well – tell her I'm an anti-monarchist. I'd like to kick the whole crew of Windsors in the bloody backside and send them to . . .' (I could think of no place that deserved them) '. . . St Helena.'

'But they crucified her,' was his memorable conclusion.

'Pia,' I said, replacing the receiver. 'It's official – there's been a crucifixion.'

Pia was stuffing toast in her mouth, wriggling her feet into shoes, off to 'a witchy meeting of radical feminist lesbian Christians at Hebden Bridge'. 'Perhaps she stands for something, something we've all lost,' she suggested compassionately.

'Our reason, you mean?'

She was out of the door and fleeing down the path.

I pottered around all morning, the television on, drinking coffee and mindlessly watching the coffin removed from the plane, decked in the royal colours. When Pia returned I had been watching on and off throughout the day.

'Was this the face that launched a thousand ships, and burnt the topless towers of Ilium?' I asked her.

'Poor perdue,' was all she said.

I was hooked. So much beauty (and she was beautiful) to die so young (and thirty-six was young these days, though an average life-span in the past). So much filthy lucre (and she was a millionaire), and such confusion of soul, whose need expressed itself in offering magic to the needier. Crowds began to flow toward Buckingham Palace and Kensington in quiet tides, carrying flowers, more flowers, and most of all portraits of that face.

The face haunted me, against my better judgment. It went to bed with me. Lines of Keats popped up in my brain as I tried to sleep:

> She dwells with Beauty, Beauty that must die,
> And joy, whose hand is ever at his lips,
> Bidding adieu...

That she was perishable no one had divined. Could they have imagined then that she was an immortal? So the celluloid had affirmed. What state was the face in now? We were told the coffin was heavy because it was lined with lead. Was the face even now decomposing? The photographers who saw her slumped in the crashed car had assured the public that her face, apart from one small bruise, had been intact.

Her body was colossally haemorrhaging but the face remained undamaged. What myth were these millions groping for, in this cultic materialism? The magic of intercessive Mary,

Persephone, Elizabeth, Evita, ravished the stiff-upper-lipped Brits to a new code: he who can't cry's a sissy.

For miles along the way, the weeping crowds threw flowers in silence. As if Persephone were passing.

'Great is Diana of the Ephesians,' I said to Pia. She was impossible to nettle.

'St Paul had a lot to answer for,' she replied.

Her burial on an island in a pond at Althorp, strewn with flowers, was not the end of her for, now that the original had been annihilated, her likeness multiplied on a diversity of planes and surfaces. In virtual space, eyes roved her beauty at a much-visited website shrine. She wasn't going to go away.

✳

My father was greyer and leaner, 'as fit as a flea', he said. 'But an out-and-out loafer. We just lie in front of the pool like a pair of seals basking in the sun and occasionally slip in for a bathe. We live like gods beside a field of sunflowers, with our own cherry orchard: there's a much better quality of life out there, of course. And sunshine. You ought to come out and try it sometime. And Thérèse cooks as well as paints: she is a genius.'

'Flatterer,' said Thérèse. 'You are too charming to me.'

'He's always been charming,' I told her, in a quietly spiky voice.

'Ah, but not charming alone. He is ... a lovely man.'

He had the grace to look embarrassed. I observed, 'So my stepmother liked to think.'

Dad's eyes watered. He said, with every appearance of sincerity, 'I do miss her, Olivia. Jean was a good, kind person. But she wanted me to remarry. She told me so many, many times. She made me promise.'

'Now where have I heard this before?' I enquired. 'It does ring a bell. Oh yes, it all comes back to me. My mother (a person you might vaguely remember?) used to say that a wife could manage nicely without a husband but a husband was unthinkable without a wife. A bit like replacing a car.'

'Ah,' countered Thérèse, in a purring voice. 'He is such a sweetie. Don't tease him. Just a little boy at heart.' And she reached over to ruffle her husband's hair, which, thankfully for his youthful image, he had mostly retained. It had a silvery sheen. His years in France had given him style and his wardrobe looked as if it had cost a franc or two. Still, at fifty-seven how had he landed such an elegant young woman? It was the strongest temptation to call Thérèse 'Mother' or 'Mum'. I bit back the urge, not out of generosity but in order to conserve the pleasure of springing it like a rat-trap at some future time.

'Have some funeral baked meats,' I invited them. 'Do help yourselves. Don't stint.'

Pia looked sharply startled. 'Olivia!' she whispered, and dug me with her elbow. Her raised eyebrows enquired, 'Why are you being so nasty?'

My father bowed his head, as if to receive the thud of a blow he remembered but had forgotten how he came to merit it. That feeling of *déjà vu* arose in the air between us, as we simultaneously relived the strange recovery of one woman in the earth as we relinquished my mother there; and the rapid substitution of his second wife for his first.

'This is a very sad time for us all,' said Thérèse, lifting a shred of lettuce to her lips. She began to prattle wistfully about the tragic loss of The People's Princess. I didn't have to reply to her at all, Pia doing duty by drawing her out. Forgetting his uneasiness, my father sat transfixed by Thérèse's face, as if he could never have enough of tracing her features. He gazed at her with the fascinated reverence one accords a favourite portrait.

'We'll give you the king-size bed,' I told him.

'Oh. Right.'

'We usually sleep there.'

'You – oh.'

'Pia and me. Together.'

He coughed, flushed. A pang of embarrassment passed through him. 'Yes, right. Of course.' Then he said, with repressed fascination, like a fish nibbling suspect bait, 'You never did go much for men, did you, Olivia? Your stepmother used to get quite het about it.'

'Oh, I've got a male lover as well.' Might as well give him something to chew over.

151

'Really?'

'Sure. I'm not fussy. You might as well enjoy yourself, mightn't you?'

'Ah. Right.' This was all too much for my father to cope with.

'Doesn't she – Pia – mind? She seems such a...spiritual young woman.'

'Spirit*ed*. I expect she just accepts I take after my father. Having your cake and eating it.'

The hollow feeling as my old embittered self spat anachronistic grudges at him was desolating. I didn't retract but retired to my room. No, it was not anachronistic. The sadness you buried still endured, marked by some dolmen of flinty asperity over the place of denial.

They were off to London the following day, to pay 'homage' to Diana. They must, they said, be there where, in the wake of the funeral, crowds were still milling with their mourning offerings. They did not seem sorry to leave or eager to prolong their stay in my emotionally draughty quarters. Perhaps Thérèse did not care for the king-size bed that had accommodated not only her two predecessors but the unrepentantly transgressive love-making of me and Pia. As for my father, I realised with dawning surprise that, epicure, gastronome as he was, he was also intensely conservative. To him it seemed only right that a man should rove from woman to woman: that was the natural order.

No sooner were they settled on their southbound train than Pia boarded a northbound one. She was off to Iona with a chattering band of sweet-eyed young people to enter into contemplation of radical spirituality. What radical spirituality entailed I had not been able to elicit clearly. Was it to do with the emotions? Not exactly. Motivations? Well, you could say that. Intuitions, impulses? In a way. Language, it seemed, could not explain it. 'Is it the part of you that prays?' I pressed her.

'Well, yes, I suppose so. You can't really say *what* it is, Livvy, not like a solid object. You just know.'

I'd had the same trouble with logarithms at school: wanted the teacher to show me one. I was the Doubting Thomas of mathematics.

'I don't,' I said.

'That doesn't matter,' said Pia, with a hug. 'I can see it in you.'

Something in me resisted this condescension; assimilation to the cosying-up community of the spirituality-mongers. As far as I could see, mine was a sort of black hole, like a sick joke, mirthless and sarcastic.

I was alone with myself again.

*

The transcription of Hannah Emanuel's *Wilderness of Women* came into my hands through the simplest means possible: repentance.

I had given her up for lost; and was reconciled with my loss. After all, I told myself, in the light of the Diana furore, hadn't there been something wilfully hallucinatory about the passion that gripped me for a face I had never known: a random face, after which I hankered because I was bereft of attachments in daily life? Just because they are not present, and never will be, the dead enthrall us. The ghostly essence of Hannah had made my hair stand on end, my spine tingle, my palms and insteps prickle. Had she lived next door, would I even have given her a second thought?

But when I read her *Wilderness of Women*, I knew I would have.

John Hale was at my door, carrying a brown envelope and looking sheepish.

'Have you got a moment, Olivia? I've had something on my mind.'

'Of course.'

'The thing is ... Do you remember our last meeting? I'm afraid I was rather abrupt with you. You asked me, as you had every right to do, whether I had heard of an early member of the Society.'

'Hannah Jones.'

'Hannah Jones,' he echoed back to me. 'Or Hannah Emanuel was, I think, the name you initially gave, which rather wrong-footed me, as I recall, at the time.'

'Yes?'

'It's a difficult thing, perhaps, for you to understand how your question caught me on the raw.' He was looking around the unkempt room, as if to settle on some object which would anchor the telling of his story.

'No, I think I do understand,' I tried to help him out. John had the brown envelope on his lap: it aroused my burningly impatient curiosity. 'From what I've been able to gather, Hannah was a renegade who went around calling the leaders of the movement whores, and had an illegitimate baby which she claimed was the daughter of God – herself being, of course, God. From there it was only one step to proclaiming God female. Anathema to the leaders and, presumably, to the Hesketh community, on which she brought opprobrium. And then there was her terrible death – her crucifixion, as she would have seen it. The final insult. She was never forgiven. Or forgotten. Which is why they – should I say *you*, plural, which is to say singular, because of the unity that binds the group – had to suppress the memory. Because, of course, it's family stuff too, isn't it? Family feuds.'

'Did your mother ever tell you ... ?' he asked.

'No. Nothing.' I'd spoken at length in order to show how much I'd picked up; was taken aback to think that my mother had long possessed the knowledge I was digging about for.

'Ah.' Infuriatingly, he removed his glasses from his nose and proceeded to polish them.

'What should she have told me?'

'Last week,' he digressed, 'I had rather a shock.'

'Yes?'

'I was looking round the Manchester Museum with my nephew and his family and I came upon the waxwork head of "The Hesketh Maiden". I came, as it were, face-to-face with Hannah Jones. That very nice Alex Sagarra was there – he filled me in on how you'd done the reconstruction together. He sends you his best, by the way.'

'So,' I went on recklessly, 'you came face to face with the Movement's ugly little secrets – their complicity with the authorities in covering up her death, censoring her ... '

'I wouldn't put it like that,' he said mildly. 'But I can

154

understand your feelings. You have to grasp that in those early days, the Movement was so young and tender; so appallingly persecuted. They couldn't risk tolerating people running wild.'

'I understand that perfectly. It's one of the great historical paradoxes, isn't it, that idealistic movements tend to beget monsters in the form of mirror-images of their enemies – Marxism begat Stalinism; the French Revolution begat the Terror; the Quaker democratic freedom begat uniformity and repression. Especially of women.'

'Yes. Well, we have had our...regrettable phases. Of course. I don't quite see how Stalinism and mass-murder come into it – seems a curious analogy, given our peace-principle, but we'll let that pass. What I must emphasise is that all movements must be pragmatic to survive. We learned that. It was hard knowledge.'

'But do go on. You came to say...?'

'I should have given you this when you asked. It's yours to have in any case: you are a descendant of Hannah, at least your mother, who went into the genealogy, believed so. And she was the soul of exactitude. Hannah's daughter Grace rebelled against her mother's...waywardness...by growing up sober and pious. She married back into the movement: Abraham Cooper of Manchester Meeting. They had five children, of whom only the youngest daughter survived, Mary. She moved back to Chedle Holme and married into Hesketh Meeting, the Mather family who farmed at Pinfold. Your mother was a descendant of Mary.'

Leaning forward, I held out my hand. John appeared to have trouble parting with the envelope. I stood up, would certainly have snatched it, had he attempted to leave without yielding it up. Alex had modelled us both, Hannah and Olivia, and set us spinning on our plinths like planets in bondage to different systems; now in my mind's eye the twin heads were coming to rest, aligned, alike, children of the one line. I reached for the letter.

'I don't know what you intend to do with it?' he enquired.

'Read it.'

'And then?'

'I've no idea.'

'Your mother's belief was that publication of this kind of material would not be in the interest of Truth.'

I had the document in my hand. Could not get him out of the door quickly enough. I stepped aggressively towards him, invading his body-space, but he held firm.

'She felt,' he went on, 'that individuals were not important: it was the great unity of Truth that mattered. Not the ego but the whole. It was she, in point of fact, who gave me this testament for safe-keeping.'

'When?'

'The year before she died. When she knew about the cancer.'

I gasped for air as if he'd swung a hook on that last word and landed me back on the terrible strand, not of loss but of the era leading up to the loss, when I tried not to notice how my mother was fading and ageing in front of my eyes, never losing control, though her skin was parchment and the unsmiling eyes appalled me, pale blue, large and staring. Never for a moment did her rigour lapse. It was inhuman.

'But why?' I puzzled. 'Why give it to you and keep it from me?' The testament had travelled largely in the female line for generations, and my mother had carefully tried to ensure (without actually destroying it) that it missed me. She had arranged an abortion. My mind sang with shock, as if it had been dealt a blow from an unsuspected quarter. She had attempted to disinherit me.

'I think she felt that this Hannah Emanuel was a fairly unbalanced character,' said John. 'A judgment in which, when you read it, you might think any reasonable person would concur. A sort of dangerous stray. A stray cannon.'

'But, for goodness' sake, that was all of three hundred and fifty years ago!'

'Precisely. And she knew the glamour of distance.'

'It's ridiculous.'

Even so, recognition glimmered. My mother had seen and regretted in me the same inability to toe the line. Only my backsliding did not consist in denial of the Father God and a pregnancy, so much as a more modern apostasy: denial of any good God. Hannah and I, for all our differences, were all too alike.

As I closed the door on John, it seemed as though Hannah had come home. He went out; she came in.

Two

WILDERNESS OF WOMEN BY H.E., *who am sent out into the wastes and commons to be a scapegoat & wanderer on the face of the earth, but* GOD *shall judge ye, filthy people of Lancashire & Cheshire*

This was the title, written in gall but copied out in the Withington Girls' Grammar School neat copperplate of my mother's handwriting.

For a moment this stunned me. I imagined her sitting at...that *escritoire* over there, with the many forbidden compartments that had so fascinated me as a child, into which I would insert my fingers for trove of pencil-sharpeners and sealing wax, string and my mother's venerable fountain pens and inks. The desk had a wooden panel which could be brought down and locked: a lock at which my never-say-die fingers had fiddled, with intent to pick. The desk, with its lid drawn down to hoard in shadow many secrets, had impressed me as a sort of external mind.

And, yes, she'd slide down that panel sometimes, when she heard me coming. The ever-open door was at once an advertisement of perfect accessibility and an early-warning device through which that most private of women could detect imminent invasion. Rushing in, I'd quail and retreat before her patiently welcoming smile.

So here she had sat (I sat down in her place), copying Hannah's testament – but why? Why copy it? What had she done with the original? Surely so scrupulous a woman would not have taken it upon herself to destroy a vagrant outsider's sole mark upon the world?

No: I looked up at the oil-lamp, under its coating of dust. No: she wouldn't have destroyed it without substituting a copy. But, in making a copy, she might well have satisfied her conscience by censoring the original. Would she have done so without noting the places where she had hacked out exceptionable material? That was doubtful.

I shuffled through the sheaf. Sure enough, there were conscientious hiatus-signs, rows of asterisks where she had made her judicious cuts.

How could you do that? I asked my mother silently. *How could you be so ruthless, so . . . wicked?*

She looked up from her work in my mind's eye. *It was a difficult decision. I made it a subject of particular prayer. I saw eventually that it was right and necessary.*

What could Hannah possibly have said that would seem so incendiary to a rather straight-laced but earnestly liberal Quaker in this century? How often had I seen my mother hearing fools and asses out, fixing them with listening eyes that filled the fools and asses with certainty that at last they were braying to some purpose? Determination swelled within me to heal the wounds in Hannah's text. Like a shattered skull such as I had seen Alex working upon with finesse, I would fit the whole together in a manner so cogent that the holes would define the shape of what had been lost. In response to that licence-to-speak, the bridle would shatter.

I am one that walks alone, with my loving yoke-fellow in the wild places of the earth and is of no sect or gathered people whatsoever; I am one that like Christ wanders the wilderness and has fellowship with them that live in caves & dens & desolate places of the earth, of whom the world was not worthy.

Know, Christian locusts, that you are judged by the Most High God. The beggar that you whip at cart's tail & toss out of your towns is your Judge, & the Poor Woman in the stocks for taking a half a loaf of bread, is standing in Judgment at the right hand of God. Who then will intercede for you, men of

Lancashire & Cheshire, when the Woman is sent out into the Wilderness, a woman clothed with the sun & the moon under her feet, & upon her head a crown of 12 stars? And she being with child cries, travailing in birth, & brings forth a girl child, who will rule all nations.

Think you not that God will feed the Woman in the Wilderness, yea, with honeydew, & a handful of berries sent he to her & to her handmaiden, saying, Take, Eat.

And LOVE is the ONLY LAW.

Hear this now, ye doctors and ministers & great ones of the earth. Hear it professors & prophets, whoremasters & Judases all, whose Tongues pollute the world with filthy speech: I, a woman of Wales, am come to bring Christ to you: & LOVE is the ONLY LAW.

I am the daughter of Edward Jones of Wrexham, who, being a tanner, made money & built a great stone house near the river, & I was the firstborn of eight girls & two boys. From the first I was one that could not sit still, but must be busy & haring round the house from morn till night, a racing child like a fast beck, streaming with syllables & bubblings of spirit. I could say 150 words by the time I was a year & a half. My mother indulged my love of all knowledge but my father, seeing my ready wit & quick answers, said, 'Keep thy tongue locked up between thy teeth, or thou'll trip over it one day.'

'It's not that long, father,' I protested.

He said 'I see it coming out of thy mouth, child, as long as a snake.'

It troubled me, to think my tongue might be such a monster.

Nevertheless, I sped on, & tumbled up & down my giddy path. But, hearing one day the pastor Morgan Lloyd speak in the open air at Wrexham, I was filled with strange thoughts, &, climbing with a little pack of bread & an apple up Mount Ruabon, looked north toward Mold, & south toward Llangollen, & revolved in my childish mind the mightiness of the world. Though Mr Lloyd had told us that nothing of this world is real, I heard the sheep and lambs bleat for many miles around, & saw cloud-shadows flow over the hills, & knew that the world is real & the dear Mother of us all. While Spirit breathing in the wind fanned my hair, I stood up on a rock &, stretching out my arms, babbled to the sheep, praying & prophesying & teaching them. Although I forget what I said to the Creation, I remember ending, 'Rejoice, rejoice, O SHEEP, that ye are not created GOATS.' I copied Mr Lloyd's lilting speech which was like singing; & the Spirit carried me up as if on a whirlwind above the towns of the plain. I looked down upon the world from a height, spreading my bread & apple on my skirts. The bread came out of my pocket warm as if newly baked. The apple sparkled on my tongue like wine.

This was the first of my sojourns in the WILDERNESS.

Then returning home, my father beat me for rushing off to the hills in unfilial disobedience. I rebuked him, saying, 'I have been to my Father & Mother.'

'But,' said my father, 'I am thy father & this thy mother.'

'No,' I said. 'Thou'rt only a man.' And he beat me again.

At this God was angry; for he takes vengeance on violent men that deny His Little Ones. That night I saw in a dream that the house would fall, being built on sand, not rock, & came rushing downstairs to warn my father, 'Father, listen Father, repent or our house will fall in the night.'

But he sat feeding scraps to our little dog, & laughed, saying, 'Hear the maid's prattle' to my mother. My brothers carving sticks at the hearth hooted, but only one laughed again, for the younger's arm & shoulder were smashed when the chimney-stack on the south wall collapsed in the evening, so that holes gaped in the house-side. We could see the moon through them.

My brothers now went in fear of me, my mother (a pious woman) saying I was a Holy Maid.

'She's a vixen,' said my brothers & sisters, 'with that ginger pelt.'

'A little demon,' mused my uncle, at which they all looked at me with troubled faces, for my eyes were beech-green & my hair brazen, where I sat in the firelight. I seemed singled out from earliest days for some special work. My mother taught me to read & write, & made me write my dreams in her book, to test in case they should come to pass.

My father decided I must be married, to a widower of some property, in Myddle in Shropshire, but he being 34 years of age

161

& given to drink & gaming, & myself being only 16, I refused to have him.

'If she is a Holy Maid,' said my mother, 'She is not meant for marriage but for God.'

My father snarled, 'Woman, are thou turned Papist & thinks of Holy Women like the whore of Kent old King Henry burned?'

So I was shut in my chamber until I would consent, but I clambered out of the window on to a mulberry tree, got down & sped off, whereby I thought to relieve them of my troublesome presence.

A little way along the road to Malpas, I stopped in my tracks. It had rained & the wheel-ruts brimmed with water. Having no pattens over my shoes, to get over the mud, I made small progress, & the trees ahead thrashed the air. I thought they had cruel faces & frowned on me. Fear shook me, that I should never see my dear mother again, & heart-broken I turned for home. But a Voice said, 'Turn again. If thou return to thy mother, they will marry thee to an old man. Leave father & mother, & follow me.'

As I stood irresolute on the path, I heard hoofbeats from Wrexham-way. It was my father on the mare, who got me home & had me married to this William Williams, whose father was once shrieve of the county & had left a farm much improved, for he turned through good husbandry a farm overgrown with thorns, briars & rubbish into a thriving concern. But William his son had spared no pains to turn it back to thorns, briars etc. Having married a rich widow, William had lived handsomely, & at her death cast about for a new wife with a portion. I had £100.

'Now,' said my father, 'if thou'lt be an obedient wife, no doubt he'll be a hard-working husband, & you may live happy.'

'She has a large share of tongue, & is of a masculine spirit,' said my father to my betrothed. 'But get her with child, she'll soon quieten down.'

Williams looked upon me with doting, saying I should have my way of him, he cared not to tame a shrew if she had beauty, &, taking a skein of my hair like a child, he rubbed it between thumb & forefinger. I jerked my head away and bit my lip. My father smirked & I heard him say to his brother, 'The man has no guts in his brain, Dai, but let us hope he has gear in his breeches.'

My uncle laughed, replying, 'He has a brace of bastards in the village, man.'

I begged my mother, 'Is there no help?'

She said, & sighed, 'No help but God. And rule thy tongue, Hannah, thou may also rule thy husband.'

So I was married, & I wept to leave my mother to go away so many miles from my place of birth into an alien land. My dear mother died soon after.

We passed down through Wem to Myddle, where my husband gathered me up in his arms & spun me round outside the door until I was dizzy, then suddenly rushed into the house & up the stairs, then thrust me on the great tester bed, my skirts . . .

*   *   *

And this was a great terror to me. For he was an amorous man with sharp appetites which could not be satisfied, neither could I rule my great & deep horror.

What, through prudery or (might it be?) her own wincing recognition of the shock of deflowering, had my mother censored out? No doubt Hannah bled, as virgins do. No doubt William fucked her hard and often, as red-blooded men do. No doubt he believed this was his marital right – as it was.

Hannah's, in this respect, was an ordinary story.

Since then I have carried the mutilated imprint of this account upon my mind, as if it were a portion of my own life-story. My own thoughts flow round the wounds in the text, amplifying the words on my mother's page with my power to imagine. The stuff of my consciousness is her one retreat.

Hannah Williams (but she never once calls herself by his surname) must have awoken the morning after the wedding night, cleaned up the blood and inspected the bruising on her thighs. For she surely fought, and was worsted, every time worsted. Witchhazel would heal the black thumb- and knee-prints. The bruising in her mind she must also treat.

To each her own way out. She notes that one of her neighbours in the parish, Elizabeth Onslow, entered into a pact with her fellow discontented wives to bump off their husbands.

'I hate him,' she said.

'I loathe mine,' confessed Magdalene Baker.

'Mine's a swine,' confided Elanor Clarke.

'Let's poison the lot of them.' A dazzle of freedom flashed hope in front of Elizabeth's eyes. Whereas Magdalene and Elanor were just drunk, Elizabeth was seriously interested in getting some fun out of life before life passed her by.

'You must not have blood on your hands, Lizzie,' remonstrated Hannah. 'It's not good for you.'

'Good for him though, the arse-hole,' said Lizzie.

'Your conscience will hurt.'

'Will it hell.'

'But, Lizzie, reason more shrewdly. Husbands die naturally. You need only wait and be patient. God will take him. Is he unkind to you?'

'No,' sulked Lizzie, 'I just don't like him, that's all. I want shot of him.'

When Onslow was dead, Lizzie was aggrieved that the other girls had not kept their part of the pact. She was ethically offended.

'You promised,' she whined.

Chased by the constables over the Welsh border, she was found on a public holiday with a gang of young people on the top of a hill dancing and kissing. Her father emptied his purse getting her off the gallows.

Hannah sat brooding at her front window, chin resting on folded arms. She was learning the skills of surgeon and wise woman from an elderly neighbour, Elleanor Mansell, who had no child of her own to whom she could pass on her secrets. William she acknowledged as a good-hearted man, who denied her nothing, though he stank of strong beer, wasted money and took trivial liberties with the maid-servant, saying, 'Wash my feet, wench,' and, when the girl brought a basin of water and knelt to her task, he'd reach down inside her smock and fondle her breasts.

Hannah saw, and he saw she saw.

Little realising that his play with the maid's breasts maddened Hannah because she burned to do the same, he interpreted the smouldering in her eyes as a symptom of jealousy, rather than envy. These sparkings of desire Hannah could not comprehend in herself. She began to nag her husband, which he, being dull-witted, tolerated. She ran the farm with an iron grip and kept a book of accounts; read prayers to the servants morning and evening, the patriarch's duty which William was too fuddled and easy-going to acquit.

In due course she had constructed a network of relationships from end to end of the parish, riding between hamlets and farms with her herbal medicines and, when necessary, performing minor surgery after farm-accidents. Myddle moved over and made room for her.

The nightly maulings continued, in the darkness, and she would sometimes awaken to find her husband trying to mount her, cursing her dry, spasming body for denying entry.

She lit a rushlight when he'd dropped off, snoring softly. The bed smelt of semen and sweat. From the edge of the straw mattress, she looked back at him. His face in a smear of rush-light was a fleshy landscape at once charmless and bereft of spirit. He was lying on his front, his cheek squashing his mouth open, a little moist hole which dribbled. To this gross bundle of matter she was forever tied, by bonds of law and scripture. The experience on Ruabon, when she leapt into the misty cloud, psalming the Creation and lecturing the sheep, seemed to belong to another world.

Soldiers in russet coats swarmed through Shropshire, and a new breed of officials scouring for royalist renegades. The king's head was off. She heard rumours of the Levellers and the Diggers. They were spoken of as rogues bent on dispossessing the haves (and Williams was still just about a have) but Hannah read between the lines. The spirit in her stirred; she began to dream.

In church that Sunday, she sat not in the family pew but at

the back, in the area reserved for God's least savoury specimens: the louse-ridden, the cave-dwellers, those without patrimony, some lacking a surname. She wedged herself between a man who spoke no English and went by the name of 'Welsh Frank' and three noted female debauchees, Mary, Elizabeth and Susan Bickley, bastards born of bastards, with bastard-children of their own. She took Mary's bastard on her knee and smiled in its face, puckered up to cry.

'Welsh Frank' spent the entire service with his eyes glued to his beautiful neighbour's face in a glow of stupefaction; the lewd sorority reacted to her presence with titters and mutters, in the light of the minister, Mr Vaughan's, sermon on the weakness of the flesh.

His learned animadversions sailed over the heads of most of his listeners, who improved the time by drowsing. When Hannah leapt up, her hair hanging about her shoulders, eyes blazing, Welsh Frank was startled into squeaking: 'O *duw!*' The congregation craned round.

'Can thou not speak honest English, parson, but must jaw away in profane Latin?' shouted Hannah. 'Nobody understands thee. Nobody listens to thee. Nobody minds thee. And thy profane sleeves and surplice are an abomination to the Lord.'

Thus Hannah launched her career of church- and trial-interruption, shaking from head to foot with nervous excitement.

'Evict that madwoman,' the minister demanded.

Hannah was manhandled out, but the crew of bawds seized the chance of a little fun in the form of a skirmish with the minister, boxing his ears and peeling off his clerical collar which they denounced as a 'two-pronged tongue of Satan'. Hannah, doused in the millpond, struggled out to the sound of crowing laughter, and sloshed home through the village to catcalls. Perhaps she did not greatly relish the moral calibre of her accomplices. But within two years the minister was himself evicted, for being a non-propagator of the true gospel, and his church-door nailed shut.

'What does thou, wife, sitting in the back of the church amongst Welshmen and lewd ugly pugs?' demanded

William, storming in, having heard an embellished account of the riot at the ale-house.

Hannah slowly turned, and in an even voice, said: 'Be silent and seek for Grace.'

He stared, but no words came.

Her silence as they tangled eye-to-eye bore down his before its certainty.

'Thou never loved me, did thou?' he quavered.

'I love thee as I love all beasts of the field,' she assured him, 'that live according to their impulses and have no notion of bliss save the ram's tupping of the ewe.'

'But...I love thee Hannah, with a true love, as thou are my wife.'

'Love God, man, it's the only hope for thee.'

In 1651 she left Myddle. I followed her journey on a modern map, through Malpas, Nantwich, Crewe, Congleton and Macclesfield, eventually to alight at the Hesketh hamlet of Chedle Holme. And there, she writes, at around the same period that Isabel first came to work at Pinfold Farm, she founded the Hesketh community of Seekers.

All the way on my journey I rebuked the people as I went. I was the first to bring the message of Silence & Truth into those parts; & I was the first to reveal the knowledge of the Spirit Within; I was the chosen-of-God who came at the Almighty's leading, alone in a land of darkness, who knew the POWER. *And I taught that the only Law is Love. There is none other Law. And I was the first that brought this understanding to the people like a shepherd to her flock.*

And I was before Fox.

And I was before Hubberthorne.

And I came to Malpas before John Lawson to settle a Separatist church.

And I came to Mobberley before Thomas Holme.

And I settled the Hesketh Seekers.

Before George Fox was, I AM.

Hannah had evidently thrown that embattled line of personal pronouns on to the page on her high horse, for my mother had carefully transcribed them in letters three times the normal height. Hannah's denied 'I' towered above her enemies with megalomaniac swagger. It was only now that I began to understand the unique threat Hannah Emanuel posed; and why Friends had been concerned to expunge her disorderly record from their history. Whereas other women, renegades who cast off the chains of authority, performing miracles and tearing bibles, acknowledged themselves daughters of that movement, Hannah claimed to be its mother.

My meetings met in the way of Silence for we were Seekers of Truth, not proclaimers. Quiet & tender we sat in the open pastures, &, if one had the leading to speak, that person spoke, whether cobbler, sempstress, or the old blind woman that lives on alms in a hut on the heath, all might speak. The POWER *of the Lord came among us so that we quaked & shook, or were thrown down to the earth, where we cried like babes or roared like bulls. For we were new women & new men that walked robed in the sun, all being one & of equal say & sway, & none might usurp over another.*

One day, dressed in breeches & leather coat according to my custom when travelling, I came to bleak fields in Hesketh where a woman was spreading muck with a pitchfork. For a while, I watched her & considered in my heart what manner of people would use a woman to do the work of a beast?

For her Christ died: yet she knew no more of Christ's love than did the dun cow snorting in the field. Yet even that cow, I reflected, was the child of God & in looking upon the creature, I saw her beauty, from the blue-veined udder tense with milk to the intricate pattern on her back like a parchment map of Europe such as I have seen in my mother's book.

This being so, how much more must Christ have loved what man despised: the maiden with the map of heaven unread inscribed upon her heart, hands red-raw in the perishing-cold spring air, & her eyes pensive but, like the cow's, with no thought but present pain.

'Woman,' said I. 'Why does thou hoik this great load for an idle farmer that, I dare say, feeds thee no better than his pig?'

She looked on me with wide eyes, & never said one word, this being a question foreign to her as my Welsh speech.

'Why?'

'I must because I must.'

'Then let me help thee spread the muck.'

'Thou!' and she broke out in scornful laughter. 'Thou sparrow of a lad! Thou grasshopper! Thou cannot do a strong lass's work.'

So in pique I seized the fork & furiously spread the good dung on the earth but before long (being unaccustomed to bodily labour) I began to pant & stagger, at which she shouldered me aside & went on with her work, cursing & railing at me, & at the dung, at her master & at God – all being one to her.

Then I took off my cap & all my hair fell down, at which she was much amazed.

So I said, 'Isabel, I come for thee.'

Isabel shivered where she stood, overshoes in mud & muck, thinking me an angel or demon, in that I was a woman & knew her name, which I had caught in the flood of cursing that poured from her lips.

'Who has sent thee?'

'I am thy sister & thy fellow, Isabel, & have known thee from the beginning of time,' I said, 'and we are not to curse the good earth our mother.'

'Shit-mother,' said Isabel.

'Think thou not that God made honest shit as well as the stones of the church?'

'Shit-God made Arsehole-church,' was her opinion.

'Thou'rt a good theologian,' I said.

'And thou'rt a great louse on a small head. Come here & I'll crack thee between finger & thumb.'

I went up to Isabel & stood before her, close, my eyes gazing into her eyes, whereupon she gasped & stumbled, asking again, 'Who art thou?'

And I said, 'Thy friend.'

So I went my way; & obtained work in the house of William Hulme, teaching his three daughters to read & write. He, being a staunch, Seeking man, an Independent, was for toleration. By & by I convinced William & his whole family, save his eldest daughter, who, believing her father wished to marry me (being a widower) & breed new sons, brought the catchpoll to spy us at our silent prayer.

But I said lovingly to the catchpoll, Martin Dawes, a simple man, 'Friend, welcome to our feast. Pray sit & share our meal.'

He, gaping round the library, asks where is the food? All he can see is books & calm faces.

'We feast on the Lamb & the wine of love,' I tell him. 'And we offer it to thee, friend Martin.'

'But where is the lamb?' asks Martin. 'I smell no roast.'

Whereupon a leaden sadness laid itself upon me that the people the Lord loves live in ignorance, cursing & mindless, for ignorance is the leading rein with which rich folk drive them. Then I remembered my dear Isabel Clarke & went to Pinfold Farm, to ask after her.

The mistress not being at home, Isabel had me into the dairy, where she was turning the great cheese-press, to make the cheese for which this country is famous. This press being of massive iron, she must use her whole might & both hands to crank the screw.

'Does thou curse still, Isabel,' I asked, '& practise thy study of theology?'

'Ay,' she said. 'My learning that-road is higher nor the minister's.'

'That's nothing,' I said. 'The paid minister knows nought. God's for simple lambs to know. The foal just dropped from the mare's backside knows more of Truth than university-vermin.'

We rejoiced at Cromwell's winning the Battle of Worcester, after which fatguts Heyricke & tithe-baron Hollinworth of Manchester were clapped in prison, with other Presbyterian fleshpots; but prating Heyricke got off his execution.

'Isabel, would thou learn to read and write?'

'What-for should such as I read and write?'

She was sullen, through fear of being too stupid, since she was accounted the dregs of the vat, but I found her a better pupil than many gentryfolk's children, & to see her learn was like watching dawn break after a centuries-long night. So Isabel came out of the dark into Jerusalem.

One evening we kissed each other long & deep, between the dovecotes & the beehives in the orchard at Pinfold. In the calm

*of evening, the hives glimmered and cast long egg-shaped
shadows.*

> *Thy lips, O my spouse, drop as the honeycomb: honey & milk
> are under thy tongue; & the smell of thy garments is like the
> smell of Lebanon. A garden enclosed is my sister, my spouse,
> a spring shut up, a fountain sealed.*

*(I quote Scripture to answer anyone who dares doubt the
lawfulness of such love as ours; but even if Scripture forbade
it, the Spirit permits it, for* LOVE IS THE ONLY LAW*).*

*From that day our fingers were always laced & we walked
with our arms linked, as sisters & yoke-fellows, calling Pinfold
from henceforth* BEULAH, *which means* MARRIED. *For who
could be more married than me and my sister-spouse, needing
no half-wit priest to bless our immortal union?*

*We became pilgrims & wayfarers. We travelled the
wilderness from Chedle Heath to Shadow Moss, & crossed
Bakestonedale Moor, with the coal mines, where black-faced
men toil below ground, like slaves, shunned as devils by the folk
that burn the coal. At Pott Shrigley we saw the bell-pit, ('hell-
pit', said my yoke-fellow), where the horse lugs the wheel & coil
round all day, turning the gin to bring up the coal. Elsewhere
on the moor, men stripped to the waist work the hand-windlass
& women push monstrous heavy carts filled with coal &
cannot stand upright, but go forever bent & crooked. We
uncoupled the horse from the gin & the miners beat us away
when we pleaded, 'Let the creature rest.'*

One afternoon as they cross Lindow Moss, Hannah and
Isabel bump into a flock of fleeing women and children,
shouting 'Boggart! Boggart! Don't go uppalong, there's a
devil-woman int' Clough.'

'There's no such thing,' says Hannah.

'There be,' says Isabel, rigid with fear. Nothing will induce
her to go on.

'Are thou frightened of a bogeyman?'

'Nay. But Boggy Bo, him I conna bide.' It intrigues me to
find Isabel reverting to her native tongue. She shrinks back

into the centuries of rooted superstition from which Hannah has painstakingly drawn her.

'Who is Boggy Bo?' asks Hannah, taking her companion's hand.

'Him what can't rot int' buryhole.'

'Tis true, we saw un,' shouts one of the peat-cutting women from a safe distance. 'But warnt a man, war a witch, far wuss.' She holds her flapping apron up over her mouth as if to ward off contagion.

'They couldna hill her up, see,' explains Isabel. 'She wunna stay down int' mizzick. Dunna go, Hannah. She'll haul thee down into t'seechy bed.'

I wonder whether Hannah shares the pang of fear, as she scans the heathlands toward the peat-cuttings; whether she too is momentarily cowed by a prehistoric terror, before she asks Isabel to wait while she goes to view the woman who can't decay and won't stay down. 'For,' she chid her mate, 'our Jesu stayed not in the buryhole to rot but on the third day rose again.'

Saturated peats are piled at the edge of the cutting: rain in the night has rinsed the face and part of the torso of a woman, exposed by the cutters. At first I take it to be an hallucination. But while Hannah squats to examine the prodigy, I peer over her shoulder and Alex Sagarra looks up in my mind. He grins, just as he did in the museum inviting me to view Rostherne Man: 'Meet Old Pete Marsh.' Hannah sees a squashed face and shoulder, like an old leather jacket. The cadaver seems boneless, a leather pouch, tanned like animal hide, with long ruddy-brown hair braided into a three-strand plait and around her neck a knotted thong.

The murdered Iron Age woman lies on one side, most of her body submerged as if in the act of slumbrous swimming through the quagmire. Her right arm trails, palm-outward, fingers curled. Lashes and eyebrows can be clearly made out. A rapt expression contradicts the gash at the back of the cranium; the garotte that bites the leathery neck. Involuntarily Hannah reaches out to the cold hand, with its fingerprints, life-lines and love-lines.

A Celt, no doubt. Slaughtered in her prime as the tribe's

blood-sacrifice to the gods of the nether world. One last meal of barley-cake; as she kneels, a blow stuns her from behind; her neck is cut and the blood caught in a bowl, while she is garotted. God is propitiated; spring and harvest ensured. The remains are jettisoned in the bog. Decades pass; centuries. Saturated through and through by dark brown acid and tannin, her carcase undergoes chemical change in every cell.

I look up from the page, my mind faint with echoes.

When Friends came into Chedle, we joined them & made a barn into a Meeting House, & there enjoyed blessed meetings, on the earth floor that still smelt of hay, a sweet smell. Many a time in Manchester Old Church I lashed Priest Lyngard with my tongue & made him dance. And James Nayler came to visit us, his soul in his eyes, a tender man who could listen to a woman; & went thoughtful away.

I thought of James for many weeks, with longing, & saw him in my dreams. At this my yoke-fellow a little sorrowed, & I saw it with rue.

'May a woman not love two, three or more people, Isabel?' I asked her. 'Should I not love all those who show the spark of Jesu in their souls?'

While I spoke these words, as one willing to be corrected, I tenderly brushed Isabel's hair, which fell to her waist, hazel-brown & glossy in the evening light. When my brush tangled in her hair, I brought it away & with loving care parted the strands & undid the knots; then I kissed her cool hair & whispered words of love. All this while she sat silent, hands in her lap, eyes downcast. But then she raised her eyes, & said, 'Yea.'

'Yea?

'Love James Nayler, if thou will.'

'Not I but the spirit of love in me.'

'Yea,' was all she said. And got up from her stool, knocking the brush from my hand, her eyes streaming with tears.

'Isabel, if it be against thy will . . .'

'Thou must be free,' she said. 'For thou has freed me, thy yoke-fellow, from the burden of darkness & ignorance.' She continued, taking both my hands & speaking the words of Ruth to Naomi, 'Whither thou goest I will go, & whither thou

stayest, there will I abide. Thy people shall be my people, and thy God my God.'

This was our marriage-night, when we lay down together in her sacking bed under the attic beams at Pinfold & never turned away from one another all night. Many deep & tender kisses we exchanged, & in our ecstasy...

* * *

I leaned up on one elbow above my beloved, stroking her lips with my finger, & whispered, my breath on her cheek, 'I love thee now, Isabel, & love thee in eternity.' She spoke the same words to me, not as a vow or oath, but to state the plain Truth that Death could never part us. Then I laid my head between her breasts...

*

Here under the same roof, Pia and I have lain whole afternoons, lax from love-making, gazing into one another's eyes. What my mother's quaint pencil chastely censors from Hannah's text, I have lived and breathed, winding Pia's damp curls in my fingers, enjoying the intimate lassitude of limbs interwoven, slack mouths swollen from kissing. Nothing need be said; I'm glad she left it blank, for I shall read the forbidding silences as my holy places.

The next day, Isabel said, 'I have had a dream, Hannah, that we must go to Exeter & there meet with James, & have more talk.'

To which, laughing in her arms, I said, 'But we never slept a wink, Isabel, so how could thou have dreamed a dream?'

'Believe me,' she insisted, 'I dreamed.'

So we journeyed down to Devon, where we found James in a disquiet state, being wrought upon by Martha Simmonds, whom George Fox called an unclean spirit who had bewitched & perverted James. I set it down here that Martha was not a wicked woman. She was a firebrand of intense heat & light, wild with the love of God. When Martha stood tall & straight as a willow to speak out her message, the men put their fingers to their lips & sat like statues (I have seen them), finger-on-lips,

174

till she cried, maddened, 'Open your lugs, men, and let your lips alone.' Martha ran wild with being shushed & banished like a babe at bedtime, & then she buzzed and sang to drown the men's talk, & (since James was open to her voice) worshipped him as Christ – forgetting that Christ was in her own self.

A Word About James: James Nayler, now dead, was the most beautiful man I ever saw. I had only to see him for my heart to skip & skid, for he (though mean in attire & humble as to features) had Grace speaking in his face. His eyes rested on me as though my voice were rare music. Attentive & thoughtful, he would take my hand & smile with such openness, it seemed that I had come home.

Isabel said, firmly, 'He is a good man. Stay at his side.'

When James rode into Bristol on a white ass, we were with him, but my heart misgave me, knowing that Christ will not come again as a man. Yet I loved James, & he me. When soldiers seized my beloved, I thought, 'He will be killed.' And it seemed that, if James died, so would God. The world would be a place of darkness.

When James was tortured, my yoke-fellow & I walked alongside his tender body, & I darted in between the lash of the executioner's whip & my friend, but the soldiers kicked me back. I cried, 'Flay me! Flay me for him!' & the women cried, HOLY HOLY HOLY. Isabel wrenched the whip from the executioner's hand, shouting, 'Enough, fellow, that is enough, give over,' &, being as tall & strong as he, she prevailed, until the soldiers beat her off. When we watched James branded through his tender tongue, & on his forehead, & humiliated, the light of God went out in my soul.

Rebecca Travers went into prison to tend his wounds but, said she, no skin remained on James' back, which was ingrained with filth, & she was sure he would not live.

Later I said to Isabel, 'There is no God.'

'Say thou there is no God, when She has sent thee to me, to bring me out of the land of slavery?'

'There is no God.'

'There is a God, my lamb, and God is in thee & me. But She cannot change the actions of wicked men.'

Thus again Isabel played theologian. She comprehended

that God our Mother cannot protect her Creation from man's brutality.

I said to Isabel, 'I am with child.'

So we returned to Chedle, but now our friends' faces had darkened against us, & they said, 'Thou bears the heretic Nayler's bastard.' They drove us out on to the heath. Through all this Isabel stood constant, saying, 'Thus is the prophecy fulfilled that the Woman shall flee to the wilderness, & she shall bear a child.'

Yet now I lost all hope and faith.

I lay howling in an inner wilderness & God left me there to freeze to death as a bastard abandoned in a ditch. I said to Isabel, 'We were deluded, there is no God of love at all. God hates us & spits on us from the heavens.'

For when I looked up, the skies lowered & rains swept in. The heath lay open to wind & rain like an upturned dish, & the bracken rusted beneath a sky of pewter. The icy spikes of rain were like the spitting of God; & I cried, 'God our Mother has forsaken us.'

But Isabel was of no such mind. Covering me with her cloak, she began to cut the heath to build a wall against the weather, & in two days had built a wig-wam such as we have heard the Indians make in the wilderness of New England. I would not go in. I stood in the whirlwind & cried, 'James! James!' &, expecting never to see him again, I would not be comforted. For I said to myself, 'James has repented & will go home to heaven but I am an unclean thing that God has dropped along the way, & shall go to hell.' Not that I cared a fig for hell but only that I might never see James' face again.

My tongue was hot & sore. Night & day I thought I felt the branding spike as it pierced James' tongue & smelt the burning. I said to Isabel, 'Look at my tongue, Isabel, see if it festers.'

She peered in my mouth &, seeing that it had swollen up, smeared willow-powder on it to take away the heat. In my frantic folly I spat out the salve. Taking refuge in silence, I would neither speak nor look up when spoken to, but lay on the heather & vomited.

But Isabel was a rock. She was a heart of adamant to all endurance & love. She laid my head in her lap & dripped water on my lips (for I would not open my dry mouth, with its monstrous tongue). She told me, 'Our God that has brought us so far together will never desert us. All our pains are her pains, & in the bitterness of the pit, there She is, in the night, & amongst all those cast off & cast away.'

'But I shall never see him more,' I wailed.

'Thou has the babe,' she said. 'And I have thee.'

So she rocked me, fed me, counselled me, hiding her own tears from my sight. For I had cut her to the quick.

A wind cast down our house. And Isabel built it again. Ashamed at my peevishness, I drank water from the stream. But our bread ran out & there was bitter winter upon us. Then the Dutch Friend, Christiana Henryks, came out from Lancaster, bringing milk, eggs & bread, also a little beer.

Winter froze the bracken into a rimy forest, but us it could not hurt, sound in our heath-beds, covered with sacks. One morning the sun shone & I crawled out to piss, & stood looking at the whiteness of the world. As I walked into the heath I tumbled into a cleft in the Moss, where, clinging to the lip of the wall, grew a bank of bilberry, & on the bush a few late berries remained. Creeping in to the bank, I feasted my eyes on the impossible fruit. Blue-black they were & covered with powdery bloom & frost, & I saw that they were good. As I crouched there, I looked at the heath, which now seemed a silver forest.

'My love, come,' I said. 'Come & see the manna from heaven.'

So Isabel came & we did not so much pluck the berries as nudge them into our hands. We ate with relish, never finding any fruit as delicious. Next day the babe quickened in my womb; I laughed aloud.

Isabel was astonished. 'What is it?'

'Our babe,' I said. 'It fluttered its wings.' And because I had said, 'Our babe,' she wept.

Now the babe, which had begun as my despair, became my hope. For secretly I thought I should bear a second James, & see his darling face in my son's face. I never told Isabel of this.

As my belly grew great, we cast about where I should be delivered: & our child was born in a barn in Chedle, a daughter, whose name was Grace. I bounded up from my bed of straw & announced, 'Grace is come, & our Morning Star is arisen.' From the first our daughter looked like Isabel, her dark-blue eyes & hazel hair, so that I doubted in my mind whether she was not a miracle conceived between my yoke-fellow & myself, by God's so strange love that scorns earthly laws & teaches us the ways of a new Heaven & a new Earth. I said to Isabel, 'Surely she is thy daughter?' Isabel wept again.

And we called our name EMANUEL; God-with-us. Jones, Clarke, Nayler were names we knew no more, for we divorced our names.

Now was our blossoming time, Isabel's & mine. We had our child, who, feeding at my breast, grew strong & could clap her hands for joy by the age of five months; & behold she was a prodigy.

But Priest Lyngard put it about that I had given birth to a monster, an hermaphrodite. He published a paper entitled 'The Ranters He-She-Bastard Delivered', so that many flocked to see our babe, & once he rode to Macclesfield where we lodged with Tobias & Elizabeth Powell.

'I am here to see the lusus naturae, Mr Powell,' he told Tobias. 'And the lewd mother.'

'We have no loose natures here.'

'Speak thou no Latin, fellow?'

'Speak thou no English, friend?'

'I seek the lewd mother and her spawn, in plain English.'

'Which lewd mother seek thou, filthy Priest?' called Isabel from the top of the stairs. 'For our daughter has two.'

'The green-eyed witch's cub. The monster.'

I spoke to Lyngard charitably of his sins, saying that he was a crookedly-made, sad creature full of passions he little understood. But he, angrily seeing the perfection of our child, took hold of my breast & twisted till the milk squirted; seeing which he shot his hand away wiping it on his coat: & dashed downstairs crying 'WITCH'S MILK!' He ran off to the magistrate. Soon we were arrested & carried to the port of Liverpool, & there put aboard ship for Jamaica. Pirates took us to Turkey, & thence home. In our sufferings & travels we were full of cheer & brought many to the Light.

By Providence we returned to Bristol in 1660, where we

found the king restored, & all things overturning, this being God's Judgment on the crimes of the Protectorate. The first thing I did, unknown to my dear yoke-fellow, was to ask Friends for news of Nayler.

'James Nayler is dead,' said Sarah Briggs. 'He died at King's Repton with contrite heart.'

At this my heart quivered like a taut string, & I would have wept but (for love of my yoke-fellow) held back the tears. Three years later the letter James had written to me found me.

Beloved in Christ, Hannah my sister, I saw thee in my mind's eye last week, labouring along a noisome high road, bearing a great burden. And the burden was thyself. So it came to me to write to thee, sending these crumbs of wisdom from one who is of a broken and a contrite heart. I have fellowship with them who live in dens and desolate places of the earth, and who through death shall obtain resurrection: I go on a journey & must bid thee farewell, kissing thee with the kiss of peace. And saying, put down thy heavy burden, (that is, THY SELF), live in quiet & without contention. Speak not too much nor too loudly. Listen. Pray. Neither think thyself alone in this world. For in thine aloneness thou art not alone. He who loved thee will not forsake thee. Forgive whatever sin thy brother, the broken reed, hath committed against thee, as he freely forgives thee, for with no unclean

* * *

Now I counsel thee, Hannah, receive the healing spirit, for we have undergone travail of soul and now is the deliverance. Thy brother in Christ, JN

But I would not lay my SELF down. If I lay my SELF down, what else remains to me? My soul & self are one being. Shall I cleave myself down the centre – shall I submit to the bridle like any broodmare – shall I deny the Light that is IN ME?

I shall speak much & loudly.

I shall NOT still my tongue.

Without my tongue, I am a silent witness.

In these words, I wrestled with the bit with which James in

death would mute me, the blinkers, & leading reins that would turn me to a dumb creature.

I dreamed that James & I wrestled, hand-to-hand, a terrible conflict, for I flinched from hurting him. I saw his wounds, the bloody back, scarred with stripes of red; I heard his voice hobbled from his wounded tongue; I saw his tender skin, soft as a girl's. And this was the man I must fight.

How easy it has been to fight my enemies. God our Mother gave power to my voice. But to fight my friend –

As James prevailed, so I lost ground, & my voice was lost, as if the wind had swept it away over the barren.

But I said, 'I cannot live without my Voice.'

Mine adversary whispered, 'Melt, yield, be lost in me.'

My limbs were as liquid, flowing back where he poured me.

And he said, 'Now I have thee, & I will drink thee like wine.'

But still, though I was only a pool of water, scooped in his palm, I could not surrender; & I cried out with a loud voice, 'I MUST SPEAK!'

With a sigh, James fell away from me & turned upon me a face of reproach; and he vanished into the other world.

But I awoke. I turned to my yoke-fellow and kissed her with the kiss of peace.

Three

When the prophet Ezekiel, dragged round the visionary terrain of Ancient Israel by a haranguing God, is dumped in a valley full of dry bones, and asked, 'Can these bones live?', the shell-shocked prophet is only able to squeak the obvious, 'O Lord God, thou knowest.'

The Almighty informs the bones: 'Behold, I will cause breath to enter into you, and ye shall live.'

Having laid down sinews and added a layer of flesh, God seals the packages up in skin, breathing into them. Ezekiel gapes as he hears the clatter of bones coupling up together after their long divorce.

Shall these dry bones live? I had asked myself, doubtfully. Nothing of the prophetic strain lingered in my age: only nostalgia twinned with amnesia; the blind mouths of ferociously solipsistic disputes in the academic Babel. But I had listened to Hannah. My emotion assured me of the vitality of the remains. Only a living voice could have roused the tears that smarted as I moved toward the catastrophe of Hannah's story. In the receptacle of my listening mind, her words had become flesh, however transiently. Her 'I' had become one with my 'I' in the act of reading. I knew with gut knowledge that Hannah was my ancestor. I voiced the woman who had given voice to me.

I let slip the sheaf of papers on to my lap, deferring the conclusion, to prolong the sensation of quickening in my mind. *Listen to our babe*, Hannah had told her companion, *her wings are fluttering*. Hannah in turn lay inside me, my lively guest, a tumbling embryo whose gestation was incomplete.

Yet, how odd: I hadn't altogether liked her. That was beside the point. She didn't ask to be liked. She'd be diagnosed as a suitable case for counselling if the likes of her appeared nowadays. But she was alive: *alive* in a way few of us ever are. If we see them coming, we step off the pavement to avoid them. They have bees in their bonnets. They nourish designs on us. Hear voices. Burn with a quality of threatening intensity.

Perhaps only Isabel had ever known Hannah as well as I did now. For to know her you must touch her, taste her, breathe her in, experience her – read her.

I took a deep breath, leaning my head back and discovering that my bone seemed to have set in the one position, which had not shifted since I began to read. I twisted my neck to unlock the crick; sighed; shrugged my shoulders. Half of the copied manuscript remained to be read. I'd not read it today. When she was wholly read, and re-read, learned by heart, Hannah would turn away irretrievably into the past: the place of often-told stories and dreams hauled up to daylight. I wanted her kept in part unknown, potent in potentiality, like a lover, like a future.

Resisting the temptation to devour the remaining pages, I sheathed the whole transcript in its envelope and locked it away in my mother's desk. As I straightened up, there was the sense of a presence either inside the room or just beyond: not a haunting so much as a prosaic visitation which one had little expected. Someone's face seemed to have just been and gone at the window.

Faith?

My mind sped back to last year and my embarrassing, muddled visit to her house, when I'd spied, seeing the back of her head (could see it now, as clear as day), that indistinctly revelatory early morning. It seemed to me now that someone peered in and I caught a blur of motion as she withdrew.

Nobody there: I walked to the gate. No: nobody. It must have been a bird nesting amongst all that ivy I'd allowed to wander in shaggy swathes over the ground-floor windows. Or the shadow of an aeroplane across the sun, which makes you think the sun winked.

It felt like a face.

But there was no one.

*

She was sitting in the Christie Library in an immense leather armchair, legs curled under her, as one *didn't* in those rather august surroundings. Her face was abstracted, looking up vaguely at the leather-volumed walls, with their high Gothic windows and portraits of male Manchester eminences. The light here was smooth and pearly, falling in lozenges. A burr of conversation and muted laughter humanised the room, as did the cheerful clatter of the bistro at the other end.

Her face was pensive to the degree that she had disappeared into her own thoughts. She looked so young. Standing at the lift, I realised how little time touched her: it glanced off Faith's unassuming surface and went preying elsewhere. That aura of youthfulness, of course, was one reason why the department thought fit to exploit her willingness to labour for the common good. She looked junior; and, being single and small of stature, afforded them scope to look down on her. She was worth a hundred of them. My indignation rose. How dare they condescend to someone with more to her than they could ever imagine?

'OK if I join you? Tell me if you're enjoying a bit of privacy. You looked so far-away there.'

'Please do join me. It's been ages . . . '

I ordered coffee for myself and a new pot of tea for her: she'd have Earl Grey, she was addicted to the bergamot.

Suddenly I wanted to blurt it all out: the quest and its partial discoveries; the sense of wayfaring. I wanted her to hear the news of my foremothers and fathers; to make a name for myself beyond the name I was born to bear, which suddenly seemed to lie so lightly on my identity.

For surely I am James Nayler's last surviving lineal descendant?

And my foremother was a witch.

Instead of bragging my spurious credit of lineage, I blushed fiercely, which Faith sensitively pretended not to notice, repeating, 'It's been such ages since we talked.'

'Forever,' I agreed. 'How have you been?'

'Oh. It's been difficult. Lovely. Impossible. Perfect. Tiring.'

'Pretty run-of-the-mill then?'

She laughed. 'I wouldn't say that. How about you? How is – Pia?'

'Off. She comes and goes you know, like the moon or the tides or something. At present she's in her neap. Way-out. She's gone to the Isle of Mull to commune with the fairies – no, not really, she's on Iona with her fellow spirits.'

'And is that OK?'

'It is really. I get fairly far down into my reading, as you know, and Pia respects that. How's – Jim?'

We tiptoed round the names of our respective partners like dancers on points. I knew Jim had left his wife and moved in with Faith because it had gone the whole way round the gossip-chain, at least twice, so that, for all my obtuseness to chatter, I had had no choice but to hear it.

'Fine. We had his three children for the weekend. They are lovely. Seem to accept me really well but I am anxious not to encroach. It's most important he should have his space with them.'

She frowned and bit her lip; spoke these words of received wisdom like doctrine, but in her case an earnestly lived doctrine, which I felt she would put into practice religiously. She went on, 'I've thought so much about you, Olivia. It was strange last year. I felt we came so close, and then... events...'

'I still feel close, Faith. Do you know, I often dream of you?'

'Really?' She looked determinedly interested though I felt she froze. Faith's warm goodwill is a deep form of courtesy. It goes as deep as courtesy can. Passionate feeling threatens that soft outer covering. She pulled her long grey skirt around her knees.

'Just simple everyday sort of dreams,' I hastened to reassure her. 'You come along and wave. Or I see you at a window. And I think, *Faith*. I always wake up refreshed. Maybe it's your allegorical name.'

She shuddered. 'Awful, isn't it?'

'Think yourself lucky. Old Barebones, whose Christian name was Praise-God, called his son Repent-or-be-damned-forever. *You're* a pale imitation.'

'A remnant.'

The bible word sounded a hollow echo of the impassioned English I had been reading.

'Your name means to me . . . perhaps this is it, and why you come in dreams . . . something lost. But because you are someone I can believe in, Faith seems validated in the dream.' I was less than candid. In my dreams, it was also made plain that, though glimpsed, she was lost to me. She sped past, in transit, beckoning only to perish without trace.

'Well,' she meditated. 'It's certainly better than "You-must-have-Faith-or-God-will-strike-you-dead". How are things in the seventeenth century these days?'

'These yesterdays, which feel like todays. Well, I'm deep in some old books and manuscripts I've discovered: they are . . . thrilling, I can't tell you.'

Keep it to yourself, said the warning voice. If I divulged Hannah's story, it would lose its aura. Smoke would drift away into the haze of distance. I'd be left with ash.

'When are you going to publish?'

'*Never.*'

My ferocity at once unsettled and intrigued her. She leaned over to pour another cup of tea, which she did as she performed every action, neatly, carefully, her hand begetting a phantom hand in the glass table-top.

'Heresy, Olivia. Refuse to publish? Where is your Ambition Toward Research Excellence?'

'Well, I don't mind publishing stuff, but not this. This is too personal. It's private to my life. Does that sound weird?'

'Not at all. It sounds like you. But of course it makes one curious. Oh look, there's Jim.' She waved. 'Are you looking for me, love?'

'Darling.' He swooped down and encompassed my friend with a proprietorial arm, at which she showed shy delight tinged with embarrassment. They looked at me affably, not quite as one, for part of Faith was still bonded to me.

'So,' he addressed me. How are you, Olivia? Not seen you much around.'

'Not looking very hard?' I said.

'Why, have I ignored you?'

'No more than I've ignored you.'

We stared each other in the eyes with perfect bale. Faith uncurled from her chair, putting her stockinged feet on the wooden floor, searching about for her shoes.

'Whoops, I've got a ladder,' she exclaimed, by way of a desperately banal diversion.

We all three gaped at her feet, as they slid into her shoes. Semi-bare feet are curiously vulnerable on the parquet of a public room, where portraits of distinguished worthies keep watch and a bust of some forgotten professor peers through sculpted specs over a well-watered pot-plant.

A terrible urge welled to kneel and take those small, tender-looking feet in my palms and kiss them.

'What size are your feet?' I suddenly heard myself ask Faith.

'Three and a half,' she said. 'Small, aren't they?'

'They're lovely,' I said. Jim glared at me with real offence; bounded up and offered Faith his hand.

'Well,' he announced. 'I think that's enough discussion of my wife's feet just for the moment, Olivia, thank you.'

'Your – *what?*'

'I haven't told her,' breathed Faith, looking up at him in appeal.

'Why ever not? It's no secret.'

'Faith – are you married?'

She nodded.

'Why didn't you tell me, love?' I reached out my hand, ignoring her husband, as if Faith's marriage were an autonomous state she'd entered, to which he stood as an addendum. His hand balled into a fist, which he crushed into a pocket.

'Are you coming, Faith?' he asked, also reaching out a hand to her. She took both of our hands. We joined in a triangle.

'In a minute, dear. Just a sec. I want to speak to Olivia. I'm sorry I didn't say. I can't honestly explain. Well, I can try. Excuse us, Jim, would you, a minute?'

'On no account will I hang around pandering to this . . . dyke on heat . . . with her insulting interest in *my wife's feet*.'

'Shush, Jim, really.'

'I will not shush. I will *not* shush,' he exploded. He was a soft-spoken man, renowned for semi-audible lectures, but his raised tones were enough to turn heads and slew eyes from other enclaves of leather settees. 'I am not a baby, to be told to shush, Faith.'

'Please, dear. Don't be unnecessarily silly,' she appealed, precisely as one might address a child who has gone off his rocker. 'I'll follow you over shortly.' And, with that firmness I'd occasionally glimpsed at the core of her apparently malleable character, she did not so much drop his hand as return it to him, and turned to me.

'I'll wait for you here,' he sulked.

'May I ask you something?' I snarled up at him.

Jim averted his eyes sniffily and held the gaze of the marble professor.

'What century are you living in?' I demanded. 'I've never heard anyone claiming to own his wife's *feet* before.'

'You are a pain in the arse,' he flashed. 'Do you know how you're laughed at? Do you? Don't you know you're a standing joke? Swaggering around in your butch suits. In corners with the good-looking girl students. Do you think you're invisible or something?'

I stood up and faced him.

'What, while you poke round your mouldy Cistercian monasteries examining some perverted wanking old monk nobody's-ever-heard-of-and-nobody-ever-wants-to-hear-of's underpants?'

Aghast between the infantile pair of us, Faith stood to her inconsiderable height.

'Shut up. I'm going. As far as I'm concerned, the pair of you are welcome to one another.'

Off she stalked, dived into the perspex lift, and stood with her back turned.

I turned to Jim.

'So I am a joke, am I?' I hissed. 'OK, I'm a joke. But I do *not* mess around with students, and you'd better take that back.'

I stood on a level with him, red-faced and murderous. His resolution seemed to have undergone subsidence with Faith's withdrawal.

He muttered something indistinct.

'I didn't catch that. Speak up,' I barked, at which the gathering did not turn their heads: but the very back of their necks showed an enthralled attentiveness.

'Oh leave it,' he said, beginning to move toward the lift.

'I will not leave it. You take that back.' I had him by the sleeve of his corduroy jacket.

'All *right*.'

'And if *your wife* – which is to say, *my friend* – isn't free to talk to her friends, what kind of a life will she have with you, you pathological git?'

'You are nothing – but – a – fucking – mouth.'

I knew what he meant by mouth. He meant cunt.

I don't think he intended to strike me, but in his lunge to release his sleeve so that he could enter the lift, I was thrust sprawling back against a wooden pillar. This delighted me, as putting him publicly in the wrong.

'Are you OK?' asked a woman who came to my assistance.

'Never better.'

But as I walked back to my office, my head tolling, the frenzied triumph evaporated. They laughed at me. All of them. They suspected me of exploiting every female student with whom I discussed essays or passed the time of day. They had me down as a freak.

What if Faith only kept company with me out of charity?

This thought was piercingly painful. Opening my office window as far as it would go, I leaned out over the quadrangle, looking down on the lawns and the fine old beech tree. Yet even at its most verdant, the beech looked wan, like some caged creature sequestered from its kind.

Workmen were scooping up turf and piling it on a wagon; they had begun to build an artificial mound, to landscape the area. I trusted they had no modernising designs on the beech. It had always been there, since I began. I hoped it would go on growing after I was gone.

And now where were they, the conjugal pair?

Getting into her car, fastening seatbelts, not speaking? Was she remonstrating, placing a calming hand on that corduroy sleeve I had grasped like the scruff of the neck of some beast? I rubbed the feel of its nap off my palm. Who knew what married people did and said in private? They were unknown and unimaginable to an outsider. Perhaps they resolved the tension between them by laughing at me: my outsiderliness could be the solvent that fixed them all the more closely. A disagreeable thought, but I could live with it. I could live with 'everyone' laughing at me, should it come to that. Native truculence came to the rescue. I quit the window with an air of aggression as if I'd detected one of 'them' in the room with me; hoisted my backpack and stomped down the deserted corridor, to pause at the display of staff mugshots, intended to make freshers feel that we were all nice chaps and approachable really.

Was I really such a weirdo? Did I stand out as Hubbie had claimed. *Do you know you are laughed at? Do you? Don't you know you are a standing joke?*

My photograph showed a black-and-white likeness of a woman with spiked hair and a disrelish for cameras. She had a tapering jaw, large and rather staring eyes of a pale colour and no particular expression, a rough-textured jacket. She looked no more and no less peculiar than her colleagues. Less bald than most. No five o'clock shadow like some. No double chin. Younger. Not obviously delinquent.

Now Hannah: you'd never have caught Hannah attempting to vanish into the woodwork. And if she was laughed at (which she undoubtedly was, communally, as a taming mechanism), she would only have felt more self-justified. Wasn't Christ hissed and booed? Stigma was a sign that you were getting there: because you'd got to them. But Hannah had swung her net among the clouds drifting at the summit of Ruabon Mountain and caught the shimmering Holy Spirit in its fine mesh.

*

I could fly anywhere I wanted. So the travel agents' brochures told me. From Manchester Airport, I could join the summer thunder in the sky. From my noise-blasted garden, I viewed their trails writing in the heavens signs of their passage to Majorca, Florida, Tenerife. Why don't I join them in the sky?

But where?

Under the copper beech I sluggishly turned the pages in the inert heat: all places were the same place. Turquoise pools and matching skies and seas; pale sands from which the crowds appeared to have been shooed in order to photo-graph a solitude not yet colonised, waiting for me to fly in and take possession, at advantageous prices but with a surtax for single rooms. It was impossible to choose on any rational principle. Better to pick at random. Jamaica. Hannah was shipped off there but never arrived.

No. But I couldn't stay here, on this mainland of memory while all the couples flew off for a fortnight's oblivion.

Pia hoped I wouldn't mind but she and Louise had experienced strange and wonderful insights together on Mull: would I mind sharing Pia with Louise? She was so sensitive and intense, and besides she made Pia come over all faint when they had their strange experiences of the Goddess. Pia did not elaborate but appeared to be veering toward a Wiccan phase on her misty pilgrimage. I would adore Louise, Pia raved, Louise was overflowing with love and mysticism, besides being a brilliant water-diviner.

I went in and answered the letter:

My Dear Pia,
Please be happy. We'll still be friends and thank you for everything.
Olivia.

That felt better.

Later, as evening cooled Pinfold, and I sat in the old dairy where my mother's *escritoire* had replaced Isabel's heavy cheese-press, I began to shiver. I took myself in my own arms and rocked her like a child. Waves of shocked bereftness swept me and my skin was gooseflesh. No more to lie with Pia in our bed seemed like death. Though I'd hardly felt the lack of her, closed in with my books and my phantom broodings,

I'd known she was over there, flighty, promiscuously good-humoured, but tenderly mine. I could let her go in order to receive her back. But I couldn't share her.

Isabel screwed the cheese-press with both muscular arms on the strain. Liquid dripped from the pale compacted mass into a basin. The dairy smelled of her industrious sweat and the sweet-sour tang of white cheese. Looking up, she favoured me with a glance which carried more than a hint of contempt for my cushy self-indulgence. *If you love her*, she gave me to understand, *you will share her*.

But I didn't love Pia, did I, in that honest-to-God, absolute way: that was reserved for Faith, and Faith was out of reach. This recognition (and perhaps Pia knew it all along) was what gave me the shivers and sent me now to crouch dry-eyed beside my stepmother's imitation coalfire, longing for touch, and Faith.

*

Everyone laughs at you. Didn't you know you're a joke?

How it smarts, the poisoned arrow. I hadn't realised he'd aimed so truly, and how the dart would lodge in my tender place, and fester. I've stayed in and listened to the aeroplanes for several days. Not picked up the Hannah transcript or attempted anything except the idea of flight: all my usual activities suddenly seem symptomatic of my freakish character. I suffer a recurrent dream of opening a door which leads into an antechamber; from which I hear muffled laughter, rustling, whispering: they are laughing at me, for sure. Opening the door into my own bedroom, I burst in upon naked, entangled lovers, blonde Louise and Pia, my Pia, who holds out a hand to me and asks politely, 'Won't you join us?' And the little blonde thing titters, dragging the sheet up over her head.

Everyone laughs at you. Don't you know what a joke you are? Well, I'll give myself a day or so more, and then pull myself together.

Pia would say, *It's Jim's own damage that's showing. Take no notice. You're lovely as you are.*

I tell myself severely, washing grit off lettuce for a salad, *I will not allow myself to be made a wimp of.*

Knocking at the door; probably the milkman. I wipe my hands cursorily and rummage a fiver out of my jeans pocket.

'I thought you were the milkman,' I tell Faith. I was just about to pay you.'

'Well, OK, if you insist.'

Now that I've despaired and relinquished her, thereby attaining a certain peace of mind, of course she turns up. Better for my equanimity if she'd bolt conclusively, or just be there as a steady friend – but how could that be practicable with her husband so hostile?

'Is he with you?'

'No. Just me. Is it OK?'

'Sure. Come in. Actually I'm glad you've come, I feel there are things that ought to be said. Well, by me. Such as, sorry. To *you*, not him. Sure, I rubbed him up the wrong way, but what he said to me was *vile*.'

'He knows. He's truly sorry. It was unforgivable.'

'It was. And I'm not forgiving him.'

'No,' she falters. 'OK.'

'But I want him to know that if he spreads slanders about me messing around with students, he will pay dear for it.'

She looks pale; her lip quivers. 'Why, what did he say?' she asks in a husky voice.

'Sorry, Faith. Do sit down. It's nothing to do with you at all. I'm sorry. Except of course that you are part of him and so you get the brunt of it. And I was being vindictive. So I suppose I goaded him and got what I was asking for. Tell me, Faith,' I go on, my voice tinny with corrosive emotion, 'is it true what he said, that you all laugh at me? That I'm a joke – a freak?'

'Is that what he said?'

I nod. Her very shock is anodyne. Evidently he hasn't told her the half of it.

'No, Olivia. I don't laugh at you. Never, I've never heard anyone laugh at you behind your back. You're my friend. I admire you for everything I can't be.'

'OK.'

'Truly. Most truly. Do you believe me?'

'If you say so.' Why must I sound so begrudging, so

sullen? I suppose it is my distaste for my own display of weakness; shameful tears are sparking behind my eyes. Mother taught me to be restrained. Be controlled. I roughly roll up my shirtsleeves, forcing back the tears.

'He gets into occasional rages,' says Faith.

'Did you not know that?' I ask, my concern peeling off myself and transferring to her. 'Before you married him.'

'I knew.'

'So why...?'

'He's had a lot of pain in his life,' says Faith. 'I can help him with that.'

I can summon no reply. This seems more immature than anything I've ever heard her say. I whistle inwards through my teeth.

'No. Really. I can.' She sits bolt upright in her chair, as if pleading a case against a probing attorney. 'And we are exceptionally happy.'

'Right. Sure. I expect it's just me that winds him up.'

'He's jealous, quite simply,' says Faith. 'I haven't yet managed to reassure him. Because I had feelings for you, Olivia, which I couldn't exactly deal with...it threw me. I blame myself for not confronting those feelings and talking it through with you. But, putting that cowardliness and perplexity aside, and thinking of Jim: it's himself he thinks people laugh at. He believes, with justice, that he's been passed over for promotion just because the importance of his work is not understood.'

A dervish dance of Cistercian monks whirls across my mind, all proclaiming in plainsong the significance of their tonsures and vespers to the study of history. Jim spins along in their wake, asserting the value of the cloister to an indifferent modern world. I quash the spasm of fellow-feeling (weren't my Revolutionary women the centre of my world?) that threatens. I hold on to the seething upsurge of long-buried emotion as Faith refers back to the embrace of last year, which now seems, to my salved eye, rather stillborn than abortive. One can grieve and recover, because there has indeed been something born, a mutual love which we might still convert to friendship. Her love had stood tiptoe for my love to sweep it off its feet, in that extempore moment which now feels hallowed, ungainsayable, but bygone.

'It's OK,' I yield. 'I understand. I'm afraid I've ballsed things up good and proper. We'll not be able to see each other, will we?'

'Why not?'

'Well, if it upsets him every time you and I have a cup of coffee together...'

'Oh,' she raps back, 'I'm still a *person*, Olivia.'

*

We sit in silence, my love and I, across the table from one another, leaning forward, our hands woven lightly together. This spirit-lightness touches without imprinting a claim, or at least, if I am truthful (and here I must not fail in plainness), the least pressure possible to merely human touch. I am so grateful now for the silences of my Quaker childhood, the candle-flame of attention held through the circle of an hour that seemed over in no time yet had encompassed eternity. Was I always practising for this? This clement revelation? If I have a wish, it is that I possessed skill to record on canvas the still beauty of Faith's face, in this tempered light that reverences the equality and difference of the person. She will never be anything like me. She will never come home to me. She will always be herself, apart and other. I love her for that, and for the single tear that builds, brims and slowly overflows her lashes. The windows beside us stand wide open.

*

'I want you to see something, Faith, if you've time.'

'What is it?'

'A copy of a manuscript. No one has seen it but me.'

'What you were talking about the other day? Are you sure you want anyone to see? I realised how private and special it was.'

'I don't want *anyone* to see. Just you.'

With many murmurs and deep breaths, whispered comments and hushed exclamations, she and I bent her heads together above the second part of Hannah's *Wilderness of Women*.

Four

I prophesied & said, 'O London, London, thou art a place of terror & barbarous cruelty, filth & pride.'

Isabel & I saw the fanatic Harrison come to execution. We watched his wife clasp him in her arms, with a livid pale face. He said to her, with fierce, holy gaity, 'I shall see King Jesus within half an hour. And I'll return to thee darling tomorrow.'

They strung him up. Cut him down, still breathing. Kicked him awake. Doused his head with water. Sawed off his privates & stuffed them in his mouth. Cut out his guts. Reached up through his abdomen & tore out his heart, raising it to the roaring crowd; boiled it in a cauldron of tar. Chopped off his head & hacked his body into four quarters, & boiled the parts.

Slowly the people dispersed, while we stood gasping, & I heard one fop say to his friend, 'O Captain, you are all heart,' at which they laughed.

I lifted up my voice & cried, O LONDON LONDON, & howled. For what are we? Bags of guts, I thought. Bags of suffering guts.

My own guts churned as I retched through the streets, but Isabel said, 'Hannah, we are more than this, for we can weep, & love, & are pregnant with pity. And he has but shed a suit of clothes.'

The shrouded bodies of Cromwell, Ireton and Bradshaw were dug up & hanged at Tyburn, which I witnessed, & smelt the foul stench. Their heads were stuck on poles at Westminster Hall. On the heads, with tarred eyes & scraps of scalp, the rain drove. Carrion crows perched on the bone & pecked. Snows in winter froze them & in summer sun, beads of sweat seemed to break from their foreheads. Whenever a skull fell, apprentices played football with it.

Many times as we passed over London Bridge, I have stopped to look up at the malefactors' skulls on poles, & stood considering these remains in silence. 'The skulls do not feel pain,' said Isabel.

When Venner & the Fifth Monarchy-Men rose against the king the next year, bawling 'King Jesus, & the heads upon the gates!' there was more hanging, drawing & quartering. These foolish men were rattled along to execution on sledges, still expecting King Jesus to come. I thought of Anna Trapnel who we met at Manchester, wishing that babbling creature safe & quiet, warming her toes by some fire-side.

But now the great Persecution was upon us. Friends' Meetings were broken up, but came back together again. Menfolk imprisoned, the women came together again. Womenfolk arrested, children came together again. When their windows were stove in, their houses knocked down, they came together in the open air, worshipping in silence upon the ruins. Seeing all this, I went to George Fox & said, 'I & my yoke-fellow is drawn by the Spirit to stand with thee George in Friends' time of trial. Will thou own us again?'

He stood a while in thought, leaning against the chimney-piece, a carthorse of a man, with coarse heavy features, wearing a dusty leather jacket & breeches: but eyes of speedwell-blue & very strong & strange. A quiver passed through my body in looking at his eyes, & for the first time I understood why people shy away from my own. George's eyes scanned a person's secret places; but an intimate, speaking beauty called the spirit home.

'Art thou in the Truth, Hannah?'

'I am in the Truth.'

'Will thou accept the tender admonition of thy brothers & sisters?'

'Aye, George, if it accord with the Spirit. Will thou?'

This prickled & provoked George, who strove within himself & drew in a sharp breath, as if to rebuke me. But, uttering nothing, he turned his face all rosy from the heat of the fire, towards me, saying (but not bitterly, more as a question):

'Thou was the undoing of poor James, Hannah, thou &

Martha between you.'

'Am I so powerful, George?' I asked him, moving close &
looking up straight into his face. 'Does thou quake with fear I'll
undo thee too?'

At this he laughed & lovingly took my hand, shaking his head.

'Nay. It was the weakness of James that undid him, not thy
power.'

'That, & thy pride, George, for when he longed to make
peace with thee & offered to kiss thy hand, thou insultingly
offered him thy foot instead.'

'Well well,' he sighed, turning away. 'He pardoned me, I
pardoned him, Christ pardoned us both. We made our peace
before he died, & he said much to me of thee, Hannah ...'

'Never mind that,' I put in, for a pang wellnigh bent me
double. I dreaded to hear any words James might have said
concerning our most private bond. 'Thou loved the man & I
loved him, & he is gone, & let that stand. May my yoke-fellow
& I be accounted as one with the Seed, George, & worship with
them & suffer with them?'

'With all my heart,' he said, & took my hand. I set this down
as testament of my one meeting with George Fox, that great
spirit, which left a deep impression upon my soul.

So Isabel & I joined once more with Friends. Standing in the
rubble, we prayed in silence, a silence so vocal that it could be
heard streets way. It seemed to bring the soldiers running. Sir
Richard Browne's men (beasts rather), sword in one hand,
cane in the other, hounded us into gaol, men, women &
children. Isabel & I was in and out of Bridewell, but we took
turns for our babe's sake, to keep her out of prison.

Yet, though I stood with Friends to bear witness to the Light,
my inner being was turbulent & dark. I doubted even if there
was a soul. The skulls & quarters on the poles seemed to tell me
that all we are is bags of guts. Offal.

Through the window of Prior's Rhenish Wine House I
witnessed men filling these bags with wine & oysters. In that
very window, a plump young lecher with a wine-flushed face
was tumbling a woman. Which I watched.

While he fed the woman oysters with one hand, his other
crawled up her smock & fondled her bosom, crooning, 'O Betty

what a white, white thigh.' Which I watched.

Betty rubbed at his privy member without modesty, as if shining up a shoe. Which I watched.

When I tapped smartly on the lead-paned window, crying out, 'Friend! Why abuse the gentlewoman so?' he flapped his hand at me to gesture me away, but, when I only knocked harder, he gave over flapping & fell to straddling the woman until he was tired. Which I watched.

He went out the back way, off to Whitehall. I followed, saying, 'Friend, know thou not thy body is the Temple of the Holy Spirit?'

'Madam,' he replied pleasantly, 'you take care of your temple & I'll take care of my body.'

'I tremble for thy soul, friend.'

'Do you indeed? And many men must have trembled for those green eyes and fine hair, have they not?'

'My green eyes must melt into jelly, friend, & my hair be cut off my corpse to make false pieces for thy poor, poxed whores.'

'Ah now,' said he, 'poxed whores I do not use. Mine are clean whores.'

'How can thou know? What are we, man, under the skin?'

At this the young man looked at me with new interest. 'Come over to the bridge & I'll show thee, my pretty little fanatic.' I saw what he intended.

'Nay, friend, I mean thy eternal soul, which thou starves. It cries like a babe within thee.'

Then he began to ask me in which organ or member of the body the soul lived. He had seen a cadaver, he said, dissected at the Surgeons Hall. 'And I could scarcely resist touching. My hand sneaked out – like this – & I touched the skin. Not like yours, soft and warm, but cold as mushroom. It excited me strangely to see his inside opened up.'

He stood brooding, hand over his small, moist mouth. 'I saw the whole inside world of man. But…no soul. No room for a soul.'

'Friend, the soul was flown.'

'Doubtless,' he said. 'Now will you walk with me? God does not begrudge our natural pleasures.'

'Man, give thought to thine eternal soul.'

And so I went my way, my heart bursting for the ills of LONDON. *I longed for the green fields of the little town of Manchester, the sweet air of the Irwell & the red sandstone cliffs. As I walked away from this man through the sour crush of bodies, blank sadness clutched my heart as if the soul-candles of this great city were snuffed out, in a new night. Only body remained. Body & no soul. And money & shops, shops & money. For all things & most people were for sale.*

As I crept back to our lodgings along the soiled pavements, my entrails spasmed to smell the cruelty & carnality of LONDON. *My head pounded, for my soul was like a city in which the poor & persecuted seethed & toiled. Their cries ascended to the heavens but the heavens heard them not. The great ones fed off the mean ones. They racked their rents & ate up their lands & evicted them from their cottages so that they had no roof over their heads & must be on the road & came here to this great sewer like other vermin.*

In the night I heard the scavengers' carts grate along the cobbles. In a fever I heard them night & day, smelling a foetid smell. Clinging to Isabel where I lay imbrued in sweat, I begged her to tell me, 'Have they not yet collected all our dung? Must it go on forever?'

But the reek was myself, for I fouled the bed with my flux, & besought God that we might go home again, if I lived, to the mild airs of Stockport & the calm, gentle country of Cheshire, & to Pinfold Farm which we had named BEULAH.

Twilight surprised us. We had sat for several hours piecing the words together and, though we had not finished reading, our energy was spent. When I saw Faith to the gate, the air weighed heavily with perfume from the buddleia, compromised by car-fumes from the street. The sky was cloudless and an eggshell-blue half-moon was waning on the tip of a bough of the copper beech.

'So it was here,' mused Faith, taking in the whitewashed walls of Pinfold, greened with smears of mould, its sagged belly bolted through with an iron pin, windows messy with unpruned ivy. 'Here, in your home, that they...'

We stood hesitating, one on either side of the gate, hands

lightly linked. 'What an evening,' said Faith. Her face seemed to be fading by the moment under the dwindled light. 'Thank you for sharing Hannah with me, Olivia.' She seemed unequal to the task of finding words for the experience of becoming lost together in Hannah's book, tongue-tied as one is when the audience spills out on to the street from an absorbing film, whose colours and emotions are perishing even as one seeks words to detain them.

I turned back into myself as she disappeared.

Bags of suffering guts. The reek that was myself. Boys playing football with a skull.

Where could Hannah go from here, set down from her buoyant dream of a new heaven and a new earth, on the modern-seeming terrain of Restoration consumerism and technology; a world composed of investigable matter rather than founded on quintessence of spirit? It was the first time I had known Hannah want to run away; the first time she had expressed nostalgia for some place quitted in the course of her pilgrimage. Home-sickness shook her for the region that had stigmatised and ostracised her. In the light of the darkness of London, she ruefully forgave a Manchester whose scale she could encompass.

The sweet airs of the Irwell & the red sandstone cliffs? The mild airs of Stockport?

This Eden was beyond me to imagine. My earliest memories of Manchester are of its blackness. A foot of carbon stood on civic buildings and the Gothic university: black deposits from a couple of centuries of industrialisation. On bright days the black buildings shone like coalfaces sculpted to impressive forms against a turquoise sky. Men with masks came and sandblasted off the black crust. Hannah was prehistoric to these buildings and their coating of industrial grime. Before factories, before the 'hands'' cellar-hovels, before Marx and Engels conferred in their eyrie at Chetham's Library, before Manchester was what we understood as Manchester. To Hannah in the capital, the quiet country town and rural Stockport beckoned like a pastoral sanctuary.

I recalled a section of the sandstone cliffs, exposed beside the multi-storey car park by the River Irwell, rosy-coloured strata bearing graffiti and a line of Carlsberg cans.

*

Hannah's heart lifted as soon as they were out of London. On the road she grew hale, stepping out fast to match her smaller strides against Isabel's. They took turns to hump Grace on their backs, or threw sticks ahead for her to scamper after, sleeping rough in ditches and under ricks. In the mid-September sun, the air was balmy, with only hints of frosts and storms to come. All three wore leather jackets and breeches, as the most practical gear. New ideas bubbled in Hannah's mind, messages from the Spirit which Isabel developed. Between St Albans and Dunstable, they seem to have formulated a rule-of-thumb theory of communism, a quilt formed of common-sense, scraps of the bible and shreds of Digger belief. They tried out their theory on the burgesses of Dunstable. The borough catchpoll, sizing up the dimensions of his lock-up with the number of local dissenters already cramming it, deemed it judicious to shove the crackpot women on their way with a mere cuff on the ear. Scrumping apples and pears, they lifted vegetables at the wayside, picked pocketfuls of hazel-nuts and were sensible of the generosity of the season. Grace ate well, chewing milky corn-ears and nearly making herself sick on blackberries.

At Northampton, Hannah preached from the market cross and advertised the setting-up of a Jerusalem to be built in the North. Louts pelted her with derision, shit and stones.

'Leave father and mother, husband and brother, and follow me,' shouted Hannah over her shoulder. A scarecrow group of paupers and drunks tagged in her wake. These are named as Susan Piper, a beggar named Jane, and a black-haired woman who did not seem to speak English, but what language she did speak no one could tell. Hannah took her to be a gypsy, separated from her group.

Outside Leicester, they held a great meeting in the open air. All the town's Quakers and some of the other dissenters came. 'A new heaven and a new earth is coming,' she promised the crowd. 'In Stockport, or the wastes and commons thereabouts.'

Three more pilgrims upped sticks, prepared to forsake not just husband but, between them, a brood of ten children.

'Bring the little ones along,' said Hannah.

At Derby, the magistrates were awaiting the group, now swollen to seventeen, with writs to commit them straight to the House of Correction. It seemed to Hannah and Isabel prudent to skirt the town. The clemency of the harvest season was yielding to frosty nights. They improvised a form of sleeping bag, all huddling together for body-warmth.

The children dragged their feet on the Derbyshire hills; grizzled and fretted. Isabel gave donkey-rides.

Just below Stockport, the group rested, scanning the vista to the hill on which the remains of the Norman castle had been blown up at the beginning of the Civil War. The peace and beauty of the scene calmed them all. Red deer paused in the woodlands, quiveringly timid, looking out between the tree trunks. Tilting their heads, the women followed a flock of a hundred or so geese wheeling in an arc before flying away north-west. The gleaming Mersey, teeming with salmon, lay before them; a black-and-white huddle of houses, old-fashioned and built to a human scale. I imagine especially Isabel's sense of home-coming to this country of abundance.

I see them climbing up to the market place, to proclaim the New Jerusalem: the death of private property; the reclamation of the commons by persons of good faith, new Eves and any Adams who wish to learn the ready and easy way back into Paradise.

The bell is rung for trading to begin. Live pigs and dead calves pass hands, cheeses are bartered, cream-coloured and crumbly, with their ammoniac scent. Meal is weighed.

The women cluster in the market in Quakerly silence, like dingy sepals centred by the brazen-haired stamen. The sharp air is tinged with woodsmoke. Hannah clears her throat and begins, in her most strident voice,

O STOCKPORT, FOR THEE HAVE I TRAVAILED! SELL NOT THY GOODS, BUT FREELY GIVE & SHARE WITH THE POOR & WIDOWS & ORPHANS.

Grabbing a massive round cheese from a stall, she makes good her words by breaking off generous hanks and looking round for widows and orphans amongst whom to redistribute it.

Perhaps she has not sufficiently explained her theory, for the entire market sets upon her.

'We come in peace,' Hannah keeps insisting, between blows, oblivious to the inflammatory nature of her proceedings. 'To teach you better, more Christian ways.' Thumped in the breast. Pitched backwards. 'Doesn't Jesus say, in your bibles...' Punched in the belly. Bent double. Fights for breath to continue her sentence... 'in your bibles, friends, give all that you have to the poor?' A storm of slaps round the ears.

'Hit me, strike me, I care not,' bawls Isabel; and gets precisely what she asks for. She could squash some of these little runts, as she knows, but both hands are tied behind her back by the covenant of peace.

Hannah is silenced; Isabel scarcely knows what she is saying as they are dragged into the handy nearby lock-up along with those women who have not run away.

*

On Mealhouse Brow, curving steeply up from Little Underbank, one can still see the small door of the dungeon into which Hannah, Isabel, and four of the women were thrust, into a low-arched cellar, 12-foot long by 6-foot wide. I have haunted the place since and run my fingers over the oak door, double locked, studded with nails and fitted with an iron grating. I stared in through the grating and my eyes met darkness. Whereas she was locked in, I, it seemed, was to be locked out.

'Oh you can't go in there,' the Town Hall told me. 'It's not open to the general public. What do you want to go in there for anyhow?'

'Historical interest?'

'Well, as far as I know, it's just the same as any cellar. Used for storing cheeses when they stopped banging poor sods up.'

I didn't want just any cellar. I wanted the one Hannah and Isabel had been incarcerated in. Returning, I pressed my forehead against the grille.

The dungeon, I knew, had been en-suite to the Court Leet that must have sentenced Hannah. Just up Mealhouse Brow stands the old market mealhouse beneath which the baronial court met, in whose bowels is a spiral stair leading to the dungeon.

Like some love-sick teenager adoring from afar, unable to credit that my puerile vigil could fail to conjure a glimpse of the beloved, I prowled the narrow way, which seems to squirm its way up the cobbled hill but in that period acted as main thoroughfare. Up there the pack-horses lumbered, laden and straining; the soldiers marched south-to-north, north-to-south. Inside these blind spaces Hannah Emanuel was sentenced to fifty strokes of the lash, ducking and the brank.

And for bringing the Good News of the new Jerusalem to the people of Cheshire, this was all the thanks I got from the lewd burgesses of Stockport, to be sentenced to barbarous punishment. I laughed in their faces whereat they held their ears.

'Be silent, woman.'

'I will NOT be silent.'

'We'll have to cut her tongue out,' mused Master Lumb. 'By the roots.'

'Thou would not dare.'

'The law against scolds allows it as a final remedy. Nevertheless we'll try the others first.'

So first they ducked me in their filthy pool. Because I showed no panic, but took a deep breath each time I went under & let it out when I came up, they said I was a witch & should be swum. My left thumb would be tied to my right toe & I would be plunged in the Mersey. If I floated or whirled on the water, I would be proven a witch; but if I drowned I would be innocent (but, unless they dragged me up in time, dead).

'Tedious fools,' I said, 'don't you know that CHRIST could walk on water?'

Then they tied me at cart's tail & their constable wrenched my bodice off so that my breasts were bare to public view; & I saw the greedy eyes of men and boys roving my breasts. I huddled my elbows over my breasts to shield them but my arms

204

were roped behind my back. I hung my head so that the hair might cover my nakedness.

Then an apprentice cried, 'One o' 'er didd's bigger nor t'other! Give us diddy, mother, give us diddy!' Though such laughter scorched my very soul, I was able to tell them in an even voice that I did indeed come here to nurse them, in the sweet milk of the Holy Spirit.

A lad darted up & battened on my nipple (the others roaring him on) till I screamed, for he bit the tender place with his teeth. He was chased away, the constable half-laughing saying, 'None o' thy kinkum crankums here, lad.' The rude sot, bawling that my milk was bingy & made him boke, made as if to vomit over his fellows.

At this cruel usage I was much distressed. I had trouble in holding back my tears. Courage forsook me. But when the constable whipped me through Stockport, I chanted, 'The Spirit, she is in me, the Spirit she's in me, Spirit's me, Spirit's-she's-me, she's-me, she's-me,' which carried me through. By & by I became numb to the bloody strokes, & quietly turned my head as the constable paused to shake his aching arm, looking him in the eyes with a smile & saying in a gentle voice, 'I forgive thee, friend, & will pray for thee.'

At this he was agitated, & forbore to strike so hard, seeing that I went patient as a lamb, until presently he offered mere taps on my bleeding back. People murmured, 'He is bewitched.'

When I was returned to the dungeon, Isabel cleaned my wounds & smeared a paste of willow on the cuts & hazel on the bruises. Lying on my side, I saw that, as she ministered to the cuts on my breasts, tears blinded her eyes. She shook her head, saying nothing, &, having covered me up gently, turned away to the wall, her shoulders shaking with silent howls. I was hot & delirious that night, & within a week, my back was a mass of green pus. When they came to put me in the brank, my dear yoke-fellow leapt up & begged, 'Take me for her. She cannot stand.'

But they would not.

Now I shall tell of the worse-than-Turkish tyranny of the borough of STOCKPORT, which I, who have travelled to Smyrna and met Infidels, may justly do.

They took me into the market-square & stood me before the people, at which I, reviving in the sweet air that blows in from the green pasture all around, thought fit to speak to the people & urge them to give all they had to the poor. For their eyes, I thought, were not unkind, only hollow & blank, in need of the delicious milk of the Spirit.

So I stretched out my arms & said to the people, 'My friends, we are the Lord's babes. So let us love one another.'

Not a word did they say. I thought they appeared anxious & abashed, some fiddling with the brims of their hats, others shuffling from foot to foot. But before I could continue to unfold Truth to them, the brank was brought & shown to me by Master Lumb.

'A hat for the head of Mistress Tongue.'

'It would suit thee better, friend, being made to a foul design. It is made in the devil's forge. Therefore put on what thy hands have made.'

'I did not make it, I make nothing.'

'No, thou Gentleman, thou makes nothing. Takes all. Takes bread from the starving & toil from the wage-slave.'

'Dost thou THOU me, witch?'

'Ay,' I said, 'and I have thou'd mightier than thee. The king himself, was quiet to receive correction.'

'Be silent.'

'I will not be silent. Think thou that THOU can silence the Spirit when she speaks in woman?'

'I will fit the crown on thy head myself.'

I shrank when I saw the bridle they keep in this Christian town for Christian women who tell the gospel truth. As he advanced toward me, holding out the monstrous implement, I weakened.

The brank at Stockport is an iron cage, a stone in weight, with a bit two inches long, ending in nine iron pins with sharp points.

I whispered, 'I cannot take that in my mouth.'

'It will muzzle thee, rabid bitch,' he said, and with two others shoved my head into the cage, until I was forced to open my mouth to receive the spikes. Blood filled my mouth & throat.

The crowd was silent. No one moved, no man insulted me

while I stood there & bled. All afternoon I stood, & women came & sponged my face clean of blood and vomit, through the cage, until at four the constable led me around the square, at which I, for anguish, swooned, & our women held me up at either side.

And they called, HAIL CHRISTA, QUEEN OF THE JEWS.

And some of the crowd called, 'Shame, in a Christian country.'

And the cry went up of, SHAME, SHAME!

But I, fainting, thought that the call was JAMES, JAMES, & in my trance of pain I believed James Nayler to be nearby, come back from the dead, or that I had gone to him, through that same door of humiliation.

James came to me radiant, his face just as it had been, tender as a mother to her babe, & with delicate care he lifted off that cage of pain & infamy, replacing it with a crown of light, identical to that on his head. He showed me his tongue, with the wound closed. And lifted me with his strong arms out of the mire, so lightly, saying, 'We are safe now, Hannah, we are across the river, my lamb, & the white shining people await us. A little way, & we are in Jerusalem.'

But when I saw Isabel's face over me in the hell pit, I wished her away, for it was James I longed for, not Isabel.

But he was dead.

I knew that I too must die, to be with and in him. The pain in my mouth was beyond anything, & seemed to boil. I could not move my head for the intolerable weight of that cage had locked my neck & shattered my back teeth on one side. So after that I had trouble in eating solid food & have lived on slops since. But this disturbs me very little.

My loving friend ministered to me night & day until I could be moved. Our daughter Grace, being cared for by Susan, was brought to the grille each day to see me, but spoke few words all the time I was in that place. She seemed angry with me at my plight.

'Why cannot we live in a house & play at tops?' she asked.

'Thy mother is chosen of God, Grace.'

'I wants to play with tops & puppets,' was all she would say; & shook her head like one demented, thrusting out her tongue.

'*Thou must obey the Spirit, Grace.*'

'*Shan't, nohow,*' said Grace.

Then said I, the first words almost I spoke since I was bridled, with thick, pain-bloated tongue, 'It is good, daughter, that thou'rt defiant, but defy the bad, not the good.'

However, she said no more, and was from that time waywardly dumb.

The remnant of the band of women and children limped out of Stockport, travelling north-east. Several, daunted, had slipped away south to their homes. Isabel half-supported, half-carried Hannah, whose shattered jaw juddered with every step. Sometimes she must have felt she was nothing but that pain. Susan Piper dragged the reluctant, squirming Grace along by the hand. Jane of-no-known-surname carried in her bundle a great round cheese and a stock of rye-bread given them by the compassionate stallholder from whose stock 'poor Hobby the Hoyden', as he called Hannah, first saw fit to grab the cheese.

It was cold but at least it seems to have remained dry. Their feet smashed along through the wreckage of banked leaves under the great oaks on the track to Bramhall. Past the oatfield at Linneys Tenement, they crossed Ladybrook, passed stealthily through the Catholic demesne around Bramhall Hall, and followed Carr Brook into the wood.

'Here,' decided Hannah. Isabel set her down on her feet.

'It's marshy-like,' Susan pointed out. 'Whose is it anyhow?'

'Ours,' stated Hannah. 'Commons.'

'Don't like it here!' shrieked Grace. 'Don't like the boggarts. Is boggarts in this wood.' She seemed impotent to discern any benefits in being born the daughter of the new Christ.

'There is no boggart,' said Isabel patiently, crouching to the child. 'There's no boggart. No sin. No hell. No devil. All these things was invented to terrify poor people into obeying their gaffers. Help Izzo collect leaves and wood, Grace?'

Dry leaves were bagged into sacks for mattresses. Practised hands wove brushwood together, securing it with hemp ropes to construct a cluster of shelters. Hannah was laid gently down on the most comfortable of the makeshift pallets. Isabel did not believe she could live long, and saw little hope of the community's survival. Winter, however, seems to have proved clement, and Pinfold, deteriorating with the master's drinking, eagerly accepted the illicit labour Isabel and Susan could barter for twopence a day. No questions asked. Isabel was twice picked up as a vagrant; whipped and let go. One of the children died and was buried in the woodland. Nobody penetrated into the depths of Carr Wood. Even their fires attracted no sustained notice.

Once a man with a smoking gun and a hound came plunging down into Carr Wood. The children ran to the dog and fondled away his growls. Looking round coolly, the intruder nodded his head as if assessing numbers. Without speaking, he crashed off out of the wood.

'Trepan,' said someone, panicking. 'Informer.'

They waited edgily for ambush. Nothing.

A maid kicked out of service for being pregnant by her master arrived to join them, as did two male vagrants and a pickpocket fresh from the stocks in Macclesfield.

'I must write,' says Hannah. She is given pen and paper and begins to write *Wilderness of Women*.

And so we have come to this blessed sanctuary, outside the law, where we is one seed & one heart, & picks the fruit and enjoys the ancient rights of the commons, where in the waste wilderness, Eden is to be built, the New Jerusalem, the land that flows with milk & honey: for here we bide in leafless winter, pray & know that soon the Spirit will announce the Change that is to come. And my loving yoke-fellow, helpmeet & marriage-partner, as she has been for so many years, remains my shield and defence, my mother, sister & my eternal love. For as Christ & the Spirit is one person, so Isabel & Hannah Emanuel is one seamless unity.

Hannah Emanuel

Beneath this, my mother had written:

Here the testament of H. Jones ends. The manuscript continues in another and less educated hand, which I take to be that of Isabel Clarke, as follows. Some of the words could not be transcribed, the whole of the remainder of the document yielding the impression of haste and extreme emotion. Lacunae have been noted & possible variants supplied at the foot of each page. I have supplied punctuation where necessary to maintain the sense of the text.

Soul of correctness till the end, my mother's intolerance sanctioned itself as a tidy instinct, conscientiously polishing and civilising the crude raw material she was allowing through the inquisitorial Vatican of her mind. I thought, with venomous indignation, *Why could you not leave us the original manuscript, mother, so that we could decipher for ourselves?* I thought of Hannah's daughter Grace, retreating from her mother's hair-raising instability to take sanctuary in the docile bonnet of second generation Friends. Who could blame her? Perhaps we were destined, generation by generation, to repeat the oscillation between wild mother and tame daughter; piety and licence; the hearth and the bonfire? Childless I was; childless I would remain. That was a comfort. I read on.

Came the men like wolves into the fold. Came with knives & ropes & pitchforks, & smashed our homes to pieces. Took my beloved from my kiss.

I fought. Hannah said USE NO VIOLENCE *but I fought. I seized a great hurdle of birch and stood before my family & I battled with the regions of hell & they prevailed.*

And they took Hannah Emanuel captive to Chester.

And I stole a horse from Syddal House stable & rode to Chester.

And they tried my beloved for witchcraft & I [beat] the witchtryingwoman with my own hands, till her face was bloody-black so they whipped & stocked me & they said of my yoke-fellow she had a Dog possessed by a devil in likeness of a Black Man & a Magpie who sucked her private parts.

In that dungeon was priest [Lyngard] the great whore who was held for conventicles & he said to Hannah confess, confess, beautiful but ruined creature, confess you have bewitched me from the first, but she said, 'Yea MAN *I confess* THOU *art a* WITCH *& has a coven at Lower Peover.'*

And they hanged my beloved & I took her body from the hole where they buried it with an old rusted bridle on her head in mockery, which I removed. I carried my soul-fellow in my arms, keening, reeling & washed her in the stream & all the filth came out of her bright dimmed hair, her mudded beautiful green eyes her [ ] & wrapped her in a mantle of green linen & buried her body in a dell near to Pinfold, so that I might visit her daily & wait for her to awaken for I thought, 'She must & will return, she must & will.'

Where I had hilled her over in the buryhole, each dawn I crawled back & threw myself upon the mound. As she lay under the clay, I lay over the clay. But anger rose against Hannah & I said, 'I would have died for thee Hannah but thou had no mercy on me, thou loved James Nayler more nor thy yoke-fellow that was tenderly one with thee & had no other thought or desire but thee Hannah, THEE ONLY. Why did thou breathe life into my dull clay & betray thy handiwork, running away into the grave?' Then I took to desolate wandering. I went to Chester where they hanged her, looking for a Sign. I went to Lindow to seek the moor-maiden but she had rotted away into the peat.

And now little better than an ox I ploughed, yelved manure, washed clouts in the pond, cut wood & digged, for two years or more, & still she did not come my garden enclosed my sister, my spouse, but lo I dreamed & saw Hannah Emanuel in bright radiant robes with hair blazing like forest trees in autumn, not here in the nether world of filth but above in a ring of light.

Whereupon she looking down upon me where I worked like a beast in the fields, never speaking to no one nor praying to the No-God, sweetly asked, 'O Ishbel, O my heart, why came I to thee with gifts thou has thrown to swine?'

I cried out to her, saying, 'Come again, come again, I cannot live without thee.'

Ashamed of my feebleness, she said, 'I am here with James. I am in the light. My mouth is healed. Would thou have me go through that travail again who am delivered & with my love?'

Crying louder, I fell on my face in the ploughed field, asking, 'Am I not thy love?'

'Yea, Ishbel, thou art.'

But I was not satisfied, I ground my teeth pleading my own cause, complaining, 'I have served for thee in the fields twice that time Jacob served for Rachel & I have thee not.'

But she, stooping from the glowing sky, held with one hand to James & with the other (her hair falling forward) reached down to me, saying, 'Take hold, dear heart, we'll pull thee up between us.'

But oh, the gulf that lay between, & Hannah got down on her knees to reach far out but if she had reached any further she'd have tumbled down to earth, to suffer over again, so I ceased to plead & said, 'Stay where thou are, wait & I'll come to thee.'

'Entreat me not to leave thee, neither forbid me from following after thee, for thy people is my people & thy God my God,' were our parting words as they were our marriage words here at Pinfold Farm.

So I went to the mound where she is buried & lay for the last time upon the grass body-to-body as close as earth could suffer; and then went my ways, & William Hulme takes Grace to his household & I move on from hamlet to hamlet, telling of Emanuel's work and words.

I.E.

Five

You nesh lass, I remember the dental nurse chafing me when I winced at the removal of a wisdom tooth. I cannot imagine undertaking one tithe of the risk Hannah courted, or enduring five minutes of that pain. As I witness Hannah's Calvary, I sigh, hold my breath, swivel in my chair, reading with my nerves. The bit that enters her mouth, causes me to shift my weight and turn my head, conscious of the cavity of my own mouth: inside-cheek, floor and palate, so tender and intimate a place. Moist and networked with nerves, the mouth is made for tasting, sucking, kissing, speaking, a place of innermost sensation, ripe for pleasure and suffering. I run my fingertips over my lips; place them over eyes which backtrack to hers. Hannah lived her life in a state equivalent to rapid eye-movement dreaming – but awake. And the truths our dreams tell us, she lived out.

What was the point of it, Hannah? I ask. *What did you achieve?* You had your say, you swung, were buried and forgotten. The farmer ploughed above you; cattle cropped the grass above your shattered face.

How long did it take for your slender nape to snap, tongue extruded obscenely from the blackening mouth, blood-engorged, the slight frame dangling? All that beauty, intelligence and vitality to be hung like meat from a hook.

Beauty that believed that not even meat should be hung from hooks.

Then Isabel's unbearable-to-read bereavement. The disciple took refuge in the dumb and mindless toil of a working animal, from which Hannah had liberated her. Isabel knew (had understood all along) the division of Hannah's heart between herself and James. Tears break from my eyes to imagine the horror that shook a woman so staunch.

If I am Hannah's child, I also feel that I am Isabel's. Bone of their bone, clay of their impassioned clay.

*

That owl is here again...a barn-owl, would it be? I took it for a cat the first time it perched on the cherry tree looking fixedly at me through the window: such a solid bulk could hardly be a bird? How could such weight take wing? Then I caught sight of it with its mate soaring from tree to tree and dropping plumb down on its prey, and heard the pair one night, crying like babies.

There she sits and comforts me with the substantiality of her body, as I wrap myself in the old green dressing gown and put on the kettle. She is only an owl; not an omen. Her life is lived in the here-and-now, striking for prey, mating, raising ullets, seeing in the dark.

This stone jug is a cold weight in the hand. It too belongs to the world of the ordinary, the here-and-now, where I suddenly yearn to live my life. Somewhat dusty, I notice, and likely to remain that way.

Dust; dust everywhere. Pia wrote her name in the dust on the mantelpiece: *Pia Pia Pia Pia Pia*, like the transcription of birdsong. In my infatuation I vowed, I'm going to preserve that signature.'

'You can't. Even more dust will fall and cover it up.'

'Then you'll just have to keep rewriting it, won't you?'

'I've never seen such a dusty old house as this.'

'We aim to please.'

'Don't you ever dust?'

'It's clean dirt, Pia. Anyhow dust it yourself if it bugs you. Feel free.'

'I wouldn't go that far.'

Pia Pia Pia Pia Pia. She left her tracks like the footsteps of a bird along the shore, sea-washed by morning. What I loved about her was the wanton levity of her flight, which lightened my spirit's sombre exactions. Her incorrigible curls, hard to put the comb through, all-over-the-place when she took off her floppy hat. No one in this house had ever worn such a daft hat since the beginning of time. Her kindness. Her slender arms, bare in firelight or sunlight. I could have Pia back, if I were willing to share her with all and sundry.

Pia, don't leave me to myself and Hannah. All the sensitive places in my mouth are aroused and wincing. Imaginary, proxy pain. *You nesh lass,* chid the dental nurse. *This won't hurt,* vowed the dentist

A book is a fickle object, unlike the owl, the jug. I try to tell myself that, in reading Hannah, I have suffered not viscerally but in a space of the mind reserved for surrogate emotions. The space will soon clear to make way for a new experience. The glow will pass off like the aura of a dream; within a day, these living testaments will have lost the warm patina of intimacy and lie lifeless in my hand. The bloom goes off the fruit because such fruit was never edible in the first place. Hannah will quit me too, within a few days. I just have to wait.

Yet I dread to lose her and am bereft at such solace. I find myself sobbing into the cushion. Imagine a neighbour roused by these sounds of anguish, knocking to ask what the trouble is.

Oh, I'm crying for a witch hanged three-hundred-and-fifty years ago.

Very right and proper, dear.

She means the world to me.

Only natural.

She was crucified, dead and buried.

I'm sure that in time you'll get over it. Time is a great healer.

...Dead and buried. But then I dug her up.

✳

I take up the jug again, to regain balance in the here-and-now; and remember the hands of my grandparents coated in wet clay, kneading the clay's dark dough, wedging and balling it into a strange shape between a loaf and a head, to remove all the air. Air bubbles popped out with delicious audible cracks.

215

Want a go, Olivia?

My fingers thirsted after the clay. They lusted to delve into its innards and monkey around in a spree of virtuosity in its depths. Other children just had plasticine and playdough: I had the smelly, brackish stuff of creation. We kept a squidged block with my childish fingerprints all over it, poked-in eye holes and a bashed fist-mark.

Use your hands as eyes, Olivia. Never bully the clay. The clay doesn't like it. Has a life of its own. That's right, an egg-shape. Now use your fingers as eyes. Pretend you're blind. Let the clay tell your hands what shape it wants to take. Be tactile, touch, feel, stroke, coax.

Centring the clay, they gradually went in with the three middle fingers, collared in, pulled up the wall rhythmically, so that a moist wave travelled up the pot. Jugs were my favourite pots and I'd whine to 'do the lip'.

Pull her out, yes, with your forefinger, said Grandpa. *Now pinch the dear little thing back into the rim. Slightly, not too much.*

The jug in my lap is a cold amber weight on my own belly and thighs. Our pots were russet, green, blue, grey, glazed with iron oxide, pure of decoration. But this must surely be one of my collaborations, for look at the mouth of the jug: protuberant, defiantly lippy.

Mother would gravely remark on the frequency with which God the Father is compared with a potter.

Remember, I beseech thee, that thou hast made me as the clay: and wilt thou bring me into the dust again?

Poor old Job. I know my bible as well as she did and have often noticed God's vandalistic propensity for smashing what his own hands have made. I rest the earthenware against my belly, cousins, two kinds of clay. The incorporation of the living with the dead comes home to me as a fact to be lived with. I return the jar to the table; switch on the television to the Learning Zone, which Faith recommends as therapy for insomnia.

I half-doze during a programme on computers. As the programme recedes, faces slip in under my eyelids, shifting just out of focus as I hover on the edge of sleep. An indefinite series of these faces seems latent in that talking screen. The faces chatter in outlandish dialects and without significant expression, as if resigned to a limbo of futility.

When I come to, he is there, Alexander Sagarra, and the faces are of his making.

There he stands, green-aproned in his studio surrounded by his reconstructions, being interviewed. I realise, blearily, what a celebrity Alex has become, jetting between conferences, called in to perform conjuring tricks on television. Even for me, there is a weird little thrill in seeing on the box the very Alex who modelled my life mask, and said of my face, *If I sculpted you, there'd be a tempest in that face.* I can't deny I was gratified.

'Your work,' suggests the interviewer, 'does it ever strike you as . . . a tad . . . ghoulish?'

'Not a bit. It's just work. Manual labour. According to scientific laws.'

'You don't fear disturbing the dead?'

'How would they feel disturbed?'

He goes on to demonstrate his craft, giving a methodical commentary. In that studio Alex set the symmetrical heads of Hannah and myself spinning on twin plinths, when we first divined the affinity. Even he was startled, unnerved. As the camera pans the organised chaos of Alex's studio, where representative heads of all the tribes of the world clutter shelves, as if he were gathering in a diaspora for the end of the world, I am sure I glimpse the terracotta Hannah, or was it myself? *Go round again, damn you,* I urge the cameraman; but I doubt if he will. The lens hovers on a tray of jawbones. The studio where Alex called up the apparition of my soul-mate now strikes me as a cannibal's store-room.

'Many laymen,' suggests the interviewer, 'would feel it a desecration to tamper with graves.'

In the programme, Alex hums to himself at this point; he doesn't even bother to answer the question, so engrossed is he in getting the proportions of nose to forehead correct. Somehow it is that humming that does it. He can hum over Rostherne Man if he likes. He can jest over his colleague's reconstruction of one-eyed Philip of Macedonia. But he isn't going to hum over the effigy of my Hannah.

Isabel buried her. So must I. My own raising of the dead face to an effigy now hits me with the force of the heinous. Like anyone you truly love, she's in your soul. You don't want a waxwork stuck up on the mantelpiece. Imagine if anyone did it to me: a lifelike bust of Olivia Holderness, taken from my exhumed skeletal remains. Granted, I wouldn't be around to feel disturbed, but still, the thought is unwholesome. How much more so when it involves someone whose life had been spent destroying graven images.

＊

I phone the university and museum: Alex is glad to hear my voice but admits to being distracted as he is supervising the packing of heads in boxes to take on his forthcoming trip to South Africa.

'I saw you on TV last night.'

'Oh. Right. Made that a while back. What did you think of it?'

'Not much.'

'Ah.' He tries not to sound disconcerted but my bluntness has caught his attention as flattery would never have done.

'Still the same sweet-talking Olivia, I see.'

'Not quite the same, no, Alex. I didn't mean to be rude. Well, not particularly. You're quite a celebrity these days.'

'Actually, Olivia, believe it or not, that isn't the point. The idea is to generate income for research.'

'Sure. Anyway, that's not why I'm ringing. I need something from you.' He listens respectfully to my request that I be allowed to bury all the remains.

'But why, Olivia?'

'It suddenly strikes me as sickeningly wrong.'

'It didn't before.'

'I didn't know her then – personally. Now I do.'

'Couldn't you perhaps think of this as something distant from the person you...er...' (he coughed) 'know? Just a memento?'

'*Memento mori*. It makes her more dead. Whereas, in fact,

she's alive. If it were a portrait, that would be different. I'd be able to see her eye-to-eye, face-to-face, with my Rembrandt-vision.'

'Pardon me?'

'Oh – sorry, that doesn't make sense. Well, it does to me. Can I come and see you, Alex?'

'Certainly. I'm off to London tomorrow, and then South Africa, but perhaps we could have a good yack when I get back?'

'When will that be?'

'Two months.'

There was no way I could wait two months. It was urgent that my mistake be rectified. But if he was clearing off, presumably I must acquiesce.

'OK. Have a good trip. But can I pay her a visit in your studio?'

Short pause. 'Do. Yes, of course.'

*

Graven images. Idols. Relics. I had been brought up to abhor the worship of icons, just as intransigently as had the Puritans and Quakers of old. I was of the true old enthusiastic breed, a zealot with a hammer. Smashing images in churches would have been a joyful job to me, defacing plaster angels, and decapitating idolatrous Marys. I could imagine being one of Cromwell's soldiers, purging the sanctuaries of beauty. False, painted beauty.

Hadn't I always loathed (with fascinated horror which declared my own implication) the dummies in shop windows, plastic effigies of nothing remotely human? Barbie dolls, fashion models?

Proud little prude, my father had called me. And I rounded on him with a fanatical anger he could not begin to comprehend. He backed off, into his lackadaisical easy-goingness, sure that the tomboy would find out sooner or later that the world was as it is, men and women were as they were, looks meant a lot, and idealists never yet changed the world for the better.

Yet I, the iconoclast, had desecrated the grave of Hannah

Emanuel by having her physical likeness – itself a falsehood, by her creed and mine – fabricated on the foundation of her skull. I had made of her truth a lie; of her light a dark simulacrum. The scope of this betrayal will perhaps not be understood by anyone not brought up in a mental world that prefers inwardness to surfaces.

As an ex-Friend, I should have taken the quietest way, obtaining permission to remove the bones and restorations by legitimate channels. But it seemed to me that I owed a debt which could not wait to be repaid. It would take muscle and attack. I extracted the hammer from the tool box and set off for the university.

Imagine the churches when the iconoclasts got in there, the noise of shattering as the stained glass smithereened. The colourful panes had intervened for centuries between the individual in his pew and the heavens, throwing from the Virgin's mantle patches of sky-blue on to upturned faces; from archangelic halos aureoles of gold. Then the soldiery, government officials or populace assaulted them: the figures cried out as they buckled. Some relic-hunting Puritans filched from the debris glowing fragments of saints or angels and squirrelled them home in their pockets as keepsakes.

Altar rails next: uproot the lot. Purple drapery over the altar: bundle it into bags. Chalices of gold and precious artefacts. The heights of dim, vaulted rafters echoed to the stoving-in of rapt faces, the unwinging of angels, axe-assault on saints in wood smooth with kisses through centuries of veneration. Into the organ loft: a sigh and groan as the music died a violent death.

Until all you were left with was white space. Indistinguishable from nothing.

Plain tabernacles with transparent windows. Quiet architecture of simplicity and symmetry. Spirit-space, democratic space. The minister kneeling to you, in the posture of Christ as he washed the disciples' feet, rather than you to him. But for Hannah, even this purge was insufficient: the church itself, with its lewd bells and arrogant steeple, was an idol. She must demolish all material shrines until only naked spirit remained.

*

I'd never approached the university in the bus with a hammer in my briefcase rather than books and papers. It didn't feel quite real.

Porters and technicians were enjoying a smoky tea-break in Alex's building. I softly passed the room where muffled gusts of laughter leaked out into the corridor. The door of his studio was open: I slipped in and, avoiding the eyes of the two reconstructed heads, placed them carefully in a binbag, and departed. It could not have been easier.

The museum was the more difficult problem. How do you get an exhibit out of a glass case without smashing the case? This was what the hammer was for. All the way there, I imagined the glass exploding, shards flung in every direction; the alarm going off; myself arrested and my hammer confiscated.

I passed the yellow-haired, horned Vikings, who were represented in the act of being about to ravish and pillage an Anglo-Saxon family; passed Greek vases and Etruscan grave-statuary; found myself in the room where Hannah's waxwork reposed. Rostherne Man was still there, his pitiful head tucked under its wing. But Hannah's case was empty, except for the brank.

'Where is the Hesketh Maiden?' I asked the official.

'Are you Dr Holderness?'

I clutched binbag and briefcase in a spasm of apprehension. The room turned nightmarish. I was expected. They knew I would come in with my hammer. Was I really such a known and predictable lunatic?

'Dr Sagarra says to tell you the wax has degraded: the head's been put aside. You can take it away if you wish.'

'Yes. I wish.'

I am led through into the bowels of the place and wait in a dingy little room; a study stuffed with papers and computer equipment, whose dimensions are those of a cupboard. I sit, twitching.

A note from Alex: 'I don't know what bee you've got in your bonnet, dear Olivia, but anticipating that you might wish to reclaim the remains and reconstructions during my absence, we've taken the head out of commission and the bones will be released to you at the same time. They are, as you know, of scant intrinsic archaeological or scientific interest. If you so desire, you may reclaim the other head from my studio. You'll find it on the left hand bench as you go through the door.'

Thank you. I already have.

There is a hot sense of embarrassment, as though I had been seen through all along. Relief and gratitude: could I really have brought myself to sledgehammer that glass case? Queasy distress as I sign for Hannah's bones and agree to collect them when I have deposited the three heads in their binbag in my study.

I carry the remains of Hannah Emanuel down Oxford Road in a long cardboard box, such as one might bring away from a department store. Isabel once carried her, tears streaming down her face, from one burial-site to another. The nerves in my scalp and teeth tingle; my breath comes fast and shallow as I struggle along. It seems so far. The bones in the box shift slightly, with every pace. Traffic rushes past but its sound is not enough to account for the uproar in my brain.

'Faith,' I ask her quietly, 'there's something... in my room. Please... would you come and see.'

'Oh, Olivia,' says Faith, dumbfounded. The first thing she saw was not the heads or the bones but the hammer in my gaping briefcase. 'What have you done?'

When she sees the heads and the bones, she sits down weakly; then says, practically and bracingly, 'Right. Let's get it all into the car, shall we? We'll take her home.'

*

'Should we say anything?' Faith wonders, when we have laid everything in the trench, including the terracotta head Alex made from my life-mask, and tenderly covered the whole with the green towelling dressing gown of my childhood. It is finished. The mortal part of Hannah Emanuel is given back to the earth; the empty simulacrum of myself accompanying her as grave-goods. I straighten up, taking hold of my shovel. She is free. My tears run steadily down. We shower the earth with pale petals, where later I shall plant rosemary and rue.

'No,' I reply. 'We should be silent.'

The Characters of this Book

CHETHAM, Humphrey (1580–1653). Founder of Chetham's Hospital for the education of poor boys – now Chetham's School of Music – and Chetham's Library, Manchester, 'for the use of scholars and others well affected', the oldest surviving free public library in England, containing a matchless archive of manuscripts and sixteenth- and seventeenth-century printed books, pamphlets and broadsheets.

CLARKE, Isabel/Ishbel (fictional, c. 1635–1707). Modelled on the heroic Quaker women of the lowest orders, like Jane and Dorothy Waugh, who emerged from servitude and illiteracy, learning to write in prison and taking the Friends' message through the known world. Isabel's loyalty to her 'yoke-fellow' is an imaginative development of same-sex spiritual 'marriage' between Quaker couples such as Katherine Evans and Sarah Chevers, who spent three years as prisoners of the Inquisition in Malta from 1659 to 1663.

FELL, Margaret (1614–1702). Quaker, converted by George Fox in 1652. A formidable gentry-figure and administrative genius, she became the 'nursing mother' of Quakerism, turning her home at Swarthmoor, Cumbria, into the hub of the movement. She interceded with Cromwell and Charles II against the persecution of Friends; wrote *Women's Speaking Justified* (1666); suffered brutal imprisonment, and married Fox in 1669, chiefly living apart from him, to continue her radical activities into her eighties.

FISHER, Mary (*fl.* 1652–97) Selby servant who became a Quaker and travelled alone to convert Sultan Mahomet IV of Turkey. Her interview with the Sultan is related by George Bishop in *New-England Judged* (1667 edn). Mary maintained that the 'Infidel' Turks were far more humane and rational than the 'Christian' rulers of Britain.

FOX, George (1624–91). Founder of the Society of Friends (called 'Quakers' in mockery because of their convulsions of ecstatic 'quaking', when 'The Power' overcame them). Fox emancipated thousands of men and women by his emphasis on the 'Inner Light' of each believer. The early movement was militant rather than quietest and specialised in refusal of deference through 'hat-honour' and insistence on equality of address; 'thouing' those of higher rank; verbal attacks on priests and magistrates; 'running naked for a sign'; refusal of tithes and resistance to injustice to the poor. Fox supported the spiritual equality of women and their right to speak and travel as 'apostles'. Friends suffered brutal persecution, flogging, imprisonment and punitive fines; women Friends suffered additionally sexual harassment, bridling, ducking and stigmatisation as witches.

HEYRICK, Richard (1600–67). Proselytising Presbyterian Warden of Manchester Collegiate Church during the Revolution, imprisoned for plotting against the Commonwealth in 1651, conformed to the Anglican Church in the Restoration. It was Heyrick who called Manchester to arms in 1659 'upon the score of the Quakers being up' (ie, in armed rebellion), though Newcome argued that despite being 'very insolent and troublesome, yet [I] was unsatisfied that the thing was true that they were up in arms'.

HUBBERTHORNE, Richard (1628–62). Respected and much-loved Quaker apostle who wrote widely and died in Newgate.

HULME, William (fictional, *fl.* 1650–90). Moderate and respectable Quaker of Chedle Holme. The area of Cheadle and Stockport was known as a nest of Quakers and Dissent.

JONES, Hannah (fictional, 1630–65). Aspects of Hannah's rebellious and heretical character have been borrowed from renegade Quakers like Martha Simmonds, Mary Howgill, Ann Blaykling and Joan Whitrow, who rocked the movement by claiming spiritual authority within the group. Hannah's development of the theology of a female god recalls Jane Lead (1623–1704), the Philadelphian mystic, and Ann Lee, the eighteenth-century Manchester factory hand and renegade Quaker who became the American 'Shaker' spiritual leader, 'Mother Ann'; also Mary Anne Girling (1827–86), a 'reincarnation of the Deity' who founded the 'People of God' community in the New Forest. Hannah Jones's claim to have borne a new Christ in her daughter, Grace, recalls the various 'mothers of God' who mushroomed during the fertile days of the Revolution, eg, Joan Robins and Mary Adams. Hannah's social concern is a development of Quakerism, in combination with the fruits of the brief springtime of Christian communism of Gerrard Winstanley and the Diggers. Her hanging as a witch recalls the visionary Anne Bodenham, and the Quaker martyr Mary Dyer (executed in Boston in 1659). Hannah's supposed 'monster' child recalls both Mary Dyer and the case of the Antinomian Anne Hutchinson (c. 1590–1643), whose thirty abortive births were accounted evidence when she was condemned for heresy by ecclesiastical synod in 1637 and banished from Massachusetts; she was murdered in an Indian raid. My account of Hannah's 'bridling' is based on the account of the Quaker, Dorothy Waugh. The Stockport bridle may be viewed in the Manchester Archaeological Collection and the Macclesfield bridle is in the West Park Museum.

LYNGARD, David, (fictional, *fl.* 1640–70). His diaries are indebted to the diaries of Manchester Presbyterians Martindale and Newcome but his character as a Scots Calvinist is full of Knoxian sexual spleen. He owes much to my reading of the bilious works of the misogynist Presbyterian divine, Thomas Edwards, heresiographer and author of the notorious *Gangraena* of 1646, with its pathological fear of women preachers and the lower orders.

MARTINDALE, Adam (1623–86). Presbyterian divine who preached at Manchester, and vicar of Rostherne, Cheshire, from 1648. Evicted in 1662, he scraped a living before becoming chaplain to Lord Delamere in 1671. His autobiography is a richly personal source of material concerning Manchester in the Revolution. His debate with 'the famous Richard Hubberthorne' at Knutsford Heath and that with 'ramblers & railers' at Shadow Moss, 'that gang', have been conflated in the account of Lyngard's debate with Hubberthorne and Hannah Jones at Shadow Moss. After the Revolution, he was courageous enough to preach against maypoles, one of which his wife and her friends cut down with a saw.

NAYLER, James (1617?–1660) Charismatic Quaker leader who attracted many women disciples, including Martha Simmonds. He challenged Fox for the leadership. The culmination of his tragic career was his ride into Bristol on an ass in pouring rain in 1656, acclaimed by his followers with palms as the Messiah. He was arrested and punished by Parliament for 'horrid blasphemy' by flogging, pillorying, the piercing of his tongue by hot iron and the branding of 'B' on his forehead. On his release from Newgate, Nayler made peace with Fox and died shortly thereafter, the author of many beautiful works. Nayler's defection was blamed by the scathed movement on the women surrounding him.

NEWCOME, Henry (1627–95). Presbyterian preacher at the Collegiate Church, Manchester, from 1656, evicted in 1662, but continued to preach around Manchester. His diary should not be missed, not least for his debate with Warden Heyrick in 1658 on whether it was Christian to go and view a performing horse. 'Mr Heyricke sent to me to go with him to see him; and unless I went, he would not go. I seriously considered . . . ' but decided against, on the grounds of vulgar gawping which might lead to worse inclinations; though 'the creature's sagacity and docibility' were not in doubt, it might be 'unlawful'. Finally, '[t]his I thought of – To go, might be a sin; not to go, I knew was no sin.' Neither went. Newcome winced from bloodshed, and was politically equivocal, having a moderate mentality that preferred persecution by the king than by 'a giddy, hot-headed, bloody multitude'.

SIMMONDS, Martha (*fl.* 1654–66). A turbulent, audacious spirit, Martha (along with her fellow women, Hannah Stranger, Dorcas Erbury, Judy Crouch and 'a woman called Mildred') was loaded with blame for scandal caused to the Quaker movement by the downfall of Nayler. Burrough wrote to her that 'you are out of the truth, out of the way, out of the power, out of the wisdom and out of the life of God ...and are become as goats, rough and hairy'. Martha published tracts, preached and filibustered male leaders with an excoriating 'buzzing-singing' she had invented for this purpose. Her love of Nayler was close to worship. Martha had been a Seeker who walked in sackcloth barefoot through Colchester 'as a sign' of the world's corruption. Stigmatised as a witch ('all her witchery & filthy enchantments is set at naught' wrote Quaker leaders), she sought an authority equal to that of the males. Martha died reconciled with Friends, on a ship bound for Maryland. Modern Quaker historians like Mabel Brailsford still vilify her three hundred years after the event as 'the villain of this piece', 'immediately responsible for his downfall', the 'fountain and origin of the evil', so sharp was the wound sustained by this opprobrium.

STUART, Charles, king of England (1630–85). Exiled, after his father's execution and his army's defeat, in Paris from 1651 to 1660, when he was restored to the English throne. Forced to violate his promise of religious tolerance made in the Declaration of Breda, Charles was an unwilling party to the Act of Uniformity (1662) and a sequence of severely repressive laws against dissenters. Charles' love of luxury, science and women is legendary.

TRAPNEL, Anna (*fl.* 1642–60). Daughter of a Poplar shipwright, this vociferous rhyming prophetess of the Fifth Monarchist movement was associated with John Simpson's revolutionary church at All Hallows the Great in London. Her spiritual and political extemporisations flowed forth in trances and were transcribed in shorthand. She achieved notoriety through a twelve-day ecstasy at Whitehall attacking Oliver Cromwell's Protectorate, after which she travelled to Cornwall, was arrested on suspicion of sedition and committed to Bridewell, a journey she recorded in the vividly autobiographical *Anna Trapnel's Report and Plea*. Anna Trapnel published six inflammatory pamphlets in 1654-8. She did not (so far as I am aware) ever go to Stockport.

The author would like to acknowledge the debt to John Prag and Richard Neave's *Making Faces: Using Forensic and Archaeological Evidence*, British Museum Press, London, 1997, a magisterial work on facial reconstruction.

Established in 1978, The Women's Press publishes high-quality fiction and non-fiction from outstanding women writers worldwide. Our list spans literary fiction, crime thrillers, biography and autobiography, health, women's studies, literary criticism, mind body spirit, the arts and the Livewire Books series for young women. Our bestselling annual *Women Artists Diary* features the best in contemporary women's art.

The Women's Press also runs a book club through which members can buy, every quarter, the best fiction and non-fiction from a wide range of British publishing houses, mostly in paperback, always at discount.

To receive our latest catalogue, or for information on The Women's Press Book Club, send a large SAE to:

The Sales Department
The Women's Press Ltd
34 Great Sutton Street London EC1V 0LQ
Tel: 020 7251 3007 Fax: 020 7608 1938
www.the-womens-press.com

Sue Woolfe
Leaning Towards Infinity

A passionate and daring exploration of motherhood, genius, love and betrayal, *Leaning Towards Infinity* tells the story of three generations of women, bound together not only by the inescapable ties of family but also by the mysterious and intriguing world of mathematics. Witty and exciting, this novel was the winner of both the Commonwealth Writer's Prize and the Christina Stead Prize for Fiction.

'Extraordinarily rich . . . Woolfe's name can sit beside Gabriel García Márquez's with barely a blush' **Daily Telegraph**

'What a glorious and tumultuous novel' **Fay Weldon, Mail on Sunday**

'Written with the clarity and elegance of a numerical theorem' **Literary Review**

Fiction £6.99
ISBN 0 7043 4658 3